A Betrothal Agreement

by

Caitlyn Callery

A Betrothal Agreement

Cover Art by *Debbie Taylor*

The Wild Rose Press, Inc.
PO Box 708
Adams Basin, NY 14410-0708
Visit us at www.thewildrosepress.com

Publishing History
First Edition, 2023
Trade Paperback ISBN 978-1-5092-5055-4
Digital ISBN 978-1-5092-5056-1

Published in the United States of America

"Ed means well," she said. "I'm not altogether certain all his ideas are well thought out."

"Sometimes they need refining."

"Please tell me we're not going to announce a betrothal?"

Kit smiled and nodded at the driver of a carriage coming in the other direction, then saluted a couple of gentlemen as they passed on horseback. "Not unless it becomes absolutely necessary," he said.

Sophie stared at him in disbelief. "You're not actually considering…?"

"Smile. People are watching."

She glanced around and saw people trying to seem disinterested as they watched every move she and Kit made. Her heart sank. "By dinnertime, everyone in Town will be talking about us."

"Yes."

"Saying you're courting me."

"Yes."

"Oh, my." She struggled to catch her breath.

Kit laughed. "Should I feel insulted?"

Sophie felt her cheeks heating. "I'm sorry. I didn't mean—" Desperate to change the course of the conversation, she latched on to what he had said moments before. "You said Ed's ideas occasionally need refining. How exactly do you intend to refine this one?"

Quietly and as quickly as interruptions from passing friends and acquaintances would allow, Kit told her his version of the plan.

"If your uncle sees me—and others—showing an interest in you, it should make him think again about forcing the match with Pinkerton."

Dedication

To Sharon Howell,
who encouraged my writing
in the years when no one else did.
Thank you.

Chapter One

London, 1817

Kit Thomas entered the crowded ballroom beside his eager friend, Ed, and wondered what on earth had possessed him. He never attended these functions and never offered to dance with ladies of the *ton*. Yet here he was, having agreed to do both.

"Just one dance," Ed had pleaded. "Stand up with m'sister, get her out of wallflower's row and give the other chaps the opportunity to notice her. That's all I'm asking."

Kit's first instinct was to say no. At the best of times, coming to Lady Fortescue's ball would hold no interest for him whatsoever, and this was most certainly not the best of times. This summer evening was muggy, in want of a good storm to clear the air. To Kit, this meant the ballroom would be hot and stifling, and the noise level such that he wouldn't be able to hear his own voice, let alone what anyone else might say, while Society matrons strutted like brightly colored birds of prey, their dutiful chicks trailing them, looking for the juiciest title, or the fattest purse, or both.

As the Earl of Markham's second son, Kit had no title and, until he was thirty and able to collect his grandfather's legacy, no fortune of his own either, but he did have the next best thing—connections. For some of the Season's hopefuls, that would be enough. Even his efforts over the last three years to paint himself as the ne'er-do-well spare who spent his time gambling and drinking didn't deter them. They batted their lashes and fluttered their fans as they gave him their most practiced come-hither smiles and plotted ways to bring him up to scratch, until the only safe course of action was to avoid the dances altogether.

"I don't attend balls," he'd told Ed, pouring them each a drink and taking a seat by the fireplace.

"You can't make an exception? Please, Kit. I'm begging you. Just one dance."

"What good do you suppose that is going to do?"

Ever the optimist, Ed smiled. "If they see one man—you—dance with her," he said, "they, too, will be emboldened to stand up with her."

Kit doubted it. If those other men hadn't shown an interest before now, they were unlikely to change their opinion because of him. Truth was, she was probably plain as a pikestaff, clumsy, and with a laugh like a braying donkey. Since, from what Kit had heard, Ed had no fortune, his sister probably had no dowry either. All in all, she was beyond hope.

However, Ed was a friend, and friends did favors for each other, no matter how unpalatable they may be. "Just one dance," he'd eventually agreed.

Now, in the crush of ball-goers, he wondered if he could claim temporary insanity. The ballroom itself was not large, although the mirrors lining the walls at each end gave an illusion of space, and it helped that the doors to the terrace were open, allowing the overflow of people to spill out. Dozens of candles burned in the chandeliers, their flames combining to keep the room well lit and far too warm. People stood in small groups, shouting at one another, gazes darting about to find the next person about whom they might speculate. Ladies flicked fans in carefully choreographed movements while gentlemen stood by, their expressions a mix of interest and fashionable ennui.

"I have died and gone to hell," muttered Kit.

"Come and meet my sister," Ed shouted into his ear.

"Definitely hell." Kit followed his friend and pushed through the mass of bodies.

He was aware of the hopeful glances of the debutantes and the more calculating stares of their mothers as he passed by, but he kept his own gaze on Ed's back, determined to give no one an excuse to approach him. Bad enough he had to show an interest in one lady tonight. He'd be damned if he embroiled himself with any others.

On the far side of the ballroom, a group of ladies sat watching the goings-on. Some were clearly chaperones, older women with heads wrapped in silk turbans or sporting ridiculously colored ostrich feathers that wafted as they nodded at the latest morsel of gossip. Younger women sat near them, silent, dull, hands demurely in laps, and utter misery on their faces.

Which one was Ed's sister? Was it the short girl with the wide hips and ample bosom? Or the tall, thin lady who couldn't hide her impressive height, though she rounded her back and slouched her shoulders? Perhaps his sister was the girl with the broad brow and large nose, or the one who couldn't seem to sit still but squirmed in her seat, readjusting her dress in full view of everyone. She sniffed and rubbed the end of her nose with the back of her hand, and Kit prayed it was not her.

To his relief, Ed passed them all and headed for two ladies sitting a few feet away, deep in conversation. The one facing him was older, plump, with a generous bust and several chins. Her blue eyes sparkled with humor and her lips curved up as she listened to something her friend said.

This second lady had her back to Kit, although he could see she was younger than her companion. She was slender and straight-backed, and her hair, which was the color of wheat in sunshine, was caught up in a topknot. Ed stopped beside her. Kit braced himself to smile and seem enchanted, no matter what.

She turned, and Kit stared. Miss Wilson was beautiful. Artfully arranged curls framed a heart-shaped face, with cheeks that were an unfashionably healthy pink, and the brightest, bluest eyes he had ever seen. Her lips were full, and ready to smile. She wore a satin dress in a powder blue that matched her eyes as well as the thin satin ribbons woven into her hair. Around her throat, a two-stringed pearl choker lustered against her skin.

Obviously worried that, even at this late stage, Kit might make a dash for freedom, Ed made the introductions quickly.

"How do you do, Mr. Thomas?" Her voice was gentle, and slightly husky. It stirred something deep inside him, making his heart miss a beat. He bowed.

"Honored to make your acquaintance, Miss Wilson. And hoping there is still space for me on your dance card?"

Miss Wilson looked from Kit to Ed, and a shadow passed over her eyes. She pursed her lips and, for a moment, Kit thought she would refuse him. It shocked him to realize he did not want her to do so. Then, she smiled and handed him the card.

He let out the breath he hadn't realized he was holding, checked the card, and frowned. It was completely empty. Ed had said she was a wallflower, but this was ridiculous. Not one gentleman had penciled his name in. How could this be? Were they all blind and stupid, to overlook such a treasure?

One dance. That was all Ed had asked him for, and Kit had agreed in the name of friendship. Well, now he was going to be a very good friend indeed. He put his name against the next set, and against the supper dance too. He was pleased to see the latter was a waltz.

****

Sophie looked from Ed to his friend and back. Her lips tightened, for she knew exactly what had happened. Ed had somehow coerced this gentleman into dancing with her.

Her brother meant well, of course. It pained him to know she was passed over by the gentlemen at every ball, but did he really believe it was any better to know this man, oozing charm and acting as if she was the only woman in the room, was only doing so because Ed had asked him to?

Although asked was probably not the correct word. Pleaded might be more accurate. Begged. Forced. Or, God forbid, bought.

She felt her color rising, burning her cheeks. Tears of humiliation threatened. She blinked them away, then turned her head so he wouldn't see her discomfort as she pondered what to do. Should she rebuff Mr. Thomas and then give Ed the set-down he deserved? Or should she accept the man's offer and make him sorry by stepping on his feet at every opportunity?

5

It wasn't as if she particularly wanted to dance. Indeed, as she had repeatedly told first Papa and then, after his death, Uncle Leo, Sophie would be happy never to have a Season at all. Let the other ladies pick off the husbands milling around. Sophie had other dreams, which didn't involve parading and posturing and showing oneself off.

Her protestations were buried beneath the yards of silk and satin and tulle of her new gowns and the avalanche of invitations in every post. Her objections might as well have been in Chinese, for all the notice anyone took, as those invitations were accepted, or rejected, on her behalf. If only she were still a child, she had thought. Then she could have stomped her foot and screamed at them, "I do not want this!"

But Sophie had to admit there was a vast difference between not wanting the *ton* and the *ton* not wanting her. More, their rejection of her was all the more galling because she honestly did not know what she'd done to repel them.

The first week of her Season had been just as Aunt Jess said it would be. Her dance card was full every evening, and gentlemen called on her, asking her to ride in the park, or walk with them, or accompany them to a picnic. She'd hardly had a moment to think. And despite herself, she had enjoyed the attention.

Then, suddenly, it stopped. Nobody put their names on her card. Nobody called or sent her flowers. If she met them in the street, they were uncomfortable and remembered an urgent appointment.

At first, it had hurt terribly. Actually, it still hurt terribly, but now she refused to dwell on it. She sat with Aunt Jess, listening to her funny stories about the people in the room, and planned for the day she could return to Hamsey Hall, reopen her laboratory, and continue her work trying to increase the yields of different crops.

Last year had been disastrous. There was so much rain and cold, even in August, until people started calling it "the Year Without a Summer." The weather, the plummeting temperatures, and the lack of sunlight had decimated crops and left people starving. What food there had been was priced out of the reach of many, and it had broken her heart to see gaunt-faced children with stick-thin limbs standing, sullen, on the sides of the roads, begging for morsels.

There wasn't enough food. The harvest needed to increase, that was plain. Sophie thought about it long and hard, and reasoned that, if she could increase the amount that could be grown on individual stalks of wheat, the harvest would be bigger, and the chances of another famine would reduce.

"I can do it," she'd insisted when Ed expressed his doubts. "The Countess of Egremont did it with potatoes."

Ed had raised an eyebrow. "Hardly the most ladylike of pursuits for a countess."

"Oh, phooey!" Sophie laughed. "That wasn't the half of it. Some say she mixed paint pigments to make new colors for Mr. Turner. To say nothing of her crossbar lever to make heavy lifting easier. She won the silver medal at the Royal Society."

Ed shuddered. "Don't you go winning any medals. I'd hate to try and explain that to the world."

It had broken her heart to leave when Uncle Leo dragged them to London after Papa's death. There he'd told them, bluntly, that the family fortune was gone and everybody relied on Sophie to marry well.

Something she couldn't do if every man avoided her. Save her brother's coerced friend, of course.

Sophie turned to Mr. Thomas, still unsure how to react to his request. As she did so, she saw Baron Pinkerton watching her from the far side of the room. She shuddered. The only man who'd asked her to dance since the second week of her Season, Lord Pinkerton was also the one man she wished she could refuse. At fifty-one, he was thirty years her senior and had already buried three wives. Short and squat, he had gray teeth and tiny eyes that were hard and cruel. Any moment now, he'd make his way to her and claim the two dances propriety allowed him to take.

Suddenly, it didn't matter why Mr. Thomas had asked her to dance. Because he had done so, Lord Pinkerton's would not be the only name on her card tonight, and that was worth all the humiliation of Ed's tactless interference. She smiled at Mr. Thomas and handed him the card.

Lord Pinkerton turned and stalked away. Perhaps he'd spend the evening playing cards. Sophie could only hope.

A few minutes later, they took their places in the set for the new dance. "How do you know my brother?" she asked, for want of something better to say.

"We were at school together. He came to my home for the holidays one summer."

Sophie nodded. "I remember. He came back full of tales of all you'd done together. You went fishing and you fell into the water."

He chuckled. "If that's how he chooses to remember it."

"You didn't fall?"

"I went into the water. Shall we leave it at that?" Sophie frowned, intrigued, and he changed the subject. "Do you ride, Miss Wilson?"

"Not at the moment. My uncle doesn't keep riding horses."

"A situation easily remedied. There's a mare in my father's stables that's perfect for you. I can bring her to you on the morrow, if you'd care to ride in the park with me?"

They moved apart, dancing with other partners. It gave Sophie time to think. The invitation was the last thing she had expected.

Part of her wanted to say yes, quickly, before he changed his mind. Sophie loved riding. In the country, she'd relished the time spent on horseback, galloping through fields and sailing fearlessly over hedges.

She hadn't ridden since Papa's death. According to Uncle Leo, Papa had left them with a mountain of debts and bad investments. Uncle Leo had sold everything that wasn't entailed, including Sophie's beloved mare, to pay the creditors, and then he'd brought Aunt Jess, his sister, to Town to launch Sophie. Leo had paid for her to have this one Season, and given Sophie her tiny dowry.

So yes, she very much wanted to ride in the park with Mr. Thomas. It would be a treat to sit a horse again, and with such a handsome man! He was six feet tall, with broad shoulders that needed no padding to fill his coat. His silver silk waistcoat fitted him perfectly, showing off his sturdy chest and flat stomach, while his breeches covered slim hips and long, powerful legs. His light brown hair was carefully tousled, the ends of his curls a sun-kissed blond, and he had deep brown eyes that shone with mischief. The crinkles around them suggested he laughed a lot. Oh yes, a ride in the park with him was likely to be most enjoyable.

And yet—she barely knew him. All she did know was that he was her brother's friend, and he was paying attention to her because of that. She should say no graciously, finish this dance, and refuse to be their charity case any longer.

"She's a gray," he said about the mare as they came back together. "Her name is Dove, and she's gentle as they come. But sturdy, too, and in good need of a ride."

The horse sounded wonderful. Sophie longed to see her. And really, she'd be doing the animal a kindness. Horses needed to stretch their legs. That was why she would agree to the ride. To benefit the horse.

"I'd like to ride her, thank you," she said. He grinned. She smiled back and chose to forget, just for a moment, that Ed had engineered this.

The dance ended sooner than she would have liked. Mr. Thomas escorted her back to Aunt Jess, who smiled appreciatively at him. He bowed to them both, mentioned the supper dance, and walked away. It was only after he'd gone that Sophie looked in her card and discovered he hadn't finished with her this evening.

Moments later, her happy mood fled as Lord Pinkerton approached. He bowed and held out his hand for the next dance. Sophie wished she could say no. Then, because she had no other choice, she let him lead her to the dance floor.

****

Kit was halfway across the ballroom before he gave in to the urge to look back at Sophie. He frowned to see Pinkerton bowing over her hand. Kit knew Ed wanted gentlemen to notice his sister, but he surely did not mean that reprobate. Pinkerton had three daughters from his first three marriages, but he needed a son to inherit the barony, which meant he must marry a fourth time. Kit hoped the man wasn't considering Sophie to fill the role. Pinkerton needed someone sturdy, able to stand up to the rigors of a life that had already killed three baronesses. Sophie, while not delicate, was not of the yeoman stock needed. Besides, her eyes twinkled with mischief, and she had an air of intelligence that would be wasted on a man like Pinkerton.

Miss Wilson accepted Pinkerton's arm but did not look enthusiastic about it, which set Kit at ease. Her duenna looked none too pleased either. The older lady glowered at the baron, all trace of her good humor gone.

As the couple took their places in the set, Pinkerton glared at Kit. He seemed furious. Kit frowned. He couldn't remember crossing swords with the man, and he certainly hadn't intentionally caused him offense. Then he shrugged, thinking that if the baron scowled like that when dancing with a beautiful woman, he was a fool. Dismissing Pinkerton from his mind, Kit went in search of Ed, who was probably in the card room.

****

Lord Pinkerton appeared at Sophie's side again before the supper dance. "Miss Wilson," he said as he held out his hand for her, clearly believing her acceptance a foregone conclusion.

Sophie smiled, as apologetically as she could. "I'm sorry, my lord. This dance is taken."

His brows lowered, making his eyes even smaller, and his lips compressed in a tight line. "By whom?" The question came out on a growl, and Sophie swallowed.

"By me." Mr. Thomas stepped around Lord

Pinkerton and bowed to Sophie. "Shall we, Miss Wilson?" he asked. "Do excuse us, Pinkerton."

Feeling slightly breathless, Sophie followed him to the floor, where they faced one another, his hand on the small of her back, hers on his shoulder, waiting for the music to begin. She could feel the rise of his chest with every breath, the warmth of him, even through her gloves. His scent surrounded her, something woodsy, underpinned with the heady fragrance of clean masculinity.

His eyes creased as he smiled, and a dimple appeared on his cheek. "I apologize in advance for stepping on your toes," he said, and she gave him what Aunt Jess would call an old-fashioned look.

"I don't believe you clumsy for one moment."

"Your faith in my abilities is humbling. And slightly worrying."

Sophie laughed. His smile broadened and fun danced in his eyes. She'd thought those eyes a solid, dark brown. Now she was closer, she saw flecks of gold and green. The skin on his jaw held the slightest tinge of blue, although she was certain he would have shaved before coming here. She felt a strange urge to feel his face, to discover whether the beard shadow made his skin rough to the touch or whether the effect was just visual.

Her eyes widened in shock at her wanton thoughts. Never before had she thought of doing such a thing; it wasn't in her nature to be so brazen. Shame filled her, and she wanted to run from the dance, from him. He seemed to know what she felt, because his hand tightened almost imperceptibly around hers, and he pressed a little more firmly against her back, bringing her closer, until they felt impossibly intimate.

The room, the musicians, the other dancers seemed to fade from view as they whirled around the floor. They said nothing. They didn't have to. His gaze locked with hers and it was as if all her secrets were laid bare to him without a word being uttered. Her feet didn't seem to touch the ground. The only reality Sophie knew was his fingers wrapped around hers, his hand caressing her back.

All too soon, the music ended and he brought her to a halt. Still they stared at each other, while others pushed past, eager to get to the supper room. Sophie's heart beat erratically, her breaths shallow, as if she'd run a long way. It was gratifying to note his breathing was the same.

And then Aunt Jess was there, tapping his arm with her fan and saying it was time to escort them in to supper.

Mr. Thomas released Sophie, breaking the spell. "Your servant, ma'am," he assured Aunt Jess, offering her his other arm and leading both ladies out of the ballroom.

Chapter Two

Dawn colored the dark sky with smudges of pink-tinged white as Kit and Ed left the gambling house. Ed looked pleased, as well he might when his pockets held a thousand pounds more than they had when he'd entered. Kit had lost, though not heavily. He might wish to cultivate the reputation of a rakish man about town, but he was not stupid. He never wagered more than he could afford to lose, and he knew when to stop.

"It's been a good night," smiled Ed, swinging his cane jauntily.

"For you." Kit's words held no rancor.

Ed studied him. "Are you all right? I mean, if you're in Queer Street, I can lend—"

"I'm not in Queer Street. Not even in the vicinity. I can pay my debts."

"I meant no offense…"

"I took none." Kit smiled and lightened his tone so Ed would see he wasn't angry at him for the offer. "I can afford to pay Rivers on the morrow," he said. "Besides, my quarterly allowance is due at the end of the week, and I'll be much more flush then."

"As long as you're certain. You did me a service tonight, and I'd be honored to return the favor."

"'Twas hardly an onerous task. Dance with a beautiful lady, twice. If all labor were as pleasurable, nobody would be work-shy." An image came to him of the lady in question. Her smile was deep, making her blue eyes sparkle and revealing the mischievous dimple on her cheek. She spoke, her voice deep and throaty, drawing him in as she stepped closer, her slender form featherlight in his arms as he led her in the dance…

Ed chuckled, bringing Kit back to the present. "It worked, though, didn't it?" he said. "When we left, her dance card was full. And that rat, Pinkerton, never got the chance to mark his name more than once."

Kit sobered, hating the thought of the baron anywhere near Sophie. "He still needs an heir," he said. "Your sister should be cautious."

"She will be. Sophie's a sensible girl, and besides, she's got Aunt Jess as her chaperone. Don't let the smile on her face fool you. That woman has eyes in the back of her head, and claws worthy of any dragon. It'd be a brave man who dared defy her."

"Dragon?" Kit laughed. "You are so very gallant, sir."

"You haven't been lashed by her tongue. Her words could cut diamonds. And, you'll be pleased to know, she doesn't like Pinkerton one iota." Ed grinned. "Liked you, though." Ed's smile faltered as he changed the subject. "How go things with your father?" Kit shrugged and Ed sighed. "He is stubborn. He truly prefers to see you here in Town, squandering your life, when you could be doing so much good?"

"But that would be trade." Kit grimaced as if the word tasted bad. "The son of an earl does not engage in trade."

"I'd call it more of a craft. It isn't as though you want to run a shop, is it? You want to build better mines, save lives."

Kit had had a friend whose father owned mines in Yorkshire. He'd been staying with them when a problem was reported and Peter had gone out to deal with it. He'd been in the tunnel when it caved in. Kit knew that, if the mines could be made more sound, many lives could be saved and Peter would not have died in vain. Kit's father, however, did not agree. To him, the only work for a gentleman was overseeing his family's estates. Anything else was beneath him and not worth considering.

He pushed his bitterness away. "Enough of that. We should be celebrating your skill at the tables. What's that? Three times in a week you've relined your pockets?"

"Aye. If I can keep it up for the next three months, I may come into my inheritance solvent."

Kit started to answer, then stopped when he heard the sound of a boot scraping the pavement behind him. He glanced over his shoulder and saw two burly men. Their clothes were coarse and ill-fitting, their shoes serviceable, their heads covered with close-fitting caps; not the kind of men one would normally see in this part of town at this hour. Kit tensed, every nerve and sinew ready for whatever came next. Beside him, he saw Ed stiffen too, his fingers tightening around his cane.

They took a few more steps and Kit willed the men behind him to cross the road and walk away. They didn't.

Ahead of them, the shadows moved and a hulking figure stepped into the middle of the pavement. He was followed by a smaller man. Unlike the others, the smaller man's silhouette was streamlined, and he carried himself like a gentleman.

Kit and Ed stopped. The men behind them stopped. Kit's pulse raced and his breaths were shallow from his tightened chest. His stomach flipped and his mouth felt dry.

The well-dressed silhouette stepped into the beam of a lonely street lamp. Kit's tension rose.

"Good evening," Baron Pinkerton said. He bared his teeth in a semblance of a smile. "I've been waiting for you." The big man behind him folded his arms, which somehow made him seem more menacing.

Kit exchanged a glance with Ed. "Why?" he asked, his tone nonchalant. "Do we owe you money? I don't recall it if I do. Ed?"

"All my debts have been settled," said Ed.

Pinkerton's face darkened. "Don't try to be clever. It doesn't become you."

"Now, see here—" began Ed.

"No. You see." Pinkerton glared at Ed, and Kit used the moment to alter his stance, relaxing his knees and hips, making himself more ready.

"I know what you did, Wilson," continued Pinkerton. "I am aware it was your idea." He turned to Kit, his eyes glittering like ice. "And you should be more careful in your choice of dancing partners. Regardless of how your friends encourage you."

From the corner of his eye, Kit saw Ed shift. He kept his own expression blank, though his mind raced. There was clearly more to Sophie Wilson's status as a wallflower than met the eye. However, discovering the full story could wait. "I am always exceedingly careful of my choice of partners, but I thank you for your concern."

Pinkerton's jaw clenched and a muscle jumped in his cheek. "The last man who didn't heed my advice found himself swimming in the Thames, with a broken nose and several cracked ribs."

Kit nodded. "Doubtless you warned him to look where he was walking." He glanced at Ed again, then smiled at Pinkerton. "We bid you a good evening, sir."

The baron's eyes narrowed and his lips thinned until they were little more than a line. Ed's shoulders went back. Kit felt energy surge through him, in readiness for what was surely coming. Two of them and four opponents were not necessarily bad odds, but three of these men were huge, and looked well used to no-holds-barred brawling. Win or lose, Kit had no doubt this was going to hurt.

For a moment, all was still. Nobody moved a muscle. Kit hardly felt his breath. The breeze died. Even the candle in the street lamp burned steady, with no flicker or sputter. Then, almost carelessly, Pinkerton raised his hand and crooked a finger.

One of the men behind him grabbed Kit's arm and swung him round, while the other snatched at Ed. Ed spun and threw a punch before his attacker could hit him. Kit's man was quicker. He slammed his fist into Kit's face. Kit's head snapped back and, for a second, he saw pinpricks of orange light while pain exploded across his cheek and around his eye. He pushed the pain away and hit back, catching the man in the stomach with two sharp jabs that made him double over. A quick cut to his chin snapped back his head, and he staggered, letting go of Kit.

Kit sprang away and stood, back to the building and fists raised, ready. Ed stood beside him. There was a soft, slicing sound as Ed withdrew the stiletto from within his cane and the man who had been advancing on them hesitated.

"Get them, you cowards!" Pinkerton's order came from some yards away. His men stood, watching Kit and Ed. Kit swallowed. If they rushed forward together, Ed and he would not be able to withstand them for long, sword or no sword. They needed an escape plan, and they needed it now.

"Ho, there!" shouted a voice from along the street. "I've summoned the watch." A boot heel rang, confident and loud against the pavement, followed by the tap of a cane. Pinkerton cursed as his men turned tail and ran, and then he, too, disappeared into the shadows.

Kit let out his breath, and his shoulders slumped in relief. Beside him, Ed lowered his sword.

The man who walked into the pool of light from the street lamp was tall and lean, still spry though in his late fifties. The cane he held seemed, at first glance, no more than a fashion accessory, and his limp was barely noticeable. But Kit knew better. He was aware of the arthritis that made the man's gait unsteady and sometimes caused him to stop, gasping in pain.

"Hello, Father," he said.

"I've been looking for you," answered the Earl of Markham. "I should have known to follow the sound of trouble. Come. My carriage is around the corner. I'll take you both home."

****

Sophie arrived home happier than she'd been for weeks. She'd danced every set, and only once been forced to stand up with Lord Pinkerton. It seemed where Mr. Thomas led, others followed.

Although, she had to admit, none had danced as divinely as he did. For such a tall, muscular man, he'd been light on his feet, and when he'd taken her into his arms for the waltz, she'd never wanted it to end. Even now, hours later, she could feel the warmth of his hands on her back as he whisked her around the room, the scent of him filling her senses and blocking out the rest of the world.

He hadn't asked any other ladies to dance. Instead, he'd joined Ed in the cardroom. Quite a few of those ladies had watched him leave, then glared at Sophie, as if it was her fault he didn't mark their cards. How their annoyance would turn to laughter if they knew he'd only asked her out of pity.

Yet he hadn't betrayed that fact by so much as a flicker of an eyelid. Anyone watching them wouldn't have had the slightest doubt that Mr. Thomas asked Miss Wilson to dance because he wanted to, nor would they have been uncertain that he found her charming and enjoyed her company.

In the morning, she'd scold Ed roundly for asking his friend to dance with her. But silently, she'd thank him for such a perfect partner.

She followed Aunt Jess into their home and gave the butler her coat and bonnet as Uncle Leo appeared in the hall.

"Sophie, a word, if you please."

"What, now?" Aunt Jess was horrified. "It's almost three—"

"I am aware of the time." Uncle Leo's words were clipped, curt. "This cannot wait."

Sophie frowned, wondering what she'd done. Not only had Uncle Leo come home from his club hours earlier than usual, it seemed he'd done so expressly to wait for her.

"Pish, posh," said Aunt Jess. "Nothing is so urgent

it cannot wait until a respectable hour. Unless..." She paled and her hands fluttered to her throat, "Ed?"

The question made Sophie's breath catch and her heart missed a beat. She willed her uncle not to answer the question, yet she wanted him to answer it quickly. She couldn't bear it if something happened to Ed.

Uncle Leo raised an eyebrow. "What on earth has Ed to say to anything?"

Relief rushed through Sophie, but only for an instant. If not Ed, why did her uncle wish to see her so urgently? Had he learned of her correspondence with Jem, the boy who helped with her experiments? Was he about to forbid her from her work? The thought made her shudder. *Please, don't let it be that. I can weather anything but that.*

Aunt Jess sighed. "Very well. Let's get this over so we may go to bed before dawn." She stepped toward the study.

"You may go to bed now," he said. "I wish to see Sophie."

"I'm her chaperone." Aunt Jess fixed him with her sternest look. "If Sophie deserves your censure, I need to hear it."

"I didn't say I was censuring her."

"Good. Then you won't mind if I come." Aunt Jess sailed into the study. Clearly defeated, he gestured that Sophie should follow.

"Ordinarily, I'd wait until after breakfast to speak to you," he said as he closed the door and motioned that she should sit. She took the chair next to Aunt Jess, in front of his desk. That he'd asked her to sit made her feel better for, surely, if she'd been in trouble, he would have had her remain standing. "But I have business which requires my attention, so must go out early, and I wanted to inform you as soon as possible." Idly, his fingers stroked the pattern on his desk.

"Inform me of what, Uncle?" Sophie's voice was tiny, betraying her anxiety. Beside her, Aunt Jess fixed her brother with her beadiest stare. Uncle Leo flinched and concentrated on the dying embers in his fireplace.

"It will not be news to you," he said, "that I am disappointed with your Season so far." He rocked back on his heels and clasped his hands behind his back. "I begin to believe I was sold a pup."

"Oh, no, Uncle. Why, tonight, I—"

He held up a hand to silence her. "I was persuaded to pay for this Season for you because your aunt assured me you'd find a husband who would bring your family about."

Sophie bristled. She didn't want to marry and certainly not in order to "bring her family about." She knew Uncle Leo saw it as her duty, but Ed didn't.

"Don't worry," he'd said. "I don't need you to pull me out of the gutter. And certainly Leo doesn't. He may not be as rich as Croesus, but he's not exactly poor, either."

"I'm not worried about his fortune," she replied. "It's yours that concerns me."

Ed shook his head. "In the first place, you've no need. I've land, and rents, and if push came to shove, I'm not above working for a living. It did our grandfather no harm. And secondly, d'you think I'd want you to marry into misery for me?"

"But, Uncle Leo…"

"Ignore him. I do."

Sophie grinned at the memory of her brother's

irreverence.

Uncle Leo swore at Aunt Jess, bringing Sophie back to the present. "I make no doubt she's doing her best," he said. "But six weeks in, and not one single offer?" He grinned. Sophie didn't find it comforting. "That is," he said, looking satisfied, "until tonight."

"Tonight?" Surely Mr. Thomas hadn't spoken to Uncle Leo already? They'd only danced twice. Was that enough time for a man to know his mind?

He *had* seemed a very definite sort of person. Decisive. And he hadn't danced with anyone but her. When he left the room, had he gone to ask permission? Her chest tightened in giddy anticipation, and that made her frown. She didn't wish to marry, she couldn't, not if she wanted to follow her dream. So why was she pleased that he'd offered?

"Who on earth was in such a confounded hurry that he came to you tonight?" Aunt Jess sniffed. "'Twas lucky he found you at home."

"I wasn't at home," retorted Uncle Leo in that way brothers only ever used with their sisters. "He sought me out at my club."

Was that why Kit had disappeared? Sophie felt the smile forming, and fought to keep her expression blank. She was flattered. Even though she knew she'd turn him down, that nothing could come of it, it was pleasing to know he'd asked.

"He asked my permission, which you should know I gladly gave. You may expect him to take you for a carriage ride at two tomorrow—er, today."

Sophie frowned. A carriage ride? He'd promised her a mare. Surely he hadn't forgotten?

"Very nice of him, I dare say," said Aunt Jess in a

judgement-is-reserved way. "Of whom do we speak? What are his prospects?"

"Did I not say? Lord Pinkerton, of course. And his prospects are more than good enough, so you need make no objection, Jess."

The room spun. Uncle Leo and Aunt Jess spoke, but Sophie didn't hear them. It was as if they were at the end of a long corridor, behind a closed door which muffled their voices. A whooshing noise pounded in her ear, in time with her heart.

Lord Pinkerton had offered for her. The thought made her feel sick. Her face was clammy, her throat feathery. This couldn't be happening. She could not, would not… She took a deep breath. Then another. A third.

The nausea passed. Finally, she trusted herself to speak. For speak she must, quickly and clearly, before it was too late. "No."

There was a moment of silence. Uncle Leo stared at her, shocked, although Aunt Jess seemed happier. Sophie sat, her back ramrod straight, her heart beating eighteen to the dozen.

Uncle Leo recovered his voice first. "No?"

"No."

"You are refusing his offer?"

"I am."

"Where there is one offer," said Aunt Jess, hurriedly, "there'll be others. I refused five before I said yes to my dear Robert."

"You had a large dowry, ma'am. Sophie does not." He looked smug.

A heavy ache began behind Sophie's breastbone. Did her wishes count for nothing?

Aunt Jess looked squarely at her brother. "I had a large dowry," she agreed. "I also had the taint of the shop, whereas Sophie is the daughter and sister of barons." Sophie closed her eyes and willed Uncle Leo to concede the argument, agree to tell Lord Pinkerton that she wouldn't have him.

"Barons or not, the fact remains Sophie has had no offers, save this one. One." He held up a finger to emphasize the point. "In six weeks. And besides," he continued, "Pinkerton doesn't want a dowry. He simply wants her."

"*She* doesn't want *him*." Aunt Jess refused to give up, though Sophie wondered how much she could do. Uncle Leo was her guardian. If he said she must marry Lord Pinkerton, it was difficult to know how Aunt Jess could force him to change his mind.

"I gave the man my blessing," he said, and a quiet sob escaped Sophie. He ignored her, though Aunt Jess reached out and patted her hand. "How would it be if I withdrew it now?"

"Nobody asked you to withdraw your blessing," Aunt Jess rubbed her fingers over the back of Sophie's hand, the movement bringing comfort. "You said you had no objection, and you don't. However, Sophie does. She has every right."

He glowered at his sister, his lips pursed as if they held back angry words. His cheeks were flushed, and his neck was red.

"Please, Uncle Leo," Sophie whispered.

He turned his attention to her. "You must marry. Pinkerton is wealthy, titled…"

"Odious," muttered Aunt Jess. Uncle Leo's color deepened.

"For pity's sake, woman! If you'd listen—"

"No! You listen." Aunt Jess sprang to her feet and moved in on him. He stepped back. The desk stopped his retreat. She jabbed her finger at him and he leaned away. "This is Sophie's life we're discussing," she said. "I won't stand by while you throw it away on a detestable little man like Josiah Pinkerton! He is…oily. I don't trust him. More, he's had three wives already, each one young and healthy on her wedding day, and worn beyond recognition in a few years."

Sophie clasped her hands together and bit her knuckle. *Please God, let Aunt Jess prevail.*

"You cannot think he killed them?" Uncle Leo's voice was a shocked whisper.

"Not in the way you're thinking," Aunt Jess agreed. "But 'twas being his bride that did for them."

"Fanciful nonsense."

The two of them glared at each other. Sophie watched them and prayed with all her might that Aunt Jess would be the victor. She couldn't marry Pinkerton. She just couldn't.

Uncle Leo sighed. "Very well," he said, and Aunt Jess grinned in triumph. Sophie breathed again. "But," he held up one finger, "Sophie must be betrothed before the Season ends. I won't have my money wasted on a failed endeavor."

Aunt Jess shook her head. "The Duchess of Altrincham's ball finishes the Season, and it's only ten days away."

"Then you have ten days." Uncle Leo smiled, smugly. "If Sophie has no suitable alternative offer by then, she *will* marry Pinkerton, and her sensibilities be damned!"

Chapter Three

Someone was pounding on Kit's skull. He felt every thump go through him, and he groaned. He didn't recall drinking to excess last night, yet he had a deep headache and there was a tightness around one eye and across his cheek. Gingerly, he touched his face, felt the bruise, and remembered the fight.

The pounding began again, and Kit realized it wasn't in his head. Someone was at his door, demanding entry. The light coming through the window was a murky gray, which told him it was early, too early for respectable people to be calling.

The banging stopped, replaced by voices. One was Beeston, Kit's man. He hoped the valet was telling whoever it was to call back at a sensible hour.

Kit's door opened and Beeston peered in. The man was already dressed, and impeccably as always. It made Kit wonder how early servants had to be up to do all that was expected of them before their masters arose. And, since Beeston never went to bed before Kit returned home in the evenings, when the heck did the man sleep?

"What's to do, Beeston?" he asked. His voice was raspy, his throat dry, and his mouth tasted like brandy that had sat in a glass for a day, mixed with onion-flavored linen. He grimaced and yawned, then continued, "What was that infernal racket?"

"It was me." Ed strode into the room and perched on

the edge of Kit's bed. "I need to talk to you. Matter of some urgency, I'm afraid."

Kit sighed, noting his friend was still in the clothes he'd worn last night. Either he hadn't been home, or something had happened there to prevent him going to bed. An image of Sophie flashed into Kit's mind, and he knew an instant of panic at the thought of anything happening to her. Then he tamped down the thought. She'd been at a ball with a chaperone and a carriage to take her home. Of course nothing had happened to her.

"Coffee, please, Beeston," he said. The valet left, closing the door behind him. Kit dragged his hand over his face. Sleep gritted his eyes, and the beginnings of a beard pricked his fingers. He yawned again. "Pass my clothes, Ed. I feel at a distinct disadvantage, discussing 'matters of some urgency' while I'm naked."

Ed waited while Kit pulled on his clothes and splashed water onto his face. It was cold and helped wake him completely. He pooled some of it in his hands and rubbed them over his hair. The cold against his scalp sharpened his senses, and the wetness tamed his hair into the style he preferred.

Beeston brought in a steaming jug of coffee and two cups. Ed poured drinks for them both.

"Right," said Kit after he had drunk his first cup of thick, strong coffee and poured himself a second. "I'm awake. So what is of such great urgency that it has you at my door at—" he checked his fob watch and groaned "—six o'clock in the morning?"

Ed swallowed. He opened his mouth, closed it again, swallowed once more. Whatever it was, it had completely overset him.

Kit sipped his coffee and tried to help. "Short of

lending you money, because I don't have it myself, I will do my best to help you. What on earth has you in such a stew?"

Ed took a deep breath and blurted, "I need you to offer for my sister."

Kit blinked. There were any number of things he might have expected Ed to say. That was not one of them. "Don't you think that's doing it rather brown?" he asked. "Dancing with her was one thing, and a very delightful experience. But marriage—"

Ed waved a hand dismissively. "I don't want you to marry her. Good Lord, that's the last thing any of us wants. What a disaster that would be!"

Perversely, Kit was offended by Ed's remark. A disaster? He pictured her now, her blue eyes bright with wit, her shining hair curling round her pretty cheeks, her curves... He shook his head to clear it. If Ed had any inkling of his thoughts, it certainly would be a disaster. He'd waste no time in blacking Kit's other eye before marching him down the aisle at the point of a gun.

Ed flopped back across Kit's bed, his despair evident. "She has to be betrothed to someone before the Duchess of Altrincham's ball, and I thought, well, you're acceptable..."

"Thank you very much." Was that what they called damning with faint praise?

"I mean acceptable to my uncle. You're the son of an earl. I know you don't rank quite as high as Pinkerton, being only the second son, but you're near enough to make no never mind."

"And I have no idea what you're raving about. In fact, I'm not altogether sure whether I'm being praised or insulted."

Ed sat up. "Sorry."

"Start at the beginning?"

Ed stood and paced the room. Kit wished he wouldn't. It was far too early, and he felt far too fragile for so much movement.

"When I got home," Ed said at last, "there was uproar. Uncle Leo was in a temper, slamming around in his study, Aunt Jess looked as though she could swing for him, and Sophie was sobbing her heart out."

A dozen likely scenarios went through Kit's head, none of them good. What had Pinkerton done to make her uncle expect, even demand, an offer? Rage boiled, filling his chest and tensing his jaw. If Pinkerton had harmed that girl in any way... He could see her, those beautiful eyes filled with tears, her cheeks pale, despair slumping her shoulders. Kit wanted to go and challenge the baron. Now. He wouldn't kill him—he didn't want to have to flee the country—but he could certainly teach the man a lesson he would not quickly forget, and make sure he left Miss Wilson—and every other innocent young lady—alone in the future.

Except...Kit didn't have the right. He wasn't her brother. If he went after the baron for a lady he scarcely knew, he wouldn't be defending her honor, he'd be destroying her reputation. If anyone called out Pinkerton, it must be Ed. All Kit could do was stand his second.

Ed, however, didn't seem angry with Pinkerton. His ire was directed solely at his uncle. "Can you believe it?" he asked. "The idiot gave his permission for that—that lothario to pay his addresses to her. Then told her she must accept him, whether she wished it or no!"

"What?" Kit couldn't believe it. Even if her guardian was not aware of how nasty Pinkerton was, surely he could not wish Sophie to marry against her will. He sat back and gave Ed his full attention as his friend told him of Sophie's plight, and her uncle's ultimatum.

"So, she has to have a fiancé by the end of the Season or be forced to marry Pinkerton."

Panic surged through Kit. He could see where this was going, and it wasn't good. "But I'm not in a position to marry anybody. I want to go to University, after which the work I wish to do will be unsteady, to say the least. I may not see any return on it for years. I cannot support a wife." He held a hand up to stall Ed's protest. "And don't say I can become betrothed to her and then not marry her. I am a gentleman, and a gentleman would never cry off."

"You wouldn't need to. Sophie would. Just as soon as she was sure Pinkerton had set his interest elsewhere."

"Meanwhile, should she meet the love of her life, she would be unable to accept his offer. Is that what you want?"

"Not likely to happen. Sophie doesn't want to marry anyone. She's far more interested—"

"No, Ed. I cannot. Good Lord, man, can you picture my father's reaction to such a thing? A broken engagement and all the gossip surrounding it would give him an apoplexy. He keeps threatening to cut me off as it is, without adding fuel to that particular fire."

"I can pay you. Two hundred pounds."

"No."

"Three hundred."

"I said no. I don't want your money. And I won't offer for your sister. I will, however, work with you, and her, to come up with a better solution."

"That would make you better than me. We sat up all

night and could come up with nothing."

"We'll think of something." He checked his watch again. "Is your sister at home to callers later? My father has summoned me for breakfast at ten, but I should be free to visit at about two. Mayhap we can think of something by then."

****

Kit's visit to his father was not a pleasant family reunion. He hadn't expected it to be. He knew all too well how it would go as he climbed the steps and thanked the footman who opened the door to him. Father would say he'd heard of some of his exploits. Kit would point out that his behavior was mild, and better than some, and Father would explode and say he didn't care about some, he cared about his son, and what Kit thought mild, the earl considered beyond the pale.

At which point Kit would say, "If I were at University, I wouldn't be on the town, so I'd be unable to embarrass you."

The earl would turn puce and tell him that a *gentleman* did not become an engineer. A *gentleman* did not work, nor did he wish to spend his time underground, studying coal mines. If Kit really wanted to do something other than idling about London, frittering his allowance away, he should come home and manage one of the estates.

"I can put you on one of the unentailed properties," the earl would say. "Do well, and I will deed it to you."

The prospect of poring over ledgers, working out the price of corn and whether the sheep would be profitable this year, filled him with dread. It was why he was in London, acting the rake. He'd thought his straitlaced father would be horrified by his behavior and agree to

University as the lesser of the two evils. But it had been three years now, and the earl had not budged. They simply revisited the same argument every time they met.

Which, thankfully, was not too often.

The earl sat at the table in the small dining room, tucking into a breakfast of ham and eggs, rolls and jam. As always, the table was laid for six, although Kit knew only he and his father would be sitting down. Along one wall was a large walnut sideboard laden with dishes, steaming teapots, coffee and chocolate pots, a plate of rolls, and pots of jams and preserves, each with its own silver spoon stamped with the Markham crest. A footman stood beside the sideboard, ready to serve.

"Come in, boy. Don't stand skulking in the doorway," said the earl, and he gestured with his knife that Kit should take his place at the table. Kit did so after helping himself to several slices of bacon, some scrambled eggs, a roll, and a dish of preserves. Might as well take full advantage of his father's kitchen.

The footman poured him a cup of coffee. Kit spread the pristine white napkin over his lap.

"Thank you, Johnston. That will be all," Father said.

The footman bowed and left, and Father studied Kit for several seconds. Kit pretended not to notice, trying to seem nonchalant as he ate a piece of bacon.

"You don't look too much the worse for wear this morning, considering you were out all night," said Father, eventually.

"I was out, but I didn't have much to drink."

"Enough that you managed to get yourself embroiled in a common street brawl."

"It wasn't a brawl, Father. We were set upon, and we defended ourselves. Although," he forced a smile to his face, hiding the bitter taste the next words left on his tongue, "I thank you for your intervention. There were more of them than of us, and they were rather large."

Father broke his roll in two and slathered half in jam. "That eye's going to be a beauty. I hope the pig-widgeon who gave it to you looks as bad."

"He does."

"Good." The earl took a mouthful of bread and chewed it thoughtfully. "How have you fared this quarter?"

"Well, thank you." Kit never offered his father too much information about his life. He had learned at an early age that it gave the earl more targets for criticism. Besides, if it was bad enough, his father would learn of it without Kit telling him.

"Have you had enough wildness now?" The earl took another bite of the roll.

Kit smiled. "I was never wild, Father."

"That rather depends on who you ask."

"I do not bring shame on the family name, I'm still received in the best houses, and doting mamas don't hide their darling daughters as I approach."

"They won't. You're the son of an earl. Even the worst behavior can be tolerated. Not that that's an excuse for behaving badly. You are a gentleman, and you should behave like one."

Kit opened his mouth to speak, although he didn't know what he was about to say. His father held up a hand to silence him.

"And don't tell me your behavior would be improved by sending you to University. You don't need to go to University. You need to come home and take your place beside me and your brother."

"I'm not—"

"Managing an estate is in your blood, Christopher James Thomas. It's what you were born to, and it's high time you learned the whys and wherefores of it."

Kit gritted his teeth. The same argument, repeated like the refrains of a music hall song.

"Very little is asked of you, young man. You're privileged and comfortable, and in return you're simply required to do three things: help us maintain the family properties, marry a good woman who will give you fine children, and keep the family name clear of scandal."

"There is no scandal." Kit struggled to keep his voice even. If he lost his temper, he'd lose the battle.

"There will be if you take up a trade." The earl had raised his voice now.

"Engineering is not a trade. It's a craft." Kit echoed Ed's words of last night. "And I'll be helping to make life better for hundreds of men."

"It's not your place to do that. You need to do your duty to your family. To me!" Father's face was red, his eyes hard. He blew out a deep breath, calming himself. "All I ask is a little respect from my son," he said, more quietly.

Kit sighed. "I do respect you, sir. But—"

"In which case, you will come home, marry, and manage one of my estates!"

Marry? That was a new dimension to the demand. Kit studied his father, suddenly wary.

"A gentleman has a duty to his bloodline, to marry and produce heirs."

"My brother will do that. He's next in line."

"You both need to do it." The earl took another deep breath, a sure sign that Kit would not like what came

35

next. "I thought to give you the Martlets estate. It marches alongside Jacob Foster's land. His only child, Prudence, is set to inherit everything. If you marry her, the two estates could come together."

"Prudence Foster?" Kit was aghast. "She's a little girl." She was also plain, with stringy hair that was neither brown nor blonde, and serious gray eyes that seemed to bore through him.

"She's ten and eight this year," his father corrected him. "Marry her, and it would do both families a favor. I'd see you settled, and Foster would be spared the trouble of a Season for her."

"The cost of one, you mean," muttered Kit. Jacob Foster hated spending money when he didn't have to.

"Christopher," his father pleaded. "I urge you to give the matter some thought. I need to leave town on business now, but I'll be back for Hetty Altrincham's ball. You can let me know then."

There was no way on God's green earth that Kit would consent to marry Prudence Foster. The thought of being shackled to a woman he didn't love and tied to a greedy, grasping man like Jacob Foster was abhorrent. He'd take holy orders first. Why, he'd sooner marry anyone else than…

He stopped, his fork halfway to his mouth. Perhaps there was a way out of this. He could keep his father at bay and help a friend at the same time.

"I cannot offer for Prudence Foster," he said. To him, his voice sounded as if it came from far away. His throat was dry, and his palms were suddenly clammy. He could scarcely form the words. "I—have an—an understanding—with a young lady." He swallowed twice. The lump in his throat ached. He hated lying to his father almost as much as he hated the idea of Sophie Wilson's reputation being tarnished by jilting him.

Father stared at him. "Do I know her?"

"Hamsey's sister."

"Ah. Your school friend." Father nodded, then smiled. It wasn't something he did often in Kit's presence, and it unnerved his son to see it now. "Her father was a good man, though her mother came from trade, I believe? Still, she comported herself well enough, and I've heard nothing bad about the girl. When do you announce it?"

Not until it's absolutely necessary. "We—she—not yet."

"Making you wait, is she?" Father chuckled. "I like the sound of her. She'll make a good mistress for Martlets."

Kit frowned. Would this argument never end? "I won't be going to Martlets."

"You could be right. Be damned awkward if Foster takes offense. But there are other—"

"No, Father. I will not be managing any of the estates."

"Hah! You needn't think you're living the life of an idle man-about-town on my blunt, and there's no way you can study engineering with a wife to support." The older man's eyes darkened and a knowing look came over his face. "So that's it. You thought I'd settle something on you and you'd be able to afford to go to University."

"I thought no such—"

"Think again, boy! There'll be no settlement until you come home and take your place."

"I asked for none, sir." Anger pounded through Kit.

How dare his father think him so dishonest? A twinge of guilt made him wince. He hadn't plotted to bilk the earl of money, but he had certainly deceived him.

"Good, because you're getting none. In fact…" The earl threw down his napkin and stood, hands pressed against the table so he could lean toward his son in his most intimidating manner. "You're not getting another penny from me until you learn obedience. No settlement, no allowance, nothing!" And with that, he stalked from the room, leaving Kit shocked and speechless at the table.

****

It was almost two o'clock. The morning room was crowded with visitors, and the air rang with the rattle of cups against saucers, the trilling laughter of ladies, and the deep tones of men's voices. Sophie sat, playing hostess to her most successful At Home for weeks. Every gentleman she'd danced with last night, bar one, had called, bringing her enough flowers to stock every stall in Covent Garden. Beside her, Archie Hammond sat spouting nonsense that made her smile. He would never be a great wit, but he was pleasant company. More importantly, by taking the seat next to her on the two-seat sofa, he'd prevented Lord Pinkerton from doing so. Sophie had no wish to converse with *him*.

He hovered nearby, listening to their conversation and scowling. Archie threw him a wary glance and Lord Pinkerton gestured with his eyes, signaling that Archie should move, if not leave altogether.

Sophie was not having that. How dare he dictate the actions of her guests? She put her hand on Archie's sleeve and said, "Fascinating, Mr. Hammond. Do tell me what happened next," then laughed at the punchline of his anecdote.

"I say, Miss Wilson," he said, his face glowing an endearing pink, "do you go to Mrs. Russell's musicale this evening?"

"Indeed we do, sir." Mrs. Russell had procured the services of Giuditta Pasta, a soprano who had come to London on a tide of adulation following successful performances in Milan and Paris. It was a coup for the Russells, and an event not to be missed.

"May I sit beside you there?" asked Archie. "We can enjoy the music together and then take supper."

"I would be delighted."

Lord Pinkerton put his cup down with more force than was necessary, then strode from the room. At the door, he spoke to someone who was coming in. It did not look like a friendly exchange of words.

The next instant all thoughts of Lord Pinkerton, Archie Hammond, and musicales flew from Sophie's mind as Kit Thomas appeared.

He had a bruise around his eye that shone navy blue and violet. Since Ed had sported similar bruises this morning, they must have been out together. She hoped it was one of those boxing salons Ed was so enamored of, and not a proper fight, although that eye looked rather more sore than sparring should have left it. She sighed, wondering at the talent gentlemen had for getting into scrapes.

Although, she had to admit, the black eye gave Kit an air of danger that was—enticing. Together with his tousled hair and his tall imposing frame, the bruising suggested a roguishness that should have repelled her but which she found compelling. He wore a coat in navy superfine that clung to his broad shoulders, and pantaloons tucked into gleaming hessians that emphasized the length of his legs and the power of his thighs, something else Sophie should not be noticing about him. Her cheeks burned, and she was glad nobody else could know her thoughts.

His gaze raked the room until he found her. Several seconds passed, their eyes locked. The rest of the room was lost, the people fuzzy and out of focus, like the figures in one of Mr. Turner's landscapes. Archie Hammond spoke, but Sophie had no idea what he said.

Mr. Thomas smiled and a dimple formed on his cheek, making him seem mischievous and charming at the same time. The look in his eyes made her wonder if, perhaps, he could read her mind after all. Her face glowed hotter.

Aunt Jess greeted him. He shifted his focus from Sophie, and the moment was gone. But oh! what a moment it had been. Shocked at her own reaction, she pushed the memory of his gaze and the feelings it evoked in her to the back of her mind. She would ponder it later, when she was alone and had time to savor it properly.

Which was silly. He was no more than her brother's friend, who'd paid court to her because Ed asked him to do so. It was all she wished him to be.

Mr. Hammond stood, startling her. "Until tonight, Miss Wilson," he said. He bowed and took his leave. Before he'd left the room, Mr. Thomas occupied his seat.

"Tonight?" he asked.

Sophie smiled, in a way she hoped seemed nonchalant. "At Mrs. Russell's musicale."

"Hammond is accompanying you?" His voice was even, disinterested, but his eyes flashed with something she thought might be jealousy. She was shocked to realize she certainly hoped so.

Chapter Four

Kit tamped down his disappointment. He should be glad Hammond was showing an interest in Sophie. Hadn't that been Ed's plan? Kit should be happy that what he'd thought a harebrained scheme appeared to have worked. He should not be shooting invisible daggers into Archie's back. After all, what did it matter to him who would be at the musicale with her? Kit had had no intention of asking her. He hadn't even thought to attend. So why did the thought of Sophie sharing a program with Archie make his heart leaden in his chest?

Archie Hammond wasn't the only man showing an interest, he realized after a cursory glance around the room. In the crowd were some very eligible gentlemen, including a viscount and the heir to an earldom. In fact, Kit thought with a jolt, he was probably the worst catch here.

His heart grew heavier, and something solid stuck in his throat. For the first time in his life, Kit felt inadequate, and it hit him like a spray of cold water, shocking a gasp from him, which he covered by clearing his throat.

"Your eye looks painful, sir," she said pleasantly. Involuntarily, he raised his fingers to touch the bruise, then stopped himself and rested his hand on his knee.

"I—tripped. Hit my head. It was dark. The floorboards were uneven." *Shut up, Kit. You protest too much.*

Sophie nodded, sagely. "You gentlemen are certainly clumsy today. My brother sports a bruise on his cheek, too. He fell against the garderobe in his dressing room. Apparently." Her smile never wavered, but her eyes hardened. Kit glanced away and hoped his face was not as red as it felt.

"The sunshine looks lovely this morning, don't you think?" she asked, eyes wide with mock innocence, then she dropped her voice to a whisper. "Ed says you refused to go along with his plan. I thank you—"

"About that—" he said at the same time as she thanked him. Both stopped talking and stared at the other. Her smile wavered for an instant, then flicked back into place, but it could not conceal the anxiety in her eyes.

They really were the most beautiful eyes. From a distance, they looked a solid blue, bright as a summer's day. Up close, however, he could see flecks in them, some the color of the sky at midnight, others silver like stars. They drew him in, made him want things he knew he could not have.

Now, they were fixed on him. Suddenly, his cravat felt too tight and it was all he could do not to insert his fingers behind it. A bead of sweat trickled down his spine, making him shudder. His thighs tingled, and he hardened behind the fall of his pantaloons. He crossed his legs, hoping to hide it from her, and everyone else.

Good grief! What was happening to him? He was never like this! Even around the most alluring of females Kit had always remained aloof. Now, here he was, acting like a moon-sick schoolboy, and over Ed's sister, no less! If there was one rule Kit knew better than to break, it was the rule that said a chap's sister was out of bounds. If Ed had the slightest idea of what Kit was thinking, he'd gut him.

He took a deep breath and willed his erection to subside. Pain shot from his groin to his stomach, and he tried not to wince.

Sophie looked suspicious. "What do you mean, 'about that'?" she asked.

What had they been talking about? Oh, yes. Ed's plan. "We should talk," he said. His voice was gruff, and he cleared his throat.

"All right," she answered after a moment's thought. "When and where?"

"When we ride later?"

She nodded.

"I'll call for you at a quarter to five." He stood and bowed. The sooner he left the room, and her tantalizing presence, the better. Even though his body seemed to be back under control, his desire for her no longer evident to all and sundry, walking was still painful, and probably would be for some time.

He reached the hallway as Ed came downstairs. "Kit! Jenson said you were here." He looked and sounded hopeful.

"Just paying my respects to the ladies."

Ed's face fell. "You haven't changed your mind, then?"

Kit looked around for eavesdroppers. Two footmen stood, waiting to hand callers their hats and coats. "Walk with me." He moved to the front door. Ed followed, his mood lifted.

Outside, Kit turned to his friend. "If I offer for her, it will be as a last resort, after all other avenues have been closed."

Ed beamed. "Of course."

"I mean it. I'll court your sister, take her out driving, dance with her, do the pretty. But I will only offer for her if there's no alternative."

"Understood." Ed studied Kit for a moment. "What changed your mind?"

Kit's smile was rueful. "Your sister isn't the only one in need of a false betrothal. I spoke with my father this morning." He grimaced. "He's found me a bride."

Ed's eyes widened. "Oh, Lord!"

"When I refused her, he cut me off."

"The offer is still open. Will two hundred pounds be enough?"

Kit looked away, ashamed. The very thought of taking money from a friend was humiliating. "I'm hoping my father will relent before my bills become due."

"If he doesn't?"

He didn't want to contemplate that, but Father could be stubborn when he wanted something, and he wanted Foster's land. Kit could not be certain the earl would back down before his son was forced to flee town and rusticate. That humiliation made the shame of accepting Ed's money pale into insignificance.

"I accept your offer," he said. "As a *loan*. Then I can…" Kit stopped and held up a hand. "Did you hear that?"

Ed raised his head in a listening pose. "Hear what?"

A low moan sounded from the alleyway that led to the rear gardens of Hamsey House. Kit clenched his fist around his cane, ready to defend himself against ambush, and headed into the alley. Ed drew his sword from his stick and followed.

The alley was narrow, the tall buildings either side blocking the sun. It took a moment for Kit's eyes to adjust to the darkness. He made out silhouettes of boxes and barrels, the detritus of a busy household. And, in the middle of the path, a body, curled up into a ball. With a cursory glance at the boxes and barrels to search for any attacker who might be waiting there, Kit knelt over the injured man.

"It's Archie Hammond," he said.

"I'll fetch help." Ed started back to the street.

"Be discreet. Don't alarm your aunt or your sister."

Ed nodded. "They shan't know of it."

While Ed was gone, Kit checked Hammond over. From its awkward angle, he thought he had a broken arm, and the way he cradled his hand led Kit to believe some of his fingers were broken, too. He touched Hammond's side, and the cry left no doubt of cracked ribs. His eyes were swollen and blacking, his lip split, his breathing labored. He tried to move and moaned at the pain.

"Careful, Archie," Kit soothed. "Help is coming."

"Pinkerton," Archie whispered. "His men…" Archie struggled to take another breath.

White hot rage swirled through Kit. It was one thing for Pinkerton to take on Kit and Ed. They had enough town bronze to know how to take care of themselves, and besides, there'd been two of them. But Archie Hammond was diffident and scholarly. He could no more stand up to a bully like Pinkerton than he could fly to the moon.

"He…wants…"

"Don't talk," Kit said, keeping his voice low.

Archie grabbed at Kit's coat and cried at the pain in his fingers. "Miss Wil…Miss Wilson. He said…he…"

Kit's jaw was so tightly clenched, he heard his teeth grind. "It's all right, Archie. I'll make sure she's safe. You leave Pinkerton to me."

"Safe." Archie exhaled on the word and slumped, unconscious. Which was probably a blessing for him.

When Kit got through with Pinkerton...

Ed came through the rear gate, followed by two men carrying a trestle. "I've ordered the carriage," he said. "And sent for the doctor. Let's get him home." He frowned at Kit. "You look murderous."

Kit felt murderous. He stood and let the servants lift the injured man carefully onto the trestle.

"Lord, he's a mess," whispered Ed. "What do you think? Footpads? They don't usually chance their arm in this area, but..."

"Not footpads." Kit took a deep breath, forcing the anger down. "Let's get him home. Then you and I have someone we need to visit."

They spent the next two hours looking for Pinkerton. He wasn't at his club, nor at Tattersalls in Hyde Park Corner. Next they visited his family home in Upper Wimpole Street, an imposing building on the end of a terrace, with white marble steps leading to an imposing black door. The servant who opened the door informed them haughtily that his lordship was out and not expected back before dinner. He closed the door in their faces without offering to take their calling cards.

"I don't think much of the caliber of his staff," muttered Ed. He turned and looked up and down the street, as if inspiration would leap out at him from a neighbor's door.

"They match the caliber of the master," answered Kit. The hot temper that had sent him racing to find

Archie's attacker had cooled and was now a ball of ice inside him. If anything, this cold rage was more dangerous, because it made him more determined.

They had taken Archie home and waited with him until the doctor arrived. It worried Kit that Hammond hadn't regained consciousness at all during the ride, or when they maneuvered him up the stairs to his apartment and laid him in the bed.

The doctor had been grave. As well as a broken arm, a broken leg, and several broken fingers and ribs, there was, he said, a severe blow to the head and possible internal bleeding. The next twenty-four hours would tell.

Had Pinkerton been within reach then, Kit might well have killed him. Now, two hours later, he just wanted to teach him a lesson he would not soon forget.

Alas, it seemed retribution was to be denied today. He had started down Pinkerton's steps to the street when he heard, "Psst!"—a sound like steam escaping through a pressure valve. To the side of the house, out of sight of the door, a man beckoned to them. Kit and Ed exchanged glances, then followed him. He was dressed like a groom in nondescript homespun, and he smelled of horse sweat and saddle soap.

"You looking for his lordship?" he asked. "Owe you money, does he?"

"Something like that," Kit replied, warily. "Why? Do you know where we can find him?"

"Might do." He scratched the palm of his hand, as if he had an itch.

A guinea later, he explained this was not Pinkerton's only house. "He has a cottage in Chelsea. Goes there when he wants to enjoy himself in private, if you catch my meaning. Keeps it well hidden. Even his butler don't know about it."

"Yet you do." Kit's eyes narrowed suspiciously.

"Who do you think drives his coach out there? Got to have someone take care of the horses, hasn't he? Don't want to be doing it himself when he's got a reason to be private, and he can't leave them standing all night, can he?" He grinned. "Can't leave anyone standing all night." He chuckled at his own wit.

A second guinea secured the location and directions, and a short time later Kit and Ed stood outside a dilapidated and, to all purposes, abandoned cottage. Its roof sagged with age, pushing the upstairs wall out into a marked bow shape, the woodwork needed painting, there were gaps in the pantiles on the walls, and the garden was overgrown and untidy. The windows were black with grime. There was no sign of life.

"Cherry Tree Cottage," Kit read on a withered sign hanging loosely on the wall. "This is certainly it." He eyed the gate with trepidation. Both it and the wall looked in imminent danger of disintegrating into a pile of rubble.

"Not exactly the most romantic place for a tryst," said Ed. He reached out to open the gate, thought better of it and looked around. A few yards farther on, there was a gap in the wall where the stones had collapsed. He stepped over them and into the garden.

"He's not likely to be disturbed here, is he?" Kit followed his friend over the rubble and kicked his way through a tangle of convolvulus that snaked across the grass and up the trellis on the side of the house. The flowers that were meant to fill that trellis were long gone, strangled by the insidious weed. "Look at the place. My father would have a conniption if so much as his potting shed was neglected in this way."

The door was unlocked. The cottage was far out of the way, hidden in the trees on a barely used lane. Nobody was likely to find it unless they knew exactly where to look, so there was no need to secure it against thieves and burglars.

"Shall we?" Ed held the door open. Both men ducked to avoid hitting their heads on the lintel.

The cottage was small and dark and cramped. A layer of dust coated the table in the kitchen, and the hearth was black with soot. Black stains covered the walls where the fire had smoked. This was not a house where servants worked.

Upstairs there were two rooms, each furnished with a bed, a dresser, and an age-spotted cheval mirror. The rooms smelled musty, as if they hadn't been aired in a long time. The whole house had the damp smell of abandonment.

"He isn't here," said Ed. "So where do we look for him now?"

Kit pulled his watch from his fob pocket. "I'm afraid he'll have to keep. I'm promised to your sister in half an hour, and I still have to go home and change."

Ed grinned. "We'd better get you back to town, then. I, for one, do not want to incur the wrath of Sophie, thank you very much. Pinkerton can wait."

****

Sophie was ready and waiting at the appointed hour. She wore a riding habit in dark blue, with silver frogging down the front and silver epaulettes, mimicking the military look, as was the fashion now. Her matching blue hat was bound with a silver ribbon, the ends dangling at the back.

Kit arrived a minute before the due time. She smiled her approval at him. "I do value punctuality," she said.

"As do I." His deep, rich voice seemed to fill the room, and his smile made the air shimmer. Which was ridiculous, she scolded herself. No man's smile could do that. If the air shimmered, it was because the room was warm. She cleared her throat and pushed the nonsense from her head.

Outside in the street were two horses, a tall, sturdy bay gelding for Kit, which tossed its head and moved its feet as if impatient to be gone, and the gray he'd mentioned last night. Dove was as peaceful-looking as her name suggested, and she waited, quiet and still, for her rider to mount. The only movement she made was the gentle swish of her white tail. "Oh," said Sophie, delighted. "She is lovely!"

"She is quiet," he answered. "She won't be skittish in traffic."

Sophie hoped that wasn't a euphemism for sluggishness. While she knew she could not gallop through the park—it was frowned upon at any time but would be completely impossible at this, the fashionable hour—she also did not wish to plod along at a pace that might easily be overtaken by those on a gentle stroll.

"The park should be crowded at this time." Kit smiled as he helped her mount the little mare. "All the better to be seen together."

"Mr. Thomas, I—"

"Kit."

"I beg your pardon?"

"My name. It's Kit." She looked a little nonplussed. He grinned. "I thought we might be less formal, at least in private."

She glanced back at his groom, who rode behind them on a chestnut. "We are not in private."

"John can be remarkably deaf."

Sophie was less certain of that. Bad enough she felt forced to take part in this ridiculous charade. She didn't want to find it common knowledge throughout the servant's halls of Mayfair, too.

They reached the gates of Hyde Park and turned inside. The paths were crowded with well-dressed people, some promenading, some on horseback, most in open carriages weaving between each other, stopping so the passengers could exchange pleasantries. Couples strolled across the grass toward the river, and children played.

They rode along the paths for a while. Then, when she was certain they were free of eavesdroppers, Sophie addressed the main topic between them.

"Ed means well," she said. "I'm not altogether certain all his ideas are well thought out."

"Sometimes they need refining."

"Please tell me we're not going to announce a betrothal?"

Kid smiled and nodded at the driver of a carriage coming in the other direction, then saluted a couple of gentlemen as they passed on horseback. "Not unless it becomes absolutely necessary," he said.

Sophie stared at him in disbelief. "You're not actually considering…?"

"Smile. People are watching."

She glanced around and saw people trying to seem disinterested as they watched every move she and Kit made. Her heart sank. "By dinnertime, everyone in Town will be talking about us."

"Yes."

"Saying you're courting me."

"Yes."

"Oh, my." She struggled to catch her breath.

Kit laughed. "Should I feel insulted?"

Sophie felt her cheeks heating. "I'm sorry. I didn't mean—" Desperate to change the course of the conversation, she latched on to what he had said moments before. "You said Ed's ideas occasionally need refining. How exactly do you intend to refine this one?"

Quietly and as quickly as interruptions from passing friends and acquaintances would allow, Kit told her his version of the plan.

"If your uncle sees me—and others—showing an interest in you, it should make him think again about forcing the match with Pinkerton," he explained. "It would be precipitous of him to insist you marry the man if there are other possibilities."

"And if he doesn't change his mind?"

Kit grimaced. "Then a betrothal may become absolutely necessary."

A tingle traveled up her spine. She could not have explained it if she tried and, to be honest, she wasn't sure she wanted to examine it too closely. "But you don't want to marry me." She said it to remind herself, as much as to state the facts.

He hesitated, and Sophie bit her tongue. Had he interpreted her words as something she'd never intended?

Did he think she tried to trap him? She opened her mouth to clarify her statement, but he spoke first.

"You are a beautiful young lady, and if I were in the market for a wife, you are exactly the sort of person I'd be looking for, but…"

"You are not in the market?"

He gave her a lopsided grin that made the hairs on the nape of her neck stand to attention. That tingle traveled down her spine again. What was it about this man that the merest glance could affect her so? She had ridden with more eligible gentlemen, men who were more handsome, taller, more eager…

Perhaps that was it. He wasn't in the least bit eager to court her. This was not a man who would drag her away from her laboratory and require her to replace experiments with children, dinner parties, and embroidery.

Not only would he pose no danger to her plans, he was willing to help make sure her uncle and Lord Pinkerton did not do so either. Mayhap, Ed's silly plan had some merit after all.

"I'm glad you're not in the market," she told him, "because I'm not, either."

Kit raised an eyebrow. "You're not?"

"The last thing I want is a husband." She gave an exaggerated shudder to emphasize her point. He looked taken aback, and she felt compelled to explain. "Eventually, I suppose I shall marry, but for now, I have plans which don't fit with the picture of a wife most men hold in their heart—heads." She amended the word quickly, wondering why her tongue had formed the word "heart." She was certain her brain had intended to say "head."

"Tell me about them," he encouraged. She blushed. "I would truly like to know," he continued. His voice and the look in his eyes were sincere.

Sophie thought for a moment, wondering how much

to confide in him. The only people who knew her secret were Ed and Jem. She worried that if too many people learned of it, the news would get back to Uncle Leo and Aunt Jess. Jess would be appalled, believing, as she said, that "gentlemen do not find blue-stockings attractive." Then Sophie would be obliged to tell her aunt that she preferred study to gentlemen, and that would break the older woman's heart. She had been so kind, so supportive of Sophie, a buffer between her and her uncle, and the last thing Sophie wanted was to hurt her. She'd hoped to get through the Season without an offer and be able to go back to the country, leaving Aunt Jess none the wiser that her "failure" was what Sophie had wanted all along.

As for Uncle Leo, he, too, would be appalled, but for quite different reasons. Like many men of his generation—and younger—Leo believed a woman should accept her place and not try to emulate men. They believed women's minds were not equipped for science and study, and the sooner the silly chits accepted that, the better. Uncle Leo would probably see it as his duty to marry Sophie off as quickly as he could, so her husband could start to train her unnatural thoughts out of her.

How would Kit feel about her secret? On the one hand, he was friends with Ed, who'd accepted it and even helped her. But then, unlike Ed, Kit was not an indulgent big brother. For all she knew, he might have very definite views on the subject, views that did not match hers.

He sighed now, presumably at her silence. "What if I tell you my dream first?" he asked. He nodded at another acquaintance and waited until the rider had exchanged pleasantries and moved on before continuing. "My plans don't include being a gentleman of leisure, nor managing one of my father's estates."

Was that a trace of bitterness in his voice? He smiled, and his face softened. He was so handsome when he did that! Sophie's heart did a funny flip, and her breasts tingled, as if her nipples chafed against her shift. A strange heavy ache began between her legs. She clenched her thighs, making the mare sidestep, clearly uncertain what her rider wanted of her. Sophie leaned forward and stroked the animal's neck.

"I hope to go to University and study engineering," he continued. "It's my ambition to make mining a safer occupation."

That was not what she'd expected him to say. "Mining?" The word came out on an astonished squeak.

"Mining's a very dangerous industry," he answered, defensively. "The men go down each day, knowing they may not return. There are so many hazards—the mine shafts may collapse, trapping them, and there are gases which poison them, or even explode. Although that last danger has been significantly reduced recently, thanks to the work of both Sir Humphry Davy and George Stephenson. They've been developing new types of lamps which won't ignite the fire-damp."

"I've heard of Sir Humphry Davy," she said after a moment, because she felt she ought to say something.

"And you'll hear more of Stephenson," he predicted. "The man's an engineering genius, especially when you consider he's uneducated and completely self-taught."

"Does that hamper him?" An uneducated man was likely to have come from a poor background, and she could well imagine what those of better birth might say. They'd probably be as appalled at the idea of him taking a place in their world as they would be at her doing so.

"Unfortunately, yes. Some people are very narrow-sighted."

Interesting. Kit seemed to accept Mr. Stephenson's right to work in his chosen field, despite his lowly birth. Perhaps he wouldn't see her sex as a hindrance either?

"I'd like to work on making the mineshafts safer," he said, "both by making them less likely to collapse and by venting them to reduce the poisonous gases." He gave a wry smile. "I'm sorry. I tend to get carried away when I speak of it."

"It's your passion." For a moment, Sophie wondered what it would be like to cause that much passion in this man. She imagined him reaching for her hand and holding it, coming closer, until his lips were scant inches from hers. The scent of him seemed to weave around her, clean and fresh and enticing. His lips would brush hers, leaving the taste of him behind, warm and manly, something she would remember always. His hand would start at her waist, then travel over her body in a soft caress, leaving a trail of flame where his fingers touched her. Flames that would lick her skin, soft and delicious, over her ribs, her stomach, the soft curve of her breasts, the nipples that even now ached...

Sophie caught her breath, horrified. What was wrong with her? Since when had she become such a wanton? If her mother knew her thoughts, she would turn in her grave.

"Aye. It is," he said.

What is? What were they talking about? Oh, yes. His passion. He had confided his secret dreams. Dreams that had nothing to do with kissing Sophie, or stroking her skin. She swallowed.

"You say you don't want a husband," he said. "So

what *is* your future?"

The future. A topic that should be much safer than wondering about his kiss but which made her nerves stand on end. She chewed her bottom lip and concentrated on her hands in her lap, her fists clenched so tightly the silver gloves were stretched across her knuckles.

"I promise, what you say to me will go no further."

She relaxed her fingers and took a deep breath. "My future," she said.

Kit waited patiently for her to go on. Did he know an interruption might rob her of the courage she tried to build?

"Wheat," she told him, at last. "I believe that by blending different varieties, we can increase the yield per stalk, improving the harvest and ensuring nobody ever has to hunger again."

Would he laugh at her? The thought pained her. *Let him not mock me. Please.*

"Have you been successful?" he asked. Wary, Sophie looked at him. His eyes held genuine interest.

"It depends what you call successful," she answered. "The seeds we worked on last year did have slightly more yield than the average, but that was in the laboratory, in artificial conditions. I'd like the increase to be significantly higher, and I'd like to be able to replicate it in the fields, but it's not easy. If my uncle discovered my experimentation, he would forbid it, but so many people need... It's just that so much suffering could be ended by success in this. Last year, when the crops failed, so many starved. If the wheat that survived had yielded more..."

"More people could have been fed. It sounds a very

valuable use of your time."

Could this man be any more wonderful? Without thinking, she reached out and touched his arm. Even through her gloves and his coat, the warmth of him seemed to flow into her fingers, and a soft, delicious ache built in her chest. It was as if his very essence seeped into her. Off balance, she withdrew her hand and looked away from him.

They were on a quieter path now, and fewer people surrounded them. Sunlight dappled through the trees, making dizzying patterns on the ground and coating the lake a soft gold. Where the trees ended, the grass was bright green, dotted here and there with yellow buttercups and tiny white daisies. A small group of children sat with their nurse, making daisy chains. Sophie smiled, remembering doing that when she was a child, as well as blowing the seeds from dandelion clocks, and pulling the petals from flowers to determine if "he" loved her, or loved her not. She wondered what the flowers would tell her if the "he" was Kit. Might she have to cheat to get the answer she wanted?

Which was, of course, that he loved her not, she told herself, firmly. Hadn't they both just admitted they wanted only a sham courtship? What was she thinking? Pulling petals from daisies, indeed!

She looked away from the children and feigned interest in the park and all its busyness.

"What do you think?" asked Kit, startling her. He glanced around the park. "Do you think enough gossips have seen us together? Shall I take you home?"

She smiled and nodded, determined not to let him see her disappointment.

They turned and rode out of the park, headed for her

uncle's house.

****

When Kit returned to his apartment after taking Sophie home, he found Ed waiting for him.

"Did she agree to my plan?" he asked, as he poured himself a rummer of brandy.

"Help yourself," Kit said, and Ed chuckled sheepishly. "And yes, she did."

"Good-oh." Ed swallowed half his brandy. "So what do we do this evening? Look for Pinkerton?"

Kit shook his head. "No need. I know exactly where he will be. Shilling to a guinea he expects to take Archie Hammond's place beside your sister at Mrs. Russell's musicale."

"Lord!" Ed rubbed his hand across his face. "Sophie doesn't know about Archie—you didn't tell her? Good. But it does mean she won't be prepared for Pinkerton. What do we do?"

"*You* do nothing. In fact, unless you have a burning desire to hear Senora Pasta sing, I suggest you give the Russells' musicale a wide berth. Go to the club, play whist, and wait for me."

"Why? Where will you be?"

Kit gave his friend a mischievous grin. "Sitting beside your sister, of course. Pressing my suit, and annoying the living daylights out of Josiah Pinkerton."

"I'll drink to that," said Ed, and he raised his rummer.

Chapter Five

The Russells' drawing room was packed with people eager to hear the singing sensation from Italy. The hubbub as friends greeted one another and acquaintances exchanged pleasantries was such that Aunt Jess had to shout to have any hope of being heard. Even then, Sophie watched her lips, trying to discern the words from their shape.

"I will find us seats," Aunt Jess decided.

"Three," Sophie shouted back, holding up three fingers. Aunt Jess nodded and scurried away.

The front rows were already filled. Not that Sophie minded; one could hear the soprano as well at the back as at the front, and since her reason for being here was to listen to the music rather than to be seen by the *ton*, she would as soon sit at the back. It would be less crowded, and probably a lot less stuffy.

Somebody touched her arm, making her jump. She turned and found herself face to face with Lord Pinkerton. Sophie worked to hide her instinctive distaste of the man.

"Good evening," she said, and gave him a small curtsy. She did not raise her voice so that he might hear her. She did not wish to converse with him.

He, however, seemed to have other plans. "How lovely to see you," he said, loud enough that she heard him clearly. "I've been longing to do so."

Sophie raised an eyebrow. "You saw me earlier today."

"Hours ago. It seems like a lifetime."

She gave him a cool half smile. "If you'll excuse me, my lord," she shouted. "I must take my seat. The performance will begin soon."

"May I sit beside you?"

She tried to seem apologetic. "Alas, my lord, the place is taken."

"By Mr. Hammond, I know. But since he is unable to be here, and he didn't wish you to be alone…"

Sophie's smile slipped. Archie Hammond wasn't coming? Surely that was a lie? He'd sent no note, and he was too much of a gentleman to simply not appear. Yet she had to admit she hadn't seen him, and she would have expected him to make his appearance before now.

Lord Pinkerton's smile deepened, and his touch on her arm became a firmer grip. "My dear, we are holding up traffic. Shall we sit?"

"There you are." The voice that interrupted Lord Pinkerton was deep and rich, and it made Sophie shiver, though not in an unpleasant way. Kit stood beside her, his smile warm and genuine, crinkling the skin around his sparkling eyes. The bruising on his face had faded, and he looked every inch the gentleman about town in a coat of dark blue superfine and a blue-and-gray-striped waistcoat. His cravat was simply but elegantly tied, dark pantaloons emphasized the length of his legs, and his boots shone. Sophie could hardly take her eyes from him. She fancied every other lady in the room had the same problem.

He held out his arm for her to take.

"I say!" objected Lord Pinkerton.

Kit gave the baron an ironic smile. "Excuse us. We must take our seats before the performance starts. We don't want to cause a scene, do we?"

Pinkerton glowered at Kit for a moment, then turned and stalked away.

A mixture of relief and elation flowed through Sophie. Relief that she'd be sitting with Kit rather than Lord Pinkerton, although what Mr. Hammond would say when he finally arrived to find his seat taken, she did not know.

Elation was harder to explain, even to herself, for surely she was no more thrilled to find herself squired by Kit Thomas than she would have been by any other gentleman. What she felt was simply gratitude that he'd prevented Lord Pinkerton claiming her, nothing more.

"I thought Mr. Hammond was coming this evening," she said as they made their way to the seats Aunt Jess had saved.

Kit put his lips close to her ear so she would hear without him having to shout. "He is indisposed." His warm breath caressed her cheek and neck, and Sophie wondered, again, how it would feel if he kissed her. Would his lips be warm and soft, his kiss featherlight and tantalizing? Or would they be firm and in control?

She took a deep breath and suppressed such thoughts. Her face felt hot, and she imagined everyone in the room must know what she was thinking. "Indisposed?" she asked, and it was all she could do to squeeze out that one word.

"He was distraught at missing the evening with you."

Not as distraught as I am that we are here, in a crowded room, instead of somewhere private where you might kiss me.

"He asked me to take his place, and promises to call on you when he is better."

Better? Who? Ah, yes, Archie. She cleared her throat. "I hope his recovery is swift," she said, amazed at how steady her voice sounded. They reached the chairs Aunt Jess was guarding.

"As do I." Kit flicked up his tails and sat beside her, legs crossed. She watched, mesmerized, as the action made his pantaloons stretch tight across his thigh. Aunt Jess nudged her, startling her, then gave her a look that was half scolding, half amused. Sophie sat up straighter and faced front.

A hush came over the room when Mrs. Russell stood on the dais. The lady beamed with delight, and the feathers in her turban quivered victoriously as she thanked them for coming to her "intimate soiree," then introduced the soprano.

Giuditta Pasta stepped onto the stage. She was tiny, no more than five feet tall, and slender. She was not classically beautiful, but she was striking, with her Roman nose, bow-shaped lips, and large brown eyes. Her skin had an olive tinge, and her glossy black hair hung in ringlets down her back. For a moment, she looked around as if assessing the crowd. No one made a sound. It was as if the entire room held its breath.

The first notes of music sounded, and she drew herself up to her full height, took a deep breath, and began to sing.

She had a clear, powerful voice, unlike any Sophie had heard before. She moved easily from the shrill high notes to deep low ones, and there was a richness to her singing that others could never hope to match. One or two of the highest notes were a little strained, but the overall performance was so beautiful, those few false notes could be forgiven.

But it wasn't just her voice that held Sophie. Her face was full of the passion of the song, every emotion clearly displayed. She brought the piece to life, and the beauty of it formed a lump in Sophie's throat. She wanted the performance never to end.

All too soon, Senora Pasta took her bow. The audience applauded, although their appreciation seemed less enthusiastic than Sophie expected after such singing.

"That was breathtaking," she said. "Such quality, such—such texture in her voice."

"Hmm," said Aunt Jess. "Not to my taste. Pity. I hear they were mad for her in Paris. But then, I suppose they are French."

On the other side of Sophie, Kit chuckled, then covered it by coughing. "Allow me to fetch drinks for you ladies," he said, and he retreated into the crowd.

Aunt Jess peered around Sophie to watch him go. "Now, that," she said, "is what I call a fine figure of a man. Quite a catch, wouldn't you say?"

"Aunt Jess!" muttered Sophie.

"No sense in ignoring it, Sophie. You have to find a bridegroom, and you have to do it quickly. And you know what they say about a bird in the hand."

"He is neither a bird nor in my hand. For goodness' sake, we only met properly last night."

"What has that to say to anything? When it's the right man, time is not important."

This was disconcerting. If Aunt Jess could so readily envisage a wedding between Sophie and Kit out of this meeting, what would she think when their "arrangement" gave her cause to hope?

Sophie opened her mouth to say something, then closed it again when she realized there was nothing she could say. She and Kit had agreed to act as if they were courting. She could hardly castigate her aunt for believing them.

****

Kit stood in a queue waiting to be served. The man in front of him, Lord Neville, turned to him with a friendly smile.

"Don't often see you at this sort of gathering. Shouldn't have thought it was your thing."

"On the contrary. I'm enjoying it very much."

Neville looked over Kit's shoulder. "I see why." He frowned. "Take care though, my friend. You're fishing in shark-infested waters." He glanced to his left. Kit followed his lead and saw Pinkerton standing against a pillar, arms folded across his chest and a dark scowl on his face.

Kit shrugged, nonchalantly. "Perhaps he needs to cast his net a little wider."

Neville raised his eyebrows. "He's very territorial."

"So am I." To his surprise, Kit realized he meant it. This was no longer a simple favor for a friend, or a ploy to thwart his father's will. Although both those things were part of it, they were side issues, excuses for his actions. Nor was it because Sophie Wilson was a beautiful woman whose company he enjoyed, although he could not deny that. No. The main reason he'd agreed to this charade, the reason he would carry it through to the bitter end, was that the thought of Sophie in Pinkerton's clutches turned his stomach.

Not that he wanted her for himself. He wasn't in the

market for a wife, and wouldn't be for some years, if ever. In fact, nothing would give him greater pleasure than knowing the part he'd played in discouraging Pinkerton had given Sophie the time she needed to find someone she could truly love, someone who would cherish her, encourage her dreams, and make her happy. Someone like…

He stopped, his brow furrowed. Someone like who?

Several names came to mind, gentlemen who were looking for a wife and who might be considered a good catch. One by one, he dismissed each one. This man was too young, that one too old, they gambled too much, drank too much, or they would bore her. They were too reckless, too shy, too rakish, too prim. They wouldn't let her work on her wheat. They would spend too much time with their mistresses, leaving her alone and unloved.

He could not think of a single gentleman worthy of her. Including himself.

Reeling from that epiphany, he collected the drinks and headed back toward Sophie and her aunt. He'd gone only a few steps when Pinkerton stepped forward and blocked his path.

"Enjoying the evening, are you?" he sneered.

"Yes, thank you." Kit made to go around, but Pinkerton sidestepped, forcing him to stay.

"Make the most of it. It's a one-night-only performance."

Kit gave a curt nod and tried again to move past Pinkerton. Again, Pinkerton blocked him.

"The leading lady is engaged elsewhere," he said, quietly.

Kit regarded him for a moment. "Some shows don't make it to the opening night."

"Oh, this one will." Pinkerton's face darkened and his teeth clamped together, clipping his words. He drew himself up and squared his shoulders. Kit raised an eyebrow. He surely wasn't going to start a brawl here, in a room filled with ladies.

"If you'll excuse me, I have drinks to deliver," he said, and he slipped around Pinkerton. This time the baron didn't try to stop him, but Kit felt his glare burning his shoulders all the way to his seat.

"Lord Pinkerton looks angry," Sophie whispered.

"He wasn't enjoying the show," said Kit. "He thinks the accompanist isn't up to snuff."

"Really?" Sophie looked at the dais where the musicians were retaking their seats. "I thought the entire performance was wonderful."

Kit smiled and sipped his drink. "So did I," he said. "So did I."

****

For the second night in a row Uncle Leo waited for Sophie. This time he invited her to join him in the morning room, where she and Aunt Jess sat on a sofa, and he sat back in his chair. He struck a relaxed pose, though she had the feeling he was anything but relaxed. When he smiled, his mouth was tight, more a baring of teeth than anything else.

"How was the evening?" he asked.

"Very enjoyable, thank you," she answered. She sat on the edge of her seat, her muscles tense as she pondered what could possibly be wrong. Uncle Leo had never showed interest in the events she attended before. He'd generally ignored Sophie, leaving her to Aunt Jess.

A fire roared in the hearth, giving the room a soft orange glow. Someone had put pinecones in with the wood. The inviting fragrance and friendly light were at odds with the trepidation rising within her.

"I hear Senora Pasta has a way about her," he said. He studied Sophie closely. Uneasy, she held herself rigid so she wouldn't give in to the urge to fidget in her seat.

"You should have come with us," Aunt Jess answered, acerbically. "You could have heard her for yourself."

"I had a prior engagement." He threw an irritated glance at his sister, then schooled his features and smiled at Sophie. Sophie swallowed, nervous.

"Did Lord Pinkerton enjoy it?" he asked.

Sophie frowned. "I couldn't say."

"You didn't ask?"

"Really, Brother, what a strange question," said Aunt Jess. "Why should Sophie ask him? Do you think she should have stood at the cloakroom and asked everybody as they left?"

"Don't be facetious," he snapped. "What do I care what they thought? Once you've heard one soprano, you've heard them all."

"Well, there's your answer." Jess grinned, triumphant.

Uncle Leo glowered at her, before returning his attention to Sophie. "You didn't notice if the gentleman sitting beside you liked the performance?"

Why would Uncle Leo think Lord Pinkerton had been seated with her this evening? Surely he knew Archie Hammond had asked for that place.

Perhaps he hadn't known. Sophie tried to remember if he'd been present when she and Aunt Jess spoke of it. She was sure they'd mentioned it at dinner. Perhaps he hadn't paid attention. Or mayhap he'd heard of Archie's indisposition and assumed Lord Pinkerton would take his place.

"The gentleman beside her enjoyed the performance very much," said Aunt Jess. The tone of her voice said she drew immense satisfaction from this battle of words with her brother. "Since it wasn't Lord Pinkerton, Sophie cannot know what he thought."

Sophie thought she saw consternation in her uncle's face, but it was gone so quickly, she couldn't be sure.

"You didn't sit with Lord Pinkerton?" His voice now was quiet and calm, and it sent a shiver through Sophie. Aunt Jess must have felt it too, for she reached for Sophie's hand and squeezed her fingers in a gesture of reassurance.

"Really, Sophie," continued her uncle, "for decorum's sake, I should have thought you would sit beside him."

Sophie lifted her chin defiantly. "I have no reason to, Uncle." Beside her, Aunt Jess nodded, emphatically.

"Don't you think you should stop these silly games, sweeting?" His gritted teeth and clenched jaw made the term of endearment sound like an insult. "The man is already caught. He won't be made more eager by a show of indifference."

"I don't think it's a show," said Aunt Jess.

"He has offered for you. When you're out, it is expected he should accompany you."

"It isn't common knowledge that he made an offer," Sophie pointed out. She was amazed at the evenness of her voice, considering how she trembled inside—with anger or fear, she wasn't sure. She willed her heartbeat to slow as she continued, "Besides, I haven't accepted his offer."

"You're going to, though." It was not a question. Uncle Leo's eyes were hard, all trace of a smile gone.

"Only if she doesn't get a better offer," countered Aunt Jess. "Which she may well do."

"In nine days?"

"Oh, I shouldn't think it will take that long." Mischief made Aunt Jess's face light up and gave her voice a musical lilt.

Uncle Leo struggled to control his temper. "Who is the gentleman?" he demanded, his voice strained, as if it was an effort to keep it lowered.

"Mr. Thomas," supplied Aunt Jess, happily. "He's from a good family. His father is the Earl of Markham."

"I know who his father is!" Uncle Leo's face reddened, and his eyes seemed to bulge. He looked fit to burst. Sophie shrank back. Why on earth would he be so angry?

"He is a wastrel," declared Uncle Leo, as if in answer to her silent question. "Idle and unwilling, with no ambition, no..." He waved his hand in the air as if trying to capture the next words as they flew past.

"That's not true." The words were out before Sophie could stop them. She bit her lip. Kit might not want everybody to know of his plans for University.

Fortunately, Uncle Leo did not ask her to elaborate. He ignored her and directed all his ire at Aunt Jess. "Won't even manage one of his father's estates. The earl offered it to him and he turned it down." Sophie hadn't known that, but she wasn't surprised. Managing an estate did not fit with Kit's dreams.

"Perhaps it wasn't to his taste," said Aunt Jess. Sophie raised her eyebrows, surprised. She hadn't expected her aunt to ally with someone who turned down property. Then she saw the twinkle in Aunt Jess's eyes. The naughty woman was goading her brother. It was an effort for Sophie not to roll her eyes. Sometimes, Jess was more provoking than a child.

"He'll wish he'd taken it, want it or not. His father's cut him off. He's to go home, take up the reins, and marry some local chit—or be penniless. Still think him eligible?"

Sophie's eyes widened in alarm. *Marry some "local chit"?* Was Kit spoken for? Every ounce of energy drained from her limbs. Her stomach flipped, and her head felt fuzzy and stuffed with cotton, like it had when she'd swum underwater in Papa's pond.

It was one thing for a single unattached gentleman to court Sophie. He could become her fiancé and she could jilt him. It would cause a stir, but it was recoverable; the gossip would die once the *ton* had something else to pick at. But a man who was already promised, or one who had even given another lady reason to hope—that could ruin Sophie completely.

There must be a mistake. Kit Thomas did not seem the kind of man who would do that. Although he did have a reputation as a rake… No! There had to be an explanation.

Her heartbeat settled, and the whooshing rhythm in her ears died away. Aunt Jess and Uncle Leo were still arguing, seemingly oblivious to Sophie's distress.

"Pish-posh!" Aunt Jess said, dismissively. "Fathers say things all the time. I remember you and Papa—"

"We are not talking about me and Papa, who never threatened to cast me adrift, incidentally."

"He probably would have if he hadn't needed you to run the business." Aunt Jess's tone was matter-of-fact, and all the more cutting for that.

Uncle Leo breathed heavily through his nose, clearly trying to keep his temper in check. Sophie gave her aunt a sidelong look, meant to warn her not to push him too far. Sophie did not want Uncle Leo to be in a rage when her future was involved. Angry people said things they might not otherwise have said, and the last thing Sophie wanted was for him to decide something awful, simply because he was in high dudgeon with his sister.

And besides, if Kit truly was going to marry someone else, the whole argument was moot. Sophie would not enter into a betrothal, not even a mock betrothal, with a promised man.

As if she heard Sophie's thoughts, Aunt Jess said, "Marry some chit, did you say? Has he offered for this gel?"

Uncle Leo sniffed. "Her father's land marches beside the earl's. She's the only heir."

"Has the boy offered for her?"

When her uncle looked away, Sophie began to hope.

"The fathers have an agreement," he said.

"But not the couple?"

"It's only a matter of time. He's in town, getting his rebellion out of his system."

"Or," Jess retorted, her face shining with triumph, "he has no intention of marrying his father's choice. Mr. Thomas strikes me as a man who knows his own mind. He is nobody's lackey."

No, he isn't. Sophie let out a sigh of relief. All was well. He was not spoken for.

A feeling of shame washed over her that she had doubted his integrity for so much as a moment. He was, after all, helping her out of the goodness of his heart, with no reward or benefit accruing to him for it. She ought to have had more faith in him, refused to believe Uncle Leo's words. But then, she excused herself, she hardly knew the man. Besides, Ed wouldn't have asked him to help if Kit could not be trusted.

"Whether he'll marry the earl's choice really has nothing to say to the matter." Uncle Leo's frustration with Aunt Jess's argument was clear in his tone. "He won't offer for Sophie, so there is no sense pretending otherwise." He turned to Sophie then, his face stern. "Your father may have been a baron, but your mother was not of noble birth. You have no fortune, and you're not a diamond of the first water. You have nothing to recommend you."

"Leo! Don't speak to her like that."

"'Tis best she hear the truth. The *beau monde* is cruel, Jess. They will shred her to pieces for daring to even think she could marry the son of an earl."

"Her father was a peer," Jess reminded him, her voice icy. "and her brother is one now."

"Her husband will be one, too. Pinkerton is a baron, don't forget." He smiled at Sophie, and she shuddered. "When you marry him," he continued, "you will be a lady."

Aunt Jess sniffed. "She already is a lady. She needs no title to prove it."

"Oh, for the love of—there's no reasoning with you!" Leo stood, adjusted his coat, and gave his sister his angriest glare. "I'm going to bed. As for you, young lady, I suggest you think long and hard on the matter, and employ some common sense." He jabbed a finger in Sophie's direction. "Nine days. Pinkerton will wait no longer." He stormed from the room. Sophie jumped as he slammed the door.

She stared dismally into the dying embers of the fire. Her uncle spoke as if the betrothal to Lord Pinkerton was a foregone conclusion, but it couldn't be. Sophie would not allow it. Her uncle might be her guardian, but he couldn't force her to marry. Could he? She was sure she'd heard there was a law forbidding marriage under duress. She would ask Ed about it.

"Lord, he's a pompous ass," muttered Aunt Jess.

Sophie gave her aunt a sidelong look. "You provoked him."

Aunt Jess grinned. "He makes it too tempting to do so. I could never resist."

"You're not children brangling in the nursery. You angered him, and now he's more set in his resolve than ever."

The smile fell from her aunt's face. "My Robert used to say I was too impetuous by half. Until now, the possible consequences were not so dire, and I hurt no one but myself. Forgive me."

Sophie gave her a weak smile. "You're not the villain here, Aunt. I just wish I could show Uncle Leo how much I detest Lord Pinkerton. Then perhaps he wouldn't champion him so."

"He was ever thus. Even as a child, Leo saw one course of action and stopped his ears to all others. But never fear. We have nine days to persuade him to our way of thinking. And I can be as implacable as he." She grinned. "It's a family trait." She stood and straightened her skirts. "Now, though, I believe it's time for bed."

Sophie nodded and stood. Aunt Jess frowned. "He does have rather a bee in his head about this. I understand his desire to see you married. I share it. And I am unsurprised to learn he doesn't want to have to give you a second Season. Leo is such a nip-cheese, and a Season is expensive. But Pinkerton? I cannot see his reasoning. The man's only a baron, for goodness' sake. He's by no means the greatest catch you can hope for, yet you'd think he was the Regent himself, the way Leo is pushing the match." She winked and smiled. "Don't look so concerned, my dear. You've nothing to be anxious about. I've been on this earth a good few years now, and Leo has never bested me."

There's always a first time. Sophie pushed the unhappy thought away.

While she prepared for bed, she thought about what Aunt Jess had said. The older lady was right, and Sophie was annoyed at herself for not having seen it sooner. Something was wrong. Uncle Leo was a cold fish sometimes, but she'd never thought of him as deliberately cruel. He had to see how much the prospect of marriage to Lord Pinkerton revolted Sophie, but instead of trying to find someone else, he'd dug himself in and become more determined than ever. Why?

It couldn't be a simple desire to see her wed. He could have put her into the path of a dozen gentlemen, all of whom she could like, yet he had done no such thing. In fact, he seemed to want no other man for her, regardless of their background, fortune or prospects, for the thought of an alternative suitor had angered him, even before he knew that suitor was Kit Thomas. So it wasn't the suitor he objected to, but the suit itself.

And that made no sense at all.

It was something else to speak to Ed about. Between them, perhaps they could discover why the baron enjoyed their uncle's favor. Once they knew the reason, Sophie could fight it, and then she and Kit could end their charade.

She refused to wonder why such an outcome did not make her feel happier.

Chapter Six

The next morning Kit was about early. He called at Archie Hammond's rooms and was relieved to see him making good progress. Archie would be in bed for weeks and unable to do much even when he rose, but with time and good care, the doctor expected him to make a full recovery.

"I must apologize to Miss Wilson," said Archie. "I was promised to her last night…"

"I made your apologies to her," Kit reassured him.

He looked horrified. "She knows? What must she think of me? Injured in a street brawl like a common lout."

"You weren't injured in a street brawl, you were attacked. But you may be at ease. The lady doesn't know about this." Kit gestured at Archie, lying in his bed, his face almost as white as his sheet apart from the blackness around his swollen eyes and broken nose, and the scab forming on his cut lip. His chest was tightly bound and his hands were swathed in thick bandages, his arm was in a sling, and a cage had been placed beneath the sheets over his broken leg.

"I tried to fight back," he said. "I'm not much good with my fists."

"If I know Pinkerton, you were outnumbered."

Archie nodded but still looked ashamed.

"And he will pay," Kit added, through gritted teeth.

"Don't make an enemy of him on my behalf."

Kit smiled grimly. "He's already an enemy. Yours is just one more vile act in his debit column."

"He'll kill you."

"He may try."

"But…"

"Calm yourself, Archie. All you should worry about is healing. Do you have all you need? People to attend you? Books to read?"

"I wouldn't mind some books, actually." Archie smiled, then winced as it pulled on the scab on his lip. "I have a subscription at Hatchard's. The clerk there will know my tastes."

"Then I will go and secure you enough books to entertain you while your body repairs itself."

The clerk at the bookshop did indeed know what Archie liked to read; poetry, theology, and horticulture seemed to be his usual interests. The clerk expressed a desire for Mr. Hammond's speedy recovery and invited Kit to take a seat and enjoy a coffee while he put together a package for the invalided gentleman.

Kit wandered over to the shelves and idly perused the books. Like those crammed into the window to entice readers in, most were expensive volumes bound in Moroccan leather, their titles tooled in gilt. He picked out one or two, skimmed through them, then replaced them on the shelf.

From the next aisle he heard feminine laughter. It was filled with joy and life, unforced, unlike so many laughs he heard in the drawing rooms of the *ton*. He smiled at the music of it and reached for another book.

"You, young lady, are a minx," said an older woman. Kit cocked his head, certain he recognized the voice, hoping he had.

"You would have me no other way."

There was no mistaking that voice. Kit smiled and his chest felt lighter at the mere thought that Sophie was here, just a few feet from him. He fancied he smelled her perfume, the alluring, clean scent of lavender mixing with the smells of paper and print, leather and beeswax.

He hesitated. Part of him wanted to move round the bookshelves and into her presence. The other part, for reasons he could not explain even to himself, made him hang back, telling him to walk away, go to the other side of the store and wait for Archie's books.

He clenched his jaw, impatient with himself. "For God's sake, man!" he muttered. "You're supposed to be courting her." He squared his shoulders and took a step forward, just as the two ladies came into the aisle.

The first sight of her took his breath away. Her face shone with impish delight at whatever her aunt had said, and her laughter sounded like silver bells shaken on a soft, summer breeze.

Lord! What was wrong with him? He'd never waxed lyrical about a woman before, though he'd known plenty with beauty enough to turn a man's head. However, none of them were Sophie.

Light spilled from a high window and shone on her. It emphasized the springtime yellow of her dress and the dark gold of her spencer, and it seemed to gather around her as if drawn to her by some magic force. In that instant, Kit would not have been surprised if the full choir of Saint Paul's Cathedral paraded past him singing the "Hallelujah Chorus." He could almost hear it playing in his head. He blinked hard, told himself to breathe, and fought his way to sanity.

Sophie saw him. Her eyes flashed, and she smiled for an instant, then glanced at her aunt, blushed, and lowered her gaze.

"Good day, Mr. Thomas." Lady Jess gave him a small curtsy and a large, welcoming grin.

Kit took his eyes from her niece long enough to greet the older woman.

Sophie's aunt eyed him, her expression shrewd. Then she touched Sophie's arm. "Oh, Lud!" she said, far too loudly to be innocent. "My mind will go a-wandering. There was a book I need. I'll go and get it. I won't be long," and she scurried away into the next aisle.

Sophie glanced over her shoulder and chuckled. "She thinks she's being subtle," she whispered.

"I don't mind if you don't."

Sophie's color rose again, making her eyes shine bluer. She cleared her throat and glanced at the shelves. "Were you wanting anything in particular?"

You. I want to kiss you, to learn if your lips taste as wonderful as they look. I want to feel the silk of your hair against my skin, your breasts warm in my hands, your thighs wrapped around my hips...

Kit's body hardened, and his pantaloons became uncomfortable. He swallowed and thanked God they were black, for a lighter color would undoubtedly have betrayed his arousal.

Pushing the inappropriate thoughts aside, he said, "You are looking lovely today, Miss Wilson."

"Thank you, sir."

There was a moment of awkward silence. Voices buzzed softly in the distance. Dust motes danced in the fall of sunlight from the window. Kit tried to think of something intelligent to say. Sophie caught her bottom lip tentatively beneath her top teeth and he forgot how to think at all.

"Do you have something particular in mind?" she asked.

His mouth dried. *Pardon?*

She gestured at the shelves around them. "These are books of poetry and works of fiction. I don't see you enthralled by *The Castle of Udolpho*." Her lips twitched and her eyes sparkled with mischief. "Although, I suppose an improbable tale might suit you." She moved closer to the shelf. "There's *Pamela*, though that's a little old-fashioned. Here's one you might enjoy. Well written, by a lady author. *Pride and Prejudice*. Or perhaps you'd prefer a cautionary tale? *The Rake's Progress*?"

Kit shook himself from the trance she'd trapped him in. This was Ed's sister, for pity's sake! The *friend* he was helping, not a woman he should be lusting after. God, if Ed read his thoughts now…

"I'm merely collecting books for a friend who is indisposed," he said.

"Mr. Hammond?" Her face filled with concern. "How does he fare?"

Kit was damned if he cared at the moment. He didn't want to discuss Archie, didn't want her thinking of the other man. He mumbled some platitude about Archie's condition and changed the subject, looking at the books she held.

"*Husbandry in the Modern Age*? Are you looking at all aspects of farming now?"

Her eyes widened and she glanced around whilst bringing her finger to her lips in the universal sign for silence. "My aunt thinks it's a book on husband catching," she whispered. "If she knew I was studying farming practice, she'd be appalled."

"I see." Kit's lips twitched in amusement. "And what do you hope to find in your book on—husband catching?"

"If I knew that," she said airily, "I wouldn't need the book, would I?"

Kit chuckled. "Tell me, Miss Wilson," he said, "what *do* you look for in a husband?"

Sophie looked delightfully flustered, color high, her gaze unable to meet his. She licked her lips, and his erection became painful. Without thought, he reached out and caressed her warm cheek. She didn't shy away, but raised her eyes to his face. He could see her uncertainty, her innocence. This was a woman who had never been kissed. Kit would bet his life on that.

Suddenly, he knew he must be the one who gave her that first kiss. It was more important than anything that his be the first lips she felt on hers, that he be the first to taste the honey of her mouth, to teach her the pleasure of it, and show her what a kiss could be.

He took a half step forward, and his coat brushed against her spencer. He felt the warmth of her, the quickening of her chest as her breaths came faster. A tiny pulse flickered at the base of her throat.

She tilted her head to look at him. The flecks in her eyes seemed to dance and sparkle, drawing him in. Her eyelashes were long and surprisingly dark, and a smattering of tiny pale freckles danced across her nose. He hoped she didn't scrub them with lemon. He knew women who did that, trying to rid themselves of what they saw as a disfigurement. On Sophie, they were not disfiguring. They were charming, attractive. Beautiful.

Her breaths grew shallow. He could smell the mint of her tooth powder and the chocolate she'd drunk at breakfast.

His own heartbeat skipped when his fingers caressed her cheek. He wished he weren't wearing gloves, that he might feel the satin softness of her skin, the watery silk of her hair.

She put her hand on his chest, and he was lost. The bookshop disappeared. He lowered his head to hers, then softly, gently, brushed his lips against her mouth.

****

Kit strode along the street, berating himself. What the hell had he been thinking? Kissing Sophie was definitely not part of the arrangement he'd made. He was supposed to court her, show her uncle there was an alternative to Pinkerton and, if it became absolutely necessary, announce their betrothal. At no point had he planned to kiss her, or to hold her so close that he couldn't tell where she ended and he began. And in public, too.

He might have ruined her completely. If someone had come upon them, there would have been no false betrothal to fool her uncle, but a very real marriage. And while he'd admit that, if he had to be leg-shackled, he could do far worse than Sophie Wilson, that really wasn't the point. Marriage to anybody, however delightful, would mean going home to his father, tail between his legs and all dreams of engineering lost. Besides, the last thing Sophie wanted was marriage. Forced into it, she would be miserable. And knowing he'd made her unhappy would make Kit unhappy.

He didn't want to contemplate why that should be.

But oh! She'd been irresistible standing there, the

sunlight giving her a soft glow, accentuating every delectable curve. Her skin had been warm and soft, her breast plump and perfect in his hand. How he'd longed to put his mouth there, to taste her cherry-red nipple and...

Ed was going to kill him.

As he walked, he alternated between self-flagellation and elation, from guilt and regret to gladness, from vowing never to touch her again to wishing he could do so right here, right now. Deep in thought, he walked right past Archie's home, and it was only as he walked through the park near Hamsey House that he came crashing back to the real world and realized his mistake.

Kit cursed. It would take him twenty minutes to walk back to Archie's apartment but, resigned to it, he followed the path toward the gate. The sun was well to the west now, and it had taken on the red-gold hue of evening, while the sky had become a bright, light blue. Very few people walked in the park; the nannies and their charges had long since returned to the nurseries, and most of the *ton* were resting in readiness for their evening's exertions.

A squirrel darted across the path and up the trunk of a tree, stopping to sniff the air before disappearing into the leafy branches. A bird flew down and landed on the grass, cocking his head from side to side before flying off again as a cat came close, its body held low to the ground. It watched impassively as the bird flew off, then stalked away, nonchalantly, and disappeared into the undergrowth to look for easier prey.

The path wound round a large oak tree. Kit followed it, then stopped dead and took a step backward so he was less likely to be seen. There, on the path between himself and the gate, were Sophie's uncle and Pinkerton, deep in serious discussion.

Knowing instinctively that he shouldn't let them see him, Kit hid behind the tree.

"I'd hoped to have made my offer official by now," said Pinkerton as they came close.

"Patience, my lord," said Leo. "A week or two is nothing."

"You were too lenient with her. My daughters married who I chose and not a murmur of dissent from them." He chuckled, and the cruel sound made Kit's stomach turn. "I shall enjoy training your niece, once she is my wife."

"You swore you wouldn't harm her."

"I won't. But I will have obedience." Pinkerton clapped Leo's shoulder, and the older man winced. "Don't be squeamish, sir. Women, horses, and dogs need to be trained, do they not? Show them who's master and they're much happier for it. They like to be settled."

Kit clenched his jaw, his cheeks heated and his stare hardened. It was all he could do not to jump out and grab the baron by his throat and squeeze the vicious life from him. He remembered Pinkerton had been widowed at least twice before, and his veins turned to ice.

"You have no need to worry," said Leo. "She'll marry you. If she doesn't…"

"You will be the sorrier."

The two men walked on, out of earshot. Kit stood for a moment longer, clenching and unclenching his fists and willing his fury to dissipate.

Finally, rational thought crept back, and he frowned. Something wasn't right. Why on earth would Sophie's uncle involve himself with an odious man like Lord Pinkerton? Surely he knew Sophie could attract a much better caliber of suitor than that. How could he even think of throwing her away on such a disastrous match?

So many questions were raised by the snippet of conversation he'd overheard. Wary and suspicious, Kit determined to get to the bottom of it, because there was one thing he knew for certain—whatever they were plotting, they would not succeed. He would stop them and keep Sophie safe. Even if he had to marry her himself to do so.

Chapter Seven

Lady Pargeter's ballroom glowed. Light from myriad candles bounced from its chandeliers, reflecting a dozen times in the mirrors paneling the walls. White-and-gold curtains billowed softly at banks of open French windows, while ladies in bright gowns moved through the throng or fluttered fans suggestively at gentlemen.

Kit stood on the stairs and surveyed the scene without actually taking much note of it. There was only one guest who interested him. He knew she must be here because he'd seen her aunt, and now Ed was making his way across the floor toward him.

Golden hair caught the light. She stood beside a pillar to one side of the room, surrounded by half a dozen gentlemen. Kit tensed, wanting to plough into them, scatter them like ninepins. He told himself he was concerned for her safety—they had her trapped. It had nothing to do with the roiling in his stomach and his pulse pounding in his ear. He was not jealous in the least. On the contrary, he wanted them to pay attention to her. Wasn't that why he'd agreed to this ridiculous charade in the first place?

Now, with the plotting between her uncle and Pinkerton, it was more important than ever that Sophie find herself an alternative suitor. It couldn't be himself, he knew that, so there was no point in feeling bitter about it.

"Penny for them?" called Ed, as he climbed the bottom three steps to be beside Kit. He turned and surveyed the scene, legs apart, hands clasped behind his back, like a captain on a poop deck. The image of his most amiable and inoffensive friend, braced against the sea swell and shouting orders to his crew, made Kit smile.

"That's better," said Ed. "You looked very dour when you came in."

"I was not dour. I was...thinking."

"Don't do that. You'll frighten the horses." Ed looked over to where his sister was talking to her band of admirers, smiling and laughing as they penciled names onto her dance card. "That's more like it," he said softly.

"They don't deserve her."

Ed studied Kit for a moment, as if wondering if he was serious. Kit did not return his stare, he didn't dare, for then Ed would see just how serious he was. Kit might acknowledge to himself that he had come to care for Sophie more than he'd intended, but he was damned if he'd let his best friend know it too.

"There are three titles in that throng," said Ed. "And an heir apparent. Eligible, all of them."

A muscle twitched in Kit's jaw. "I wasn't referring to their ranks. Not one of them had the bollocks to stand up to Pinkerton until someone else did."

"That's unfair, Kit. You saw Archie."

Kit tensed his jaw. Archie was a gentle soul, more suited to the library than the boxing salon. Sensitive and studious, he wouldn't have stood a chance against any opponent, let alone a scrapper like Pinkerton. "Those young bucks are not Archie."

"Thankfully." Ed looked around the room and affected an air of boredom. "Cards?"

"I need to make my bow to your sister and claim my dances."

Ed laughed. "You may not need to. That little coterie may get you off the hook."

Kit wished the "little coterie" to the devil. He took a deep breath and forced sensible thought back into his head. "Perhaps they will, at that," he said, surprised by how even and unconcerned he sounded. "Until they do, I'm on duty."

He left Ed and approached Sophie, telling himself that duty was all there was to it.

****

Sophie gave the gentlemen surrounding her the minimum of attention. Their comments were predictable enough that she could laugh at the right moments and say the right things in response without even thinking about it. They'd filled her dance card and made her evening a success, but her focus was fixed firmly on the other side of the ballroom where Kit stood with Ed.

She'd known the moment he entered. A wave of awareness had rippled through the room, flowing over the dancers and lapping at Sophie's toes. She fancied she caught his scent on the charged air and felt the warmth of him wrapping around her like an embrace.

He saw her and nodded, almost imperceptibly. Sophie's mouth dried and she found it hard to swallow. He started toward her, every movement sleek and efficient. His coat showed off his fine shoulders and made the other men, who had seemed perfectly well made just a minute ago, seem no more than adequate.

She noted every detail, from his tousled hair and the firmness of his cheeks and chin, to the snow white of his cravat and the glittering silver thread in his waistcoat. Dark breeches showed off his long legs and powerful thighs, and the well-defined shape of his calves was completely natural, requiring no stuffing with sawdust or cotton. She imagined him whirling her through a waltz, his leg brushing her skirts, his hands on her back, holding her to him, close enough to see deep into his eyes, to feel his breath on her cheek, his lips so tantalizingly close…

The heat of a blush rose into her cheeks. If Aunt Jess could read her thoughts, she would have an apoplexy.

She licked her lips, nervously. She had taken quite a liberty this evening, and she didn't know if Kit would be angry at her for it. She hoped not.

The first thing she'd done when she received her dance card was to scribble his name against two dances. She reasoned he wanted the world to believe he was courting her, and a man who had serious intentions would have chosen those two dances. But now that he approached, she found herself wondering if she'd done the right thing.

She'd had to do it, she told herself. She didn't want to dance the waltz with anyone else, and the others had swooped before she could think. Had the waltz and the supper dance been still free, she made no doubt she would face the prospect of dancing them with a man who didn't interest her in the slightest.

Her lips tingled at the memory of his kiss. Her first kiss. She shivered at the thought of his warm lips against hers, his hands on her body, the hardening of her nipples, and the wonderful, terrible ache he'd left her with when he stopped. She could still taste him, still feel his strength as he made her forget Lord Pinkerton and the bullying bluster of Uncle Leo.

She should feel ashamed. She'd let him kiss her in public, let him take liberties that could have ruined her, had anyone seen. But she didn't feel ashamed. Truth to tell, more than anything she wanted it to happen again.

The heat in her cheeks increased, telling her that her color was rising even more.

"Good evening, Miss Wilson," Kit said, his dark, delicious voice sending wonderful shudders racing up and down her spine. "Gentlemen."

The men bowed to him, though Sophie noticed some did the smallest bow socially acceptable, their resentment of him plain. Kit ignored them and turned his attention to her, his fingers reaching for the card at her wrist.

"I set aside the dances you requested," Sophie said quickly. "The waltz and the supper dance. They were the ones, were they not?"

One of the men said that if Kit didn't want them, he'd happily take them.

"A waltz and a supper dance," Kit said. "Sounds heavenly to me."

Sophie smiled. In the distance, the musicians played the first notes of the first dance. Someone took her hand and led her to the dance floor, where she lined up with everyone else, danced and smiled, and remembered none of it. The only awareness she had was of him, watching her. She wondered what he thought as she skipped and twirled and promenaded her way around the floor. Every sense seemed heightened under his scrutiny. The air shimmered. The scent of beeswax candles mingled with the cloying perfumes of a hundred debutantes and the heady fragrance of the flowers artfully arranged in corners and alcoves about the room.

Thank goodness the dance was a simple one. Sophie went through the moves by rote, which was as well because all she could concentrate on was Kit. She felt him watching her, his gaze like a physical touch that set her nerves to tingling and made the hair at her nape stand up. She longed to watch him back, but she didn't dare. To have the *ton* view them as a possible match was one thing. To flirt blatantly with him in a crowded ballroom would be quite another.

So instead, she gave her partner a bright smile and tried to enjoy the dance to the fullest.

She promenaded up the set, whirled to come back down, and saw Uncle Leo, standing near the entrance to the card room. Sophie frowned. She hadn't realized he was here. He always said he hated these occasions, that they made him miserable. He certainly had not accompanied her and Aunt Jess this evening. Was something amiss? Had he come to fetch them home to a family emergency?

It couldn't involve Ed. She'd seen him go into the card room ten minutes ago. And since there was no one else... Aunt Jess stood with him and didn't seem anxious, which relieved Sophie. Her aunt did, however, look annoyed, and she was clearly sharing sharp words with her brother.

Sophie's spirits fell. It didn't take a genius to figure out what they were discussing. She scanned the room, looking for Lord Pinkerton. She didn't see him, but that didn't lessen her anxiety.

Get a hold of yourself! Lord Pinkerton could do nothing to her. Her dance card was full, so he couldn't demand she stand up with him, and there were too many people to see, should he try to do anything unpleasant. Besides, Kit would ensure she was safe. He'd seen the baron off before, and he would do it again.

Reassured, she took her partner's hands and skipped back up the set.

****

Kit tried not to read too much into the fact that she'd saved the waltz and the supper dance for him. The gesture meant nothing, he knew, but even so, he was ridiculously pleased by it. After all, she could have penciled him in for any two dances, yet she'd chosen those two. No dance was more intimate than the waltz, and her supper partner would take her through to the dining room and sit with her during the meal. They were perfect dances for a man who was courting her in earnest. Society's tongues would run wild with the news, and if that didn't persuade her uncle that Pinkerton was not his only choice, Kit didn't know what would.

Just then her uncle came into Kit's line of vision, as if he'd conjured him. Kit frowned. In his bid to make his father see University as the lesser evil, Kit had played the rogue at any number of events, and he'd never once seen Sophie's uncle in attendance. Yet here he was, large as life, arguing with her aunt.

Leo's presence worried Kit, especially after the meeting he'd seen in the park yesterday. What if he planned something to entrap Sophie and force her into the marriage? If he did, Kit vowed he would rue the day.

The brother and sister were most definitely arguing, although they did so in a civilized way that didn't draw the attention of most people. From the look of frustration on Leo's face, Kit thought Lady Jess might be winning.

It might help if he discovered what they argued about. He thought it must involve Sophie, which meant he needed to know more if he was to keep her safe from Pinkerton.

Kit glanced at her, still dancing with that idiot Cardew. She bestowed a brilliant smile on the man as she gave him her hands and they danced up and down the set.

A white hot spark ignited in Kit's chest, filling him with a strange rage. His stomach muscles tightened and his lips pressed together as he fought an almost overwhelming urge to stalk over there, push Cardew aside, and claim Sophie for himself.

He deliberately relaxed his shoulders and pushed away the animosity he felt for her partner. It wasn't as if Kit had any real claim on her. Theirs was a false courtship, a business arrangement, nothing more. He should be relieved that she didn't seem in imminent need of a betrothal with him.

Telling himself yet again that he was being ridiculous, he deliberately turned his attention from her and made his way, as discreetly as he could, toward Leo and Lady Jess and their argument.

The pair were so engrossed in their conversation he was able to stand behind a giant fern in a planter just three feet from them, where he could hear every word.

"All I'm saying is, she's a young lady of breeding. It isn't seemly for her to have too many suitors."

Kit frowned. He hadn't heard that concern voiced before. Young ladies seemed to collect hearts like a schoolboy collected conkers. For aught Kit knew, there might even be some contest that went on over the Season, to see which of them collected the most.

Lady Jess shared this view, apparently. "Don't be so

ridiculous," she said.

"Pinkerton couldn't even squeeze one dance onto her card," complained Leo.

"Good," said Jess. Kit agreed.

"It's not good. He's shown an interest in her, and…"

"She doesn't want him."

You don't know what he…" Leo sighed, heavily, and adjusted his coat. Kit wondered what he'd been about to say. He looked across the room to where Pinkerton stood, one arm behind his back, glass of wine in the other hand. He sipped at the drink while watching the dance. It took Kit no more than a second to verify that the baron had eyes for only one particular dancer.

What had Leo been about to say? Was he afraid of Pinkerton? Kit dismissed the thought. Leo wasn't some young buck worried about being caught alone in an alley. He was a man with the means and experience to protect himself. So why was he so keen on the match?

Extortion, perhaps? Could Pinkerton know something Leo would rather keep secret? This was a scenario that bore some investigation.

"You cannot force her where she would not go," Lady Jess said, drawing Kit's attention back to them. She spoke in the voice she might have used on recalcitrant children.

"I am her guardian," answered Leo, petulantly.

"Only for three more months," pointed out Lady Jess. "Once Ed comes of age, he takes control. Do you really think he'll force his sister into a marriage she finds reprehensible?"

Leo's face twisted in anger and he rounded on her. His eyes were so hard, his jaw so clenched that Kit worried for her safety, and he tensed, ready to intervene.

"She has to marry him." Leo squeezed the words through gritted teeth. "There is no…"

Perhaps Kit moved. Perhaps a candle, guttering in the draft, drew Leo's eye. Whatever made him look, he saw Kit, and his whole demeanor changed. His shoulders lowered and his face relaxed. He stepped back from where he'd loomed over his sister and gave Kit a smile that didn't reach his eyes.

"Mr. Thomas. Are you enjoying the evening, sir?"

Lady Jess's smile was warmer but no less strained. As nonchalantly as he could, Kit stepped into full view. "Mr. Farnham," he greeted Leo. He bowed to Lady Jess. "Lady Sanders."

They made small talk for a minute, but the atmosphere was charged and it stilted their words. When they'd covered the weather, Kit's horses, the success of the evening, and how delighted their hostess must be, there was an awkward silence before Leo said, "How goes your father?"

"He is well, thank you."

"I heard he was in town. Nothing amiss, I hope?" Leo's eyes gleamed. It was obvious he'd heard of the earl's ultimatum. Kit wondered briefly, and with some exasperation, how these stories got about. A supposedly private conversation between him and his father was now clearly in the public domain.

But not for anything would Kit confirm it, especially not to this man who aimed to make Sophie miserable for the rest of her life. "He's here on business," he said, making sure he sounded bored by the subject.

Leo nodded. "It must have been good to see him, have a talk with him?"

"Yes, it was. We shared breakfast." He turned to the

dance floor. "If you'll excuse me, I am promised for the next dance." He bowed and walked away.

Tomorrow he would talk to Ed. Then, they would investigate Leo, Pinkerton, and the connection between them—before it was too late.

****

The dance finished and Mr. Cardew escorted Sophie to her seat, then set off to fetch her a drink. Sophie peered at the corner where she'd seen Aunt Jess talking to Uncle Leo, but they had moved. If her uncle hadn't left the ball, Sophie thought, he would be in the cardroom. As for Aunt Jess, she must have gone to the retiring room, for if she'd been in the ballroom, she would doubtless have made her way to Sophie and taken up her role of chaperone.

Sophie folded her hands into her lap and watched other people meeting each other, bowing and exchanging brief pleasantries. It occurred to her that life in the *ton* was one endless dance, its moves specific and repetitive, its rhythm precise. Her lips twitched at the absurd notion and she wished she could share it with Kit. He would find it amusing, she was certain.

At the thought of him, she looked around the room again, but he too was absent. Disappointment fluttered inside her. She pushed it away. It was ridiculous to sit, vacuous as a moon calf, lamenting a lost glimpse of a man she would waltz with in a while.

"Good evening, Miss Wilson." Pinkerton's voice came from behind her and she jumped.

"Lord Pinkerton," she said, coolly.

He took the seat beside her. Although he faced front and all was perfectly proper, Sophie felt uneasy. She shifted in her own seat, putting as many inches as she could between them.

"I was disappointed not to secure a dance with you," he said.

Her smile was polite but distant. "You flatter me, my lord."

A muscle in his cheek jumped. "More than disappointed, to be honest."

Sophie deliberately misinterpreted his words. "There are other young ladies who would welcome a partner."

He bristled. She looked away, wishing she were not alone in conversation with him. Kit had rescued her at the soiree. Perhaps he might do so again.

Her cheeks heated. Of course she wasn't wishing Kit Thomas would approach her. She simply meant she wished *somebody* would do so. Aunt Jess perhaps, or Mr. Cardew with her drink, or...anyone, really, although she couldn't deny Kit had proved adept at making the baron withdraw when others failed to do so. Which was the only reason she'd thought of Kit first.

Of course it was.

Beside her, Lord Pinkerton rested his hands on his knees and massaged his kneecaps before he slapped his thighs and stood. "Very well," he said. "Have fun. That's what the season should be for a girl, after all. Once you're married, there'll be far fewer balls to attend, and even when you do go you'll be expected to eschew all partners except your husband."

Sophie felt her hackles rise. How dare he talk to her in that way? "Do you not think it presumptuous to pretend to know what my future holds?" Her voice was low and even, her ire clear. "If and when I marry, it may well be to a man whose opinions do not run alongside yours. He may enjoy dancing every night and be delighted that his friends wish to stand up with his wife."

Heart thumping madly, face hot, she turned and stared out over the ballroom, willing herself calm and wondering if she'd gone too far. She wished he would leave her alone, yes, but she'd been brought up better than to offer deliberate offense, even to one as provoking as he was.

"We shall see, shall we not?" His answer was softly spoken, giving no indication of how he viewed her outburst. He stood and bowed, wished her good evening, and walked away, leaving an undeniable chill. Sophie shuddered. Then, to her relief, she saw her aunt approaching, her arm resting lightly on Kit's. Sophie's heart seemed to swell at the sight of him. Her view of the people around him became unfocused, and she could no longer hear their chatter, nor the soft noises of the orchestra tuning their instruments.

He watched her, never taking his eyes from her as he led her aunt to a chair. The heat in his eyes made Sophie's breath quicken, and she swallowed, twice. The tip of her tongue licked her suddenly dry lips and her stomach fluttered. Her breasts felt heavy, her nipples pressing against her clothes, and she tightened her thigh muscles against the soft, squirming ache between them.

She blinked hard and tried to pull herself together. The room came back into view, and happy noise filled the air again. She forced her gaze from Kit to her aunt, and she frowned.

Aunt Jess seemed—brittle. She held herself a little too rigidly, and her arm on Kit's looked to be less a social courtesy and more a necessity, as if she needed his help to balance.

She sat beside Sophie and smoothed down her skirt. "Is all well, Aunt?"

The smile Aunt Jess flashed was too bright. "Of course it is, child. Go and dance." She waved her hands, shooing Sophie away.

"My waltz, I believe," said Kit, and he held out his hand. Sophie looked from him, smiling at her, to Aunt Jess, who was studiedly innocent. She sighed and let him lead her into the dance.

His arm was strong and warm around her, his hand holding hers generating heat that scorched her, even through their gloves. She could feel his chest almost touching hers, his strong legs moving through the steps of the dance. When she glanced up, he was watching her, smiling at her. Suddenly and inexplicably shy, she smiled back. He seemed to know how she felt, the effect he was having on her, and his eyes crinkled with amusement.

For a moment all she could think of was the kiss they'd shared. She fancied she could still taste him on her lips, still feel the roughness of his skin against hers. Her heart beat faster and louder, until she was sure he would hear it.

"Penny for them," he said, and she startled. The last thing she could tell him was what she was thinking about. Just the suggestion made her stomach swirl. Desperately, she tried to think of a suitable topic of conversation, but everything that came to mind seemed loaded with innuendo.

Finally, she settled on the only innocuous question she could think of. "What has overset my aunt?"

She thought he might say he didn't know, but he didn't. "She had a disagreeable conversation with somebody."

"Who?"

"Your uncle. I don't think he was in the mood to socialize tonight."

"He never is."

"She seems happier now." Kit turned them, and Sophie saw Aunt Jess, sitting with her friends, gossiping and laughing, her shoulders relaxed. Sophie smiled, releasing the tension she hadn't realized she held within.

"May I see you tomorrow?" Kit asked. "I have something I need to talk of with you." For an instant, he seemed troubled, but then his expression lightened. "Perhaps we can go for a drive?"

"I'd like that," she answered. He turned them again, and Sophie gave herself to the wonderful sensation of floating in his arms. It ended far too soon.

"A word to the wise," he said, as he escorted her to her aunt. "You'd do well to ensure you're not left alone with Lord Pinkerton. He seems set on marrying you, and I wouldn't want him to try and—manipulate the situation."

Sophie was horrified. "You believe he may try to compromise me?"

"It's a possibility." The humor had gone from his eyes and his mouth was set in a grim line. "I feel you should take care."

"You may be certain of that," she promised. They reached Aunt Jess, and Sophie's next partner bowed and offered his arm. She walked back onto the dance floor with him, unable to help the frisson of regret that it was no longer Kit beside her.

Only because he's such an excellent dancer. She liked to dance with someone who held her as if she were lighter than a cloud, and who didn't step on her toes, that was all.

And if she said that often enough, she might begin to believe it.

Chapter Eight

It took Kit a long time to get to sleep. So many things played in his mind, tormenting him. After they left the ball, he'd told Ed his suspicions about his uncle and Pinkerton. The two men were clearly plotting something, although what, neither he nor Ed could begin to guess.

"Perhaps we'll find the answer in Uncle Leo's study," Ed suggested. They agreed to search the study when Leo went out, and see what they could discover. Until then, they would say nothing to anyone.

Except Sophie, Kit had said.

Ed vetoed that idea. He wanted to shield his sister. Kit argued that since it involved her somehow, she had a right to know. He pointed out she wasn't a child, nor was she some delicate debutante who would swoon at the very mention of trouble. She was an intelligent young woman who could contribute meaningfully to the discussion.

Ed, however, remained adamant. Sophie would not be told, and that was that.

Kit shrugged. "As you wish," he'd said. "She's your sister." But he couldn't help thinking it was a mistake. She'd be hurt at being excluded. More than hurt, in fact—she'd be angry. Furious.

Now, it was nearly five o'clock. The gray light of dawn seeped into the room, chasing away the darkness. The strange shapes and shadows of the night transformed into everyday objects and furniture. Outside the window, a bird twittered relentlessly. The first carts rumbled softly along the street. A boot heel rang against the pavement, and there was a distant tapping as the knocker-upper rapped on a window to wake whoever had paid him for the service.

Kit stretched against his mattress, bringing his muscles to life. Twelve hours from now, he'd be at her door, ready to drive her through Hyde Park. She would look perfect, her bright eyes shining, her smile beguiling him and every other man who saw her. He imagined them glaring at him, their envy undeniable as they acknowledged that Kit Thomas was accompanied by the loveliest woman in town.

Just as they had glared when he'd danced the waltz with her. Kit clasped his hands behind his head and savored the memory. She'd been so warm and vibrant in his arms, her skin glowing, making those beautiful eyes sparkle even more. The tiny seed pearls threaded through her curls winked in the light. The lavender scent of her surrounded him. He wanted to hold her closer, to feel her against him, her soft curves against the hardness of his body.

She'd looked at him, and the pulse at the base of her neck had stuttered. Her tongue darted out to wet her lips, sending a wave of longing through Kit, hardening his thighs and making him ache deep inside, until he'd had to concentrate to stop himself doing or saying something unconscionable. In that moment, he'd been thankful his evening trousers were black. Dark clothes hid far more than light would have done.

The rest of the ballroom faded, the other dancers disappeared, and only the two of them were there, gliding around the floor, lost in each other's arms. He'd wished then that the dance would last forever, so the spell she weaved would never be broken.

Oh, for God's sake! It was five o'clock in the morning and he was in bed, lusting after his best friend's sister. He threw off his covers, stalked to the chair, and threw on his clothes. Ed trusted him and expected him to behave in a befitting manner. Which meant Kit had no right to be thinking of her in that way.

If he were on his father's estate now, he would have dived into the icy waters of the lake until his body was back under his control. Here in London, he hoped a ride along Rotten Row would suffice.

Hours later, he arrived at Sophie's home for their drive. She looked beautiful in a rose-pink dress and dark crimson spencer, her gloves and reticule a pastel pink. Her bonnet was decorated with a spray of silk roses, and her skin held a soft, healthy glow, enhanced by the colors she wore. Kit helped her up into his curricle, and they made their way through the streets.

"I thought we'd take a leisurely drive through the park, if that pleases you?" he said, and she nodded. His tiger jumped up behind them and Kit drove away.

"You said you wished to talk to me?" she asked, in her no-nonsense, direct manner.

Kit hesitated. Last night, he'd been determined to tell her of his suspicions about her uncle and to warn her to stay alert. But Ed had forbidden it, and it was not Kit's place to gainsay her brother.

She waited, expectantly. He couldn't tell her he'd been mistaken and there was nothing to say. Sophie was intelligent and quick-witted and would know he was lying.

Instead of giving her information, perhaps he could glean some facts from her, possibly even things she didn't know she knew, or that she hadn't realized held any significance to anything. The more he knew, the more likely he would be to discover what Leo and Pinkerton were about.

"I saw Pinkerton hovering beside you last night," he said.

Sophie sighed. "One would think he could discern a polite lack of interest."

"But he doesn't?" Kit kept his eyes on the road so they didn't give him away. He didn't want her to have any inkling there was more than friendly interest to his questions. He'd promised Ed, after all.

"No, he doesn't. He's relentless. I've tried to dissuade him, but he won't listen to me." She gave him a tight smile. "Last night, I was quite rude to him. I told him to find another dance partner."

Kit's heart swelled with pride in her.

"Not that it did any good. He told me how I would be expected to behave once I was married."

The arrogant ass! Kit's jaw clenched and anger set a muscle twitching in his cheek. No wonder the baron had made himself scarce when he'd seen Kit and Lady Jess approaching.

"I told him it was none of his business, because what happened after my marriage would be decided between myself and my husband, and he would have no part in it."

Kit laughed. "Brava!"

She beamed. "I was rather proud of myself. Although Aunt Jess might have scolded me for my rudeness, had she heard."

"I think she might have made an exception where he was concerned." He turned into the park and slowed the horses to a walk. The tiger jumped down and made himself scarce. "I have the impression she doesn't care for him," continued Kit. "Although, your uncle, I think has a different opinion?"

Sophie grimaced. "My uncle wants me married before I cost him another Season."

"What is it about Lord Pinkerton that makes your uncle champion his cause with you?"

"There's no mystery there. The man is willing, desperate even. He'll take me with no dowry, and there's hardly been an army of suitors laying siege to my door, willing to be his rivals, has there?"

Mostly because Pinkerton has made sure of that. Which raised a whole new set of questions in Kit's mind. It was true Pinkerton needed a wife to give him an heir. A man like him would not relish his title and property going to some distant relation he'd never met, so his foray into the marriage market was completely understandable. But Pinkerton was a rich man, and a peer. There must be a dozen young ladies willing to throw themselves in his way. So why did he insist on courting one who was unwilling?

"Did you know him before the Season?" he asked. Mayhap the man had watched Sophie grow up and become enamored of her. Kit could see how any man could fall into that way of thinking.

Sophie shook her head. "No. I believe he may have had business dealings with my uncle in the past, but I never met him until I came to London in March." She clasped her hands tightly together in her lap, stretching the material of her gloves taut across her knuckles. It emphasized the distress of her situation and made Kit more determined to help her.

"It is a lovely day, is it not?" Sophie continued, a little too brightly. She gestured at the trees and shrubs lining the path onto which he had driven. Unlike the main paths, where sparse trees sheltered well-tended lawns, the foliage in this part of the park was thick, with hydrangea bushes laden with white, blue, and red flowers plus the rhododendrons' rich pinks making it seem private and secluded. The trees were in full leaf, a barrier to the noisy busyness in the rest of the grounds. There wasn't anyone else on this path at all. In fact, it was so quiet and peaceful here, Kit could believe there wasn't another soul in the whole of London.

He thought about turning the conversation back to her uncle and Pinkerton, but the subject had clearly discomfited her and Kit had no wish to overset her. Nor did he want to ruin what was turning out to be a very pleasant ride. For now, he would forget them and be satisfied with what he already knew.

A gap in the foliage showed a narrower trail heading through the bushes and, at its end, the glint of sunshine on water. Without really thinking about it, Kit drove onto this narrower path. The branches scraped against the sides of his vehicle. He winced and prayed the damage was slight.

A few moments later, the scratches in his paintwork became worth it, when Sophie sighed, contentedly. "It is beautiful here," she said. "Almost like being in the country." There was something about the wistful way she spoke that made Kit study her more carefully.

"You miss the country?" he asked.

She looked around, taking in every inch of her

surroundings. "I like Town, but it isn't really home, is it?" She smiled, ruefully. "If I'm honest, I miss my laboratory. I wonder how things are going. But I can't write to Jem and ask for a report, can I?" She laughed. "My uncle would have an apoplexy at the very thought. His unmarried niece corresponding with the gardener's lad?"

The sound of her laughter was like silver bells. Darts of lust shot through Kit. He tried to suppress them, but in doing so, he inadvertently tightened his grip on the reins. His cattle responded with a nervous pull, and he had to concentrate for a few moments on settling them.

The jerk startled Sophie and she put her hand on his arm to keep herself steady. He felt the warmth rush through him, making every nerve buzz, from where her fingers rested to the soles of his feet. His heart beat out of rhythm. He wished the moment could last eternally.

He pulled the horses to a stop and turned to her, putting his hand over hers. A muscle jumped, making her fingers flex, and Kit wondered if she'd felt the same jolt at their touch as he had. Before he could examine that thought too closely, he cleared his throat and pulled himself back under control. *Ed's sister*.

"My apologies." His voice was gruff. He hoped she wouldn't realize the true reason for that, and cleared his throat again. "I'm usually a better driver," and he flashed her what he hoped looked like a wicked grin.

"No matter." Sophie sounded slightly breathless, too. She had lowered her eyes and seemed to be studying the folds of her dress. Her face was a soft pink, framed by the blonde curls peeking out from under her bonnet. Her lips were parted slightly, and the tip of her tongue peeped through them, the movement shy and uncertain.

He wanted to kiss each and every one of the tiny freckles on her nose. Kit's thighs hardened, and he tensed, trying to prevent his desire for her becoming even more obvious than it already was.

It took him a few seconds to realize she had not removed her hand from his sleeve, nor had she objected to his fingers covering hers. She raised her head and their eyes met. Her color deepened but she did not look away.

Kit had no idea how long they sat there. It could have been a moment. It could have been an hour. All he knew was, he was looking at her and she at him, and he wanted it never to end.

Either she moved closer to him, or he moved closer to her. Perhaps it was a little of both. But suddenly they were a hair's breadth away from each other. He could feel the warmth of her breath on his face, smell the mint of her tooth powder and the chocolate she'd drunk for breakfast mingling with the soft lavender of her perfume. The silver flecks in her eyes pulled at him and he could not resist her.

Their lips touched, tentatively at first. He pulled back a fraction and watched her face. Her eyes were half closed, hiding myriad secrets behind those stunningly long lashes. They made him want to explore, to dive into the depths and never come up for air. She blinked, languidly, and her lips formed a soft, bow shape that called to him like a siren to a mariner. He swallowed, and brought his mouth to hers once more. This time he did not stop. He deepened the kiss, tasting the sweetness of her, nibbling gently at her full bottom lip. He traced the seam of her mouth with his tongue and she opened her lips, allowing him to penetrate, his tongue dancing with hers. She groaned softly and pushed herself against him.

He could feel the heat of her body, the tiny trembles with every breath she took, the erratic stutter of her pulse when his fingers caressed her throat.

Sophie's arms wound round his shoulders and she caressed the nape of his neck. Her touch sent awareness down his spine, to his groin. His breeches tightened, and he tensed his thighs, trying to ease the ache that spread up into his belly. Her fingers played with the ends of his hair and all reason was lost to him. This woman was all that mattered.

He stroked her back, her neck, her side, his hands sliding against the soft smoothness of her dress. She gave a moan of satisfaction, and he smiled against her skin as his hand moved around, over her ribs and to the underside of her breast.

He didn't remember shedding his gloves or unbuttoning her spencer, but somehow he had, and now his fingers played with the soft curve of her breast, the delectable cushion of flesh above the neckline of her gown. He kneaded it softly, and she clung tighter to him. His hat toppled, and he didn't know or care where it went.

He moved his mouth from hers, and she murmured her objection, then groaned as he kissed and nibbled along her jawline, stopping to taste the lobe of her ear before tormenting the soft skin on her neck. He savored each moan and gasp she made, the speed of her pulse, racing so fast it seemed to be one long, quivering beat.

She came free of her bodice, and his fingers found her nipple, which pebbled under his touch. She moaned and tugged at his hair, pulling him closer to her, and he groaned his satisfaction.

As slowly as he could manage, Kit dusted her skin

with featherlight kisses, working his way down from the pulse point at the base of her throat, over her collarbone. He hoped his light and languid kisses were driving her mad, because they were torture for him, when all he wanted to do was deepen them while his body pressed into hers, relieving the aching want within him.

Finally, he reached her breast. He continued rolling one nipple between his finger and his thumb, and swirled his tongue gently around the other one, tasting it, savoring it, before drawing it into his mouth. Her moan of surprised delight sent triumph surging through him. Her breaths came in short bursts, and she squirmed in her seat, arching her back, offering herself to him. He tightened painfully, until he wanted to beg for mercy. She moaned again and he almost fell to his knees.

His mouth left her breast, and he smiled at her objection before returning to her mouth, pushing his tongue inside and running it once more along hers. She kissed him back, matching him move for move. Her lack of expertise, combined with her passion and eagerness, unmanned him, and it took every ounce of determination to stop him embarrassing himself there and then.

She cried out and clutched him tightly, her whole body writhing as she came apart. His spirits soared. To think he had brought her to this. He felt like a king, a conquering hero, even as his full balls protested that he too needed release. Release he could not take. Not here. Not now.

Kit felt the orgasm race through her, the hum of her body, the tremble of her skin, the erratic beating of her heart. He wanted this moment to go on forever. The waves within her slowed and lost their intensity, and he imagined bringing her to another climax, leaving her shattered and boneless in his arms, everything forgotten but him. In his fantasy, he ran his hand under her skirt and up her leg. She shuddered as his fingers glided up, over the cool silk of her stocking, to the soft, warm skin of her thigh, the tangle of hair at the juncture of her legs, and the hot, wet secret place beyond. He rubbed the little nub of nerves until she whimpered and begged, and then he filled her with his fingers, bringing her to the peak once more before unbuttoning his falls and settling himself between her legs and...

One of his horses snorted, and Kit came crashing back to reality.

He pulled away from Sophie more sharply than he intended. Her face was a mixture of confusion and disappointment. She made a soft, mewling sound and he wanted nothing more than to pull her close again, and finish what they had begun.

Which was the last thing he should be doing! Where was his self-control? Lost, together with his common sense, if what had just happened was any indication. He could scarcely believe what he'd done. With Ed's sister! In Hyde Park!

He had kissed Ed's sister so thoroughly he'd brought her to a climax here, in a public place, where anybody might have happened along. If that horse hadn't snorted and brought him back to sanity, he would—well, there was no telling what might have happened.

What still might happen if she continued looking at him like that.

Sophie's eyes were glazed over. Her hair was half undone and her lips were swollen and dark from his kisses. As for her clothes—Kit didn't dare to look down at them. His self-control was already hanging by a thread. He daren't risk it shattering completely.

He cleared his throat and faced front, concentrating on the path ahead. "My apologies," he said, his voice gruff. "I forgot myself."

****

It took Sophie a moment to realize he was apologizing for what had just happened. It had been the most incredible experience of her life, and he was brushing it away with words of contrition.

A wave of shame engulfed her. He had kissed her—more than kissed her—and she'd let him do so. More, she'd encouraged him, holding him close, reacting in a way that left him in no doubt that she was more than willing.

She had been startled at first, afraid even, as he moved nearer, closing the space between them until it completely disappeared. But his first kiss was so gentle, so soft, she wondered briefly if she'd imagined it. His lips touching hers were like the soft flutter of a butterfly's wing, making her long for more. Her stomach swooped and dived, and between her thighs felt…strange. She tensed her muscles but it brought her no relief, and she knew, instinctively, that only he could do that for her now.

He kissed her again, his lips playing over hers, his tongue sliding in and out. The rough skin on his cheeks tickled her, and his warmth enveloped her. She tasted coffee on his breath, fresh air on his skin, and that indefinable something that was Kit alone.

Kit broke the kiss, and she wanted to yell her protest. She settled for a tiny groan of impatience which turned halfway through to a sigh of pleasure as he moved his lips along her jawline, tasting her skin and suckling at her pulse points until her heart beat so fast she thought it might explode.

Her nipples hardened and grew, chafing against the linen of her shift until she longed for them to be free. Sophie was vaguely aware that he unbuttoned her spencer. She arched her back, thrusting herself at him, inviting him to do…she did not know what. Then his mouth was on one breast, his fingers playing with the other, and something built within her, bubbling under the surface, a delicious, frightening, wonderful, overpowering something, unlike anything she had ever experienced before. Every nerve stretched taut, every inch of her shattered into a million pieces. She cried out in ecstatic agony, pulses pounding all over her body, which jerked and bucked and writhed all on its own. She saw stars.

Afterward, she leaned into him, exhausted and happy. Every bone had turned to jelly, and a strange, sleepy peace blanketed her. She could have stayed here like this, forever.

And then he apologized!

The breeze blew across her and she realized her breasts were still exposed, her nipples, so warm from his touch just a moment ago, now uncomfortably chilled.

What a wanton he must think her! He was probably so disgusted with her that he could barely look at her. Which didn't bode well for the betrothal charade. And— oh Lord! what if he told Ed? Her brother would be so disappointed in her. Not to mention angry.

Sophie straightened her bodice and buttoned up her spencer, and reason began to permeate her brain. Kit wouldn't tell her brother how shameless she was. He couldn't. If he even hinted at what had happened, Ed would force him up the aisle so fast his head would spin. In that respect, at least, her behavior would bring no consequences.

Kit's own opinion of her, however…

She took a deep breath and schooled her expression to be politely calm. There would be plenty of opportunity to cry over his lost good opinion when she was alone. She had a feeling it wouldn't matter how many times she told herself she was to blame, that it was only her own behavior which had put her so thoroughly beyond the pale. Such a truth would not make her feel any better.

"I should like to go home now," she said, amazed to discover how even her voice sounded, although to her own ears it also sounded small.

"Sophie…"

She raised her chin, defiantly. She would not let him see how broken she felt. He wouldn't guess how much he'd hurt her. "If you please," she said, her tone like the one Aunt Jess used with recalcitrant servants and presumptuous tradesmen.

It worked. Kit flicked the reins and turned his curricle around.

Chapter Nine

Sophie didn't say a word on the way home, and Kit knew he'd upset her. He was less certain what he'd done. Was she angry with him for taking liberties? Or because he'd stopped? She hadn't seemed unwilling, holding him tightly and returning his kisses with her own sweet, inexpert ones. His apology certainly hadn't been for those kisses. He knew it should have been, but that didn't signify because he'd do it again in a heartbeat.

He was a hypocrite for apologizing about the rest of his actions, too. Because he didn't regret them, either. He had savored every moment. Telling himself she was a lady and should be treated like one, that they were on a public path, even that Ed would likely meet him at dawn if he heard about this—none of it had been enough to stop him. It was his lack of self-control—and only that—which he'd apologized for. He wished he could tell her that, but saying anything now might only make things worse.

So he, too, sat in silence as they picked up his tiger and made their way through the streets.

At her door, the tiger took hold of the horse bridles so Kit could help Sophie down from her seat. Once on the pavement, she held out her hand and said, in a very formal tone, "Thank you so much for a lovely drive, Mr. Thomas."

His jaw tightened and a muscle twitched in his

cheek. "Sophie, I—"

"I must go. My aunt will be looking for me. Good day," and she ran up the steps. The door closed behind her, and he sighed. It felt as if something had broken, and he didn't know how to fix it.

****

All the way home Sophie's anger and shame had festered until she could barely look at him, dreading to see the censure he no doubt felt. It took all her strength to remain politely neutral, to thank him for the ride as if nothing untoward had happened and she wasn't wishing she could somehow relive the day and do everything differently.

Head high, back straight, she'd walked away, not daring to chance a last look at him. Tears stung her eyes and the lump in her throat threatened to choke her. The smile she gave the footman was weak and watery at best. The footman bowed and took her coat, not betraying by so much as a wink that he noticed anything amiss. Somehow, that made Sophie feel worse.

She ran upstairs and along the corridor to her chamber. The sun poured in through the window, bathing the room in a soft, golden glow that had never failed to lift her spirits, until now. Now it dampened her mood and highlighted the folly of her actions and all they had cost her.

"Stupid, stupid, stupid," she muttered. "What did you think you were doing?" The answer came in a crystal-clear voice that rang through her. She had not been thinking at all. He had kissed her, and all rational thought had flown.

But that kiss! The warmth of his lips on hers, the taste of him on her mouth, the feel of his tongue against hers. The feathery tickle as he kissed his way along her jawline and down her throat, his lips teasing her skin, quickening her heartbeat and stealing her breath. She wanted to pull him nearer, to make him kiss her harder, to stop the torment. And when he'd put his hand on her…

Sophie touched her breast now, through her dress. It felt tender, and her nipple rose to a peak. A pleasurable ache stretched down through her, from her breast to the most private part of her. It built within her, taking her over. She had felt like this in the park, just before…*it*…had happened.

She wasn't sure what *it* was, but it had been the most exciting, the most frightening thing she'd ever experienced. Her pulse raced at the memory, and her breaths tore on her jagged emotions.

Horrified at herself, she pulled her hand from her breast, and immediately missed the touch. She folded her arms tightly across her chest to fight the temptation to feel it once more.

This would not do. Reliving the shameful moments, reveling in the way they'd made her feel was not the way a respectable young lady should behave. No wonder Kit had been so appalled!

She moved to the window and glared out at the garden, barely seeing the trees and bushes so artfully arranged there, the array of colors in the flowerbed. She turned and paced to the door, then back to the window. She reminded herself of a lion she once saw in a cage in the Tower of London. He too had paced back and forth, measuring out his tiny space. Sophie had felt sorry for the lion. Now, she felt frustration. Suddenly, her bedchamber was too confining, the powerful emotions surging through her filling the space and squeezing out all the air.

She threw the window open and leaned out, taking in big gulps of air. There was a loud, angry slapping sound as two startled pigeons flew away. The breeze rustled the leaves below her. A few gardens away, a small dog yapped and a child squealed. Life went on as it always had, unbothered in the least by the earth-shattering moments Sophie had experienced. What cared the world if she had spoiled Kit's opinion of her, just when he had made her start dreaming of forever?

Which was ridiculous! Kit Thomas was not going to offer her forever. He'd never intended to, even before today. For goodness' sake, he hadn't even offered her a real courtship. He'd played a role as a favor to a friend. It didn't matter how much she cared for him, because he did not return the feelings.

Sophie's eyes widened and her mouth formed a surprised O. She cared for Kit Thomas. In fact, despite knowing this was all a charade, she'd done the most stupid thing she could. She'd fallen in love with him.

She sat down on the stool in front of her dressing table and put her head in her hands. What a tangle! What on earth would he say? The sworn bachelor who had no interest in marriage, who needed to be free to study engineering. He'd be appalled!

But then, perhaps he already knew. Perhaps a man as experienced as he was could tell the difference between a kiss that meant nothing, a fleeting pleasure, and one that carried the heart and soul with it.

No wonder he'd been at such pains to end the intimacy. He'd been right to do so. *She* had been the one at fault, spinning yarn without wool. And then she'd compounded her guilt by refusing to speak to him, pouting all the way home at the slight she'd imagined he delivered her.

"Sophie Marie Wilson, how could you let yourself be embroiled in such a mess?"

She would have to apologize. If she wrote him a note now, it could be delivered to his rooms this evening, and she would feel better about the whole sorry saga.

She sat at her writing desk, took up her pen, and began to write.

****

Kit got back into his curricle and waited for his tiger to climb aboard. Just as he flicked the reins to move on, the front door opened again. Hopeful, he stopped his cattle and turned, a smile ready.

But it wasn't Sophie who came bounding down the steps. It was Ed, still pulling on his gloves as he approached. Kit's mouth dried and there was a lump in his throat that threatened to choke him. If his friend knew how he'd betrayed his trust today...

"Ho there," said Ed, his smile bright and open. "Thought I'd missed you."

"What can I do for you?" Kit marveled at the ordinariness of his tone. One would never think, to hear him, that anything was amiss. He prayed his demeanor would not give him away.

"My uncle's out," replied Ed. "I thought we could..." he glanced at the tiger, "...play that game of billiards?"

Kit grinned at Ed's clumsy attempt at subterfuge. "Walk the horses round to the mews," he instructed his tiger, then jumped down and followed Ed into the house. His eagerness to get inside was purely because he disliked the mystery surrounding Leo and Pinkerton, he told himself. He had no thought of seeing Sophie again. He wasn't hoping he'd be able to talk to her and repair the rift that had opened between them today.

"What exactly are we searching for?" asked Ed once they'd secured entry into Leo's study with the key Ed had pilfered. He locked the door behind them.

"We'll know it when we find it," answered Kit.

The room was dark, the walls covered in deep red silk that shrank the space. Heavy red brocade curtains hung at the windows, cutting out much of the natural light, and the furniture was dark and mismatched. The desk was mahogany and clearly old and well used, its surface scratched, with lighter patches of wood showing at the corners where the varnish had been worn away. The captain's chair behind it was old too, its seat sagging from years of service and the arms worn down and rounded. To one side of the window was a bureau, a tall piece in lacquered black, festooned with Chinese scenes picked out in a dull gold. The opposite wall was taken up with bookshelves laden with books that looked old and worthy. The fireplace was cold, although a basket of wood stood ready beside it. Above the mantelshelf hung a portrait of Leo, his chin at a haughty angle, thumbs hooked into the pockets on his waistcoat and an expression of gravitas on his face.

They searched the desk, then every drawer, cupboard and cranny in his bureau. By the time they began checking the bookshelves, Ed was despondent.

"I suppose it was a bit of a squeak, wasn't it? The chances of finding anything."

"I'd say it was evens. Your uncle strikes me as a particular and careful man. It's in his nature to write things down, even if they could incriminate him. And once written, he'd want his papers nearby, where he could find them in a hurry."

"Well, they don't seem to be in here." Ed threw himself into his uncle's chair with such force it rocked and clicked loudly. He grimaced and looked down as if he expected it to collapse on him. Kit chuckled and started searching the bookshelves.

"That's all I need, to break his chair," muttered Ed. He stood and turned the chair upside down to check for damage. "Well. That's unexpected."

Upright, the chair had looked like any other, but upturned, it was easy to see the base of the seat was deeper than it should be. More, the wood covering the base had shifted slightly, revealing the opening to a hidden compartment.

"I must have dislodged it when I sat down," whispered Ed. "I thought I'd broken it."

He rested the upside-down chair on the desk, then stood back and stared at it as if he expected something else to happen of its own volition. He glanced at Kit, then reached out and pried the secret door fully open.

Inside was a small, leather-bound book and a sheaf of loose papers. Kit took them out and laid them on the desk. Ed opened the book, a ledger, and they both leaned over it as they read. It took less than a minute before Ed swore and banged the heel of his hand against the desktop.

"That bastard! My father trusted him. I trusted him. And all the time he was bilking us." He turned and stood at the window, his frame silhouetted in the evening light.

Kit picked up the first sheet of paper and read it. It was a letter from the late Baron Hamsey to his brother-in-law. Uncomfortable at intruding on a private family matter, Kit offered the letter to Ed, who waved his hand, dismissively.

"I'm so angry, I doubt I could read it," he said, his words clipped by his gritted teeth. "Please?"

With a nod, Kit read the letter. The first few lines were pleasantries, one brother by marriage wishing another well. The baron spoke of family affairs in a light, jocular way. Then, a few lines in, the tone of the letter changed completely.

"Now, to the true purpose of this missive. You will be aware that I have no blood relatives save my beloved children. As I grow older and realize the limit of my own mortality, this has preyed upon my mind. If something should take me from them before Edward is of age, I pray you would step forward and assume guardianship of them both. It should not prove an onerous task, as they are good children. I would hate to think they would needs be cared for only by paid servants, and would welcome your acquiescence in this matter."

Kit paused, wondering why Leo had hidden this letter. So far it had said nothing secret, sensitive or incriminating. It was common knowledge that Hamsey had named Leo guardian of his children. The solicitor had produced documents confirming this. The arrangement lasted until Ed's twenty-fifth birthday, at which time, unless Sophie was already married, she would become her brother's ward, releasing her uncle from that responsibility.

"Is that it?" asked Ed, half turning from the window to study Kit.

"No. There's more." Kit scanned the letter, found where he'd left off, and read on.

"I also ask that you look after their affairs and

manage the money and estates that are coming to them. I've prepared a list of all the individual assets so you may more easily work, but you should know that, as of the last quarter, the unentailed properties, business interests, cash and other liquid assets come to a total of £150,000."

Kit read the figure twice more until it began to sink in.

Ed stared at him in disbelief. "How much?" The color drained from him and he swallowed several times.

Kit understood his friend's shock. He was in shock himself, and the news would not affect him. Ed must feel as if the world had fallen out of kilter. "There's more," he whispered, having silently read the rest of the letter. Ed looked terrified. Kit smiled, grimly. "Your father set aside £10,000 for Sophie's dowry."

Ed leaned against the wall. He looked as if his legs would not hold him without its support. His breathing was heavy, and his eyes glittered with hot rage. After several seconds, he pushed himself upright and stalked toward the door.

"Ed?"

"I'm going to kill him." Kit intercepted him before he could open the door. Ed narrowed his eyes. "Let me pass."

"That's not the way to resolve this."

Ed's voice was low and icy. "You're saying you would do differently, were it you?"

"I would want to cut his heart out with a dull and rusty knife. But what we want isn't necessarily the best way of dealing with the situation."

Ed's cheeks were flushed and his jaw so tightly clenched Kit heard his teeth grind together. His chest rose and fell too quickly, and a muscle ticked in his cheek. Kit had no doubt that, if he saw his uncle now, Ed would tear the man limb from limb.

Which was the last thing he should do. At present, Leo was unaware he'd been discovered and, Kit thought, it was better he remained in ignorance until they were ready to deal with him. Before that could happen, he explained to Ed, they needed to discover if he'd perpetrated the fraud alone or if others were involved.

Kit kept his voice soft, trying to take the fire out of Ed's anger. For his part, Ed still looked murderous, although he had now stopped trying to push past Kit and out of the room.

"There are so many unanswered questions," continued Kit. "Where does Pinkerton fit into this? Why is he so keen on marrying the unwilling Sophie when he could as easily marry anyone?"

"It's plain to see why my uncle is keen to allow the match," said Ed. "With Sophie wed, I'd have no reason to discover she'd been cheated of her dowry." He rubbed his hand across the back of his neck and his face contorted in anguish. "He's my mother's brother, for God's sake! How could he do this?"

"Greed is a powerful lure." Kit thought for a moment, then added, "There'll be a scandal."

If he'd thought Ed could look any more miserable, he'd been wrong. Absolute despair filled his eyes. "It'll ruin us all," he groaned. "Sophie won't be able to marry anyone, dowry or no."

She may not regard that as the tragedy you think. Kit bit his tongue to stop himself voicing the thought. He doubted Ed would find it helpful at this time.

Ed sighed and closed his eyes. "And as for Aunt

Jess, she'll have a conniption. The horror of it may well kill her. The tabbies will tear her limb from limb."

They stared at one another for a moment, as if each tried to gauge a solution from the other's countenance. Kit knew from the tightness of his jaw muscles that he looked as grim as Ed.

There had to be a way. Leo Farnham could not simply walk away from this as if he'd done nothing wrong. His actions had to have consequences, and he must face them. At the very least, he must restore the money he'd embezzled and ensure Sophie's dowry was restored to her.

And yet... Ed was correct. The scandal would not benefit the Wilson siblings or their aunt. On the contrary, it would probably cause them more harm than the original crime.

Much as he longed to see justice done, Kit did not want Sophie to suffer for it. Better she remain penniless than become the subject of the latest *on dit,* passed gleefully from ear to eager ear by people who loved nothing more than someone else's misery. His heart beat a painful tattoo and his breath caught in his tightened windpipe at the thought of those holier-than-thou harpies tearing her to shreds.

Her beautiful face swam before his eyes, her expression so sad it broke his heart. He wanted to reach out and hold her, shielding her from the slings and arrows of the *ton*, taking the blows himself to save her. He wanted—no, he *needed* to know she would be all right. He vowed to make certain of that, even if it meant allowing the guilty to go unpunished.

Although he was damned if he'd resign himself to that happening until he'd explored all possible paths to justice.

"What do we do, Kit?" asked Ed.

Kit glanced at his friend and was horrified at the change which had been wrought in the last half hour. Ed's eyes, usually so full of merriment, showed deep pain, and his shoulders had slumped. His face was lined, as if he'd aged a decade or more since they'd entered this room. There was a gray tinge to his cheeks, and even his hair had lost its sheen.

"Just what am I to do?" he asked again.

Kit gestured at the ledger and the letter. "Do you have somewhere to store them where your uncle will not discover them? If you haven't, I can take them to my lodgings. He cannot reach them there. We'll put the study back as we found it so he has no cause to think he is discovered and, for this evening at least, we continue as if we know nothing."

"And then what?"

"On the morrow, we find a solicitor we can trust and discover what we should do next. When we know what our choices are, we can plan accordingly."

They put the study to rights and carefully locked it behind them, then walked in grim silence along the corridor. Ed held the book, the letter tucked inside, while Kit put on his hat and gloves, then Ed handed everything to him.

"I will take good care of them," Kit promised.

Ed nodded. "I am unexceptionable as an actor. I don't know that I can sit with him and be equitable this evening."

"Then come to me. We'll dine together, then go to the club. See you at seven?"

He turned to go, and glanced up. Sophie stood at the

top of the stairs, one hand resting on the banister. She stared down at him, watching him. He stared back. Their eyes held and, in that instant, he thought he saw all the wonders and mysteries of the earth come together into one beautiful, unfathomable package. Although she was too far away for him to smell it, her soft, lavender perfume seemed to fill the hall. The color of her dress brought out the blue in her eyes and seemed to make her skin shine. His lips tingled under the phantom impression of her kiss.

Ed clapped his shoulder, bringing him crashing back to normality. He smiled at whatever Ed had said, then looked up again, ready to give her a sweeping bow.

His heart sank when he realized she had gone.

Chapter Ten

Kit called on Ed the next day, just as Ed returned from his visit to the solicitor. Ed's usual good humor was lacking, and there was a strained quality about him. Kit followed him into the morning room.

"Shall I ring for coffee, or would you prefer something stronger?" asked Ed.

Kit looked at the clock on the mantelshelf. It was just after one. He raised one eyebrow.

"I know." Ed held his hands up as if in surrender. "Slippery slope and all that, drinking this early." He ordered coffee.

"It went badly?" asked Kit. He took one of the chairs near the hearth, flipped up his coat tails before he sat, and crossed one knee over the other.

Ed shook his head. "It went well. The proof of the embezzlement has been logged and notarized, and steps can be taken both to prevent more theft and to reclaim that which is already stolen. But there's little else we can do. As you said yesterday, having Leo arrested would cause a scandal the whole family would have to weather."

Kit nodded, unsurprised. It was the way of Society. Blood mattered. And just as the family you had been born to could open doors and bring advantage, so it could drag you down. "Can you keep it quiet?"

"We must. Although," Ed's smile was wan, "Leo

131

doesn't need to know that. If he believes I'm prepared to bring him to book, he can be frightened into returning what he stole before slinking off to a quiet retirement in an isolated backwater where he can do no other damage."

"That's better than nothing." The tray was brought in with coffee and sweetmeats. They sat in silence until the maid left. The door swished closed behind her, but a small sliver of light from the hall told Kit she hadn't shut it properly. He heard her footsteps retreat along the corridor.

Suddenly Ed grinned, broadly, and when he spoke there was too much happiness in his voice. "Still, all's well that ends well, wouldn't you say? I'm not pockets to let anymore, and Sophie is safe. Leo's in no position to demand anything of her, and without his acquiescence, Pinkerton's cause is lost. Which means you're free, old chap. No more need to pretend to court her any longer." He leaned forward, poured coffee into the two cups, and handed one to Kit, then popped a sweetmeat into his mouth before sitting back, his own cup cradled in his lap.

Kit knew he should be happy at the way things had turned about. He was. He was very pleased indeed that his friend's fortune wasn't lost, and overjoyed that Pinkerton would be thwarted in his attempts to secure Sophie. At the same time, though, a heaviness hit him, weighting his chest and lowering his spirit at the thought of ending his arrangement with her.

Which was absurd. He didn't really wish the world to see them as a match; he had no intention of marrying anybody. He couldn't even contemplate it, not without giving up all chance of studying. And it was hardly fair to Sophie if her potential suitors were put off by his presence. She said she didn't wish to marry, she wanted to be free to pursue her scientific research, but if she met the right man, well, anyone could change their mind.

The thought of Sophie falling in love with another man lanced his heart. He stiffened a little and slowed his breathing until the sharp, hot pain eased. He couldn't wallow in self-pity at her loss. No, he corrected himself, not her loss. He couldn't lose what he'd never had. All there had ever been with Sophie was a glimpse of something, a life that might have been his, were things different.

He stared into the empty hearth, trying to make sense of the way he felt. That he'd come to care for Sophie was beyond doubt. He enjoyed her company, relished the moments spent with her, and he'd been miserable and out of sorts since their tiff had ended yesterday's drive. He hoped to see her when he concluded his business with Ed. Even if she no longer needed him to be her swain, he'd like to cry friends with her and be easy in her company.

But that was all. Wasn't it?

Ed poured himself a second cup of coffee, walked behind Kit's chair, and gave his shoulder a friendly squeeze. "No need to be so blue-deviled about it," he said. "Our agreement still stands. You escort my sister till Pinkerton is no longer a threat, and you'll get what I promised."

That's what Ed believed had saddened Kit? The thought of losing the payment for this charade? "I don't want your money," he said.

"Nonsense. You need to be able to live—"

"I can live perfectly well, thank you. Keep your coin."

"Don't be a damn fool. What will you use to pay

your bills? Shirt buttons? Besides, you did a sterling job. Everyone and his wife is convinced you've set your cap at Sophie. You kept Pinkerton at bay and convinced the *ton* she isn't a wallflower. All in all, you were a great investment. Worth every penny of £200. I'll bring it to you tomorrow. Or would you prefer I pay it in to your bank?"

Kit opened his mouth to say neither, but he never got the chance. The door pushed open and Sophie stood on the threshold. Her shoulders were stiff with tension, and her hands were clenched into fists by her side. Her face was dark with fury.

"You were paid?"

A feeling of despair washed over Kit. "I can explain," he began.

She cut him off. "You were paid? I thought you helped me because of friendship, and all the time, you were being paid?"

"Sophie, I…"

"Did the thought of the coins in your pocket make me more palatable?"

"It wasn't like…"

"How much extra did you get for kissing me?

"Kissing?" Ed stared, open-mouthed, at Kit. Kit didn't have time for him now.

"Sophie, it wasn't like that…"

"And for…" Sophie blushed deeply. Kit chanced a glance at Ed, who now glared at him.

"And for what?" he demanded.

Sophie lifted her chin, defiantly. "He kissed me."

"And?"

Sophie fixed him with a stare that told Kit she wasn't going to answer.

"Kit?" insisted Ed.

Kit looked away, unable to meet Ed's eye. It seemed he might have to offer for Sophie after all. It shocked him to realize he didn't actually mind. He opened his mouth to make the offer.

"He made me believe he liked me," said Sophie. Kit grimaced. This was going from bad to worse.

Ed's voice was coldly calm. "And just how did he do that?"

Sophie stepped farther into the room and gave her brother a look of contempt. "Don't be obtuse," she said. "He paid me attention. Romanced me. Kissed me. Made me feel…pretty."

"You are pretty. Beautiful." Kit hoped she heard the sincerity in his voice, and saw it in his eyes.

She didn't. "And it was all for money!"

"That's not true! It wasn't…"

But Ed was not going to let this go. "Did he do anything to—to—"

Kit wanted to shout yes. He wanted to grab Ed by the shoulders and shake him till his teeth rattled, yell that he had compromised Sophie's reputation and Ed must allow the match.

"Of course not," said Sophie, indignantly. "He is a gentleman." She gave Kit a look full of daggers. "In that way, at least."

Ed deflated with relief. "Sorry, old chap. Should've known you wouldn't…"

Anger bubbled inside Kit. He wanted to confess that he'd done what Ed suspected. He'd compromised Sophie. He would marry her. But how could he say those things now? He couldn't call her a liar.

He looked at her and winced at the disgust in her

eyes. Then, coldly, haughtily, she turned from him and gave her attention to Ed. "Make sure you give him a bonus. He earned it."

"Sophie…"

"Mr. Thomas, to my sorrow, I cannot order you from this house. Nor can I ask the servants to bar your way in future. Since you are Edward's friend, you will undoubtedly remain welcome. But don't expect to find me at home to you, for I shall not be."

"Sophie, listen to me…"

"I believe I have listened enough. I do not wish to hear more. I do not wish to ever see you again. Goodbye, Mr. Thomas."

She raised her head impossibly high and strode from the room, shutting the door firmly behind her. Kit followed her, but by the time he reached the hall she'd disappeared.

Ed stood behind him. "Sorry, old chap."

"Stop saying that. You have no reason to be sorry."

"But it seems you do. If I'd known how it was between you…" Ed stepped back. "She'll come around." Kit glared at him and Ed shut up.

"We need to decide how best to deal with your uncle," said Kit, hoping to change the subject.

"Yes, we do," said Ed. "But it can wait until tomorrow." Kit nodded, and Ed gave him a look of sympathetic understanding. "She will come around, Kit."

Kit was not so sure. Her eyes had blazed fire. He felt as if a lump of lead had been dropped onto his chest from a great height, crushing him, and suddenly he couldn't get out of this house fast enough. He'd go to his club. If Cardew was there, he could make himself feel better by thrashing him at billiards. If Cardew wasn't there, then Kit thought he might just have to get very, very drunk.

****

Sophie raced back to the safety of her bedchamber as if the hounds of Lucifer were at her heels. Her eyes burned, and there was a pounding, whooshing noise beating at her ears. She threw herself across her bed and sobbed into her eiderdown.

How could they do this to her? Oh, she was under no illusion that Kit had cared for her. She'd known from the start he was pretending because he was Ed's friend. But to discover friendship had not been enough, that he'd needed the added incentive of payment—and such a payment! Two hundred pounds! More than some people earned in a lifetime.

Had he refused to do it for less? Was courting her so onerous that only a large sum made it palatable? Considering the hesitation of other gentlemen, Sophie had to wonder.

What was wrong with her? She didn't think she was ugly. The face in her mirror wasn't beautiful, but it was passably pretty—even features, with nothing misshapen...although if she looked now, she might change her opinion. Her eyes felt swollen and raw, her cheeks chafed, and her nose running. She pulled her handkerchief from her pocket and wiped her hot face. Her skin was rough, and her breath came in gulps, as if her body tried to refuse each one entry, and there was a wet patch on the eiderdown where she'd sobbed and probably dribbled.

How charming and attractive that was! She rolled on to her back and threw her arm across her aching forehead, shutting her eyes against the harsh light of day.

If only she hadn't gone to the morning room to find a ribbon for her bonnet. It had been an unintentional interruption; she hadn't known Ed was at home, let alone playing host to Kit. The door was ajar, and as she approached she heard their voices. Her spirits had lifted at the thought of seeing Kit, even though she owed him an apology for her behavior. Having written her letter to him yesterday, she had fully intended to have it delivered, but had been unable to do so, and it was still in her pocket.

Now she had thought she could say what she needed to say and return their friendship to a steadier footing.

Ed sounded buoyant as she put her hand against the door. Then she'd heard his words.

"Everyone and his wife is convinced you've set your cap at Sophie," he'd said. "You kept Pinkerton at bay and convinced the *ton* she isn't a wallflower. All in all, you were a great investment. Worth every penny of £200."

For a second, Sophie stood, frozen in disbelief. Then a red rage descended and she pushed open the door. She hardly remembered what she said to them, but she knew she'd left them in no doubt of her feelings.

Did her own brother believe no one would even *pretend* to court her unless he was paid? Did he really think that little of her?

She tried to calm herself by doing something she'd last done as a child—dreaming up unpleasant and painful revenges on him. The technique didn't work as well as it once had, but then, learning that he had no faith in her hurt a lot more than when he'd put a toad in her boot or made a pie bed of her sheets.

Terrible though Ed's poor opinion was, though, Kit's betrayal seemed somehow worse. He had kissed her, and held her, and made her feel special. She'd truly believed he liked her, when all the time he'd been doing it for money. Hah! If he was in need of funds, perhaps he should apply to Drury Lane. His skills would be in great demand on the stage there.

Although, if she was honest, she couldn't blame him for everything. He'd never pretended the courtship was real, never led her to believe his feelings were genuine, nor encouraged hers for him. Tears slid down the sides of her face and into her hairline as she conceded that, when it came to falling in love with him, the guilt was all hers.

And that hurt most of all.

She must have cried herself to sleep, because when she next opened her eyes the light coming through the window was fading to dusk.

The room was a gray-blue now, the furniture not quite shadows but not quite visible. Sophie's back ached from lying down too long, a headache pounded, and her shoulders felt hunched and tight. She made an effort to relax them, rolled her head, then massaged her temples. Her fingers felt wonderfully cool against her hot head. Her eyes were sore, and the skin on her cheeks was taut. Even her hair hurt. She dragged her fingers through the curls and dislodged the pins, feeling relief as it loosened. If Kit could see her now, he would think he'd had a lucky escape.

The thought of him seeing her like this galvanized her. She didn't see why it should, though. Why should she care if he saw her looking like Medusa? Looking her best had failed to impress him, so perhaps he should see her at her worst.

Sophie groaned. She knew she didn't want that.

Much as it galled her to admit it, his opinion mattered. She no more wanted him to see her with her face puffy and blotched than she wished the world to know how he'd humiliated her.

No. The best revenge would be to make him realize what he'd thrown away. A diamond of the first water she may never be, but Sophie was certain she could look well enough to make him regret his actions. After all, she'd seen the desire in his eyes just before he kissed her. There'd been no pretense in that.

"I'll show you," she said. The idea of him begging for an audience while she gave him the cut direct made her feel much better.

She smiled, and the tear-tightened skin on her cheeks stretched. With a groan, she rolled off her bed and stumbled to her dresser to wash her face. Against her hot skin the cold water felt delicious.

Feeling marginally better, she went to the window and sat on the wide sill, resting her head against the pane. Like the water, the cool glass soothed her.

The bushes in the garden were black in the twilight, their shapes stark and grotesque. The grass was silvery gray, the path a pale ribbon winding through it. The colors had leached from the flowers in the borders, and the dull monochrome matched her mood completely.

"Oh, pull yourself together," she scolded herself, and she straightened, as if that could help refill her pride. "It's not as if you wanted him to care, is it? You should be glad he doesn't."

She didn't want a husband, she reminded herself. She didn't even want a beau, much as it was nice to be seen with one by people who'd given her pitying looks when she was a wallflower.

A husband would interfere with her plans for the future. He'd expect her to stay in the home, breeding his children and charming his guests, playing the pianoforte and drawing bowls of fruit. He wouldn't want her up to her elbows in earth, fingernails black and her dress ruined while she cultivated superior wheat seed to increase the harvest, help farmers, and earn a medal at the Royal Society. Even Countess Ilive had encountered opposition to her scientific endeavors, and she'd had every advantage: a tolerant husband, wealth, and space to work.

Remaining unmarried meant Sophie would at least have the latter. Ed had had the laboratory built and equipped, so surely he'd allow her to continue to use it once he came into his majority and controlled everything. Although even Ed would prefer to see her married. She must make him see that all her attention was focused on her goal, that marriage would only get in the way.

Although, she had to acknowledge, there was a great difference between not wanting a husband and nobody wanting her. She sighed, miserable.

Sudden movement in the garden caught her eye. Too big for a bird, or the neighbor's cat, which sometimes prowled the undergrowth. She concentrated her attention as the movement left the shadows and became clear— and a gasp of surprise forced from her.

Lord Pinkerton stormed through the garden, his long stride eating up the path. Even from here and in the dusk, Sophie could see he was angry. More than angry. Fury radiated from him like the heat from a fire.

What's he doing here? As she asked herself that question, Uncle Leo scrambled to catch up to him. He looked agitated, gesturing at the baron as if trying to get him to listen to something that clearly did not interest him. Sophie wished she could open the window and hear what they said, which shocked her. She'd never resorted to eavesdropping before, and now she was contemplating doing it for the second time in one day.

Besides, if she opened the window, it would make a noise and alert them to her presence. Uncle Leo would be angry at her, and worse, she'd be forced to acknowledge Lord Pinkerton. The fewer times she had to do that, the better.

Lord Pinkerton grabbed at Uncle Leo's coat and pulled him close. His teeth were bared and Uncle Leo shook his head rapidly. Sophie watched, wide eyed, as the baron reached into her uncle's pocket, pulled out a purse, and then released him. Uncle Leo stumbled back, righted himself, and smoothed down his coat. Lord Pinkerton turned back to the house, looking up at Sophie's window as he did so. She ducked out of sight.

She didn't know whether to be frightened or angry. That Lord Pinkerton was an odious bully, she'd known very well, but that he might resort to physical violence against someone older and weaker than himself made her feel sick. And if he could treat a gentleman like Uncle Leo in such a fashion, how would he treat his wife?

Sophie sat down heavily on the windowsill, shoulders hunched, elbows on knees, and hands covering her face as the implications of her fight with Kit hit her.

She'd told him she wished never to see him again, and that was true. But without his pretended courtship, what would prevent Uncle Leo's insistence upon her betrothal to Lord Pinkerton?

Oh Lord! What a tangle.

Perhaps another of the eligible bachelors would step out from the shadows and pay his addresses to her. They'd certainly been more willing to dance with her this last week. But how could she know if their interest in her was genuine or more of Ed's plotting? Who knew how many favors he'd called in on her behalf? Besides, how many of them would be prepared to announce a false engagement to help her? Most would be shocked at the very suggestion. There was only one man she knew who was willing to put himself forward for that, and he was out of the question now.

"Two hundred pounds," she muttered. She should be flattered Ed thought her worth such a sum, but all she saw was that she was such a gib-face no man would keep her company without a princely amount of coin changing hands.

Another thought struck, hard. Had Lord Pinkerton also demanded payment for the interest he'd shown in her? That would be the absolute last word in insults. She could not believe it. But then, why else would he take Uncle Leo's purse?

It could have been payment of a gambling debt, she thought, hopefully, then grimaced. Gambling debts, she knew from Ed, were settled amicably, without delay. No gentleman wanted it put about that he was unwilling or unable to make good on them; that way ran the path to social ruin.

So, not a gambling debt. But why else would Lord Pinkerton have considered he had the right to take a fat purse from her uncle?

Sophie pondered the question long and hard, but in the end she had to admit she could think of no other reason. Uncle Leo had offered money to the baron to court her, just as Ed had done with Kit.

Learning of Kit's perfidy had hurt. Discovering that the baron had done the same thing didn't hurt at all. But it did make her angry. She wanted to go down to Uncle Leo's study and ring a peal over his head, and then tell Aunt Jess what he had done so she could give him a scolding, too.

But if she did that, Uncle Leo would simply deny it. And really, what had she seen that couldn't be explained in some other way?

Indeed, Sophie hoped it could be explained. It would make her feel much better to be wrong. But even if her uncle came up with a plausible story, how could she know it was the truth?

There was only one way. She would have to find the proof before she confronted him. Then, if she discovered he was innocent, she could quietly lay her suspicions aside and he need never know how she'd maligned him in her head. And if she discovered he had indeed paid the baron to court her? Well, then she'd force him to give up his cabbage-headed schemes and allow her to return to the country forthwith so she could work on her wheat.

She nodded once, her mind set. Tomorrow, while he was out, she would look for the proof she needed. And once she had it, she would confront him and reclaim control of her future.

Chapter Eleven

Kit called on Sophie the next morning. True to her word, she had not barred his entry, but the servant informed him imperiously that Miss Wilson was not at home. He'd hoped her anger would cool overnight, but it clearly hadn't. He sighed and handed the servant the flowers he had brought.

Walking away, he glanced back and thought he saw a shadow at the window of the morning room. Was she watching him? The thought gave him hope.

Two hours later that hope withered when she returned the flowers, the card he'd sent with them unopened.

He tried again on the second day, and the third. Miss Wilson, said the servant, was not at home but thank you for calling. Each day, his flowers were returned, his missives unopened.

His mood grew blacker. He snapped at his man and was curt to the point of rudeness when Cardew challenged him to billiards. He could settle to nothing, unable to concentrate on the most mundane tasks. In the evening, his book lay unread by his chair while he stared morosely into the hearth. At dinner, he pushed his food around on his plate while he tried to come up with a way of getting her to see him. He lay in bed at night, staring unseeing at the canopy, imagining her smile and wishing it directed at him once more.

He'd visited Archie, who was mending, although it would be some time before he was fit enough to be out. His spirits had returned, however, and he talked of his plan to be bolder in future. He asked after Sophie, praising her so effusively that Kit wanted to plant the poor man a facer and yell at him to find another lady to fawn over.

Which was, Kit acknowledged, grossly unfair. Archie had every right to set his sights on Sophie, and she deserved a suitor who was decent and kind and worthy of her. Pinkerton certainly didn't fit that model, and neither did Kit.

That was the most painful part; realizing that, even if she hadn't given him his marching orders, he would not have measured up.

Today, he sat in his club, staring at the fire. An unread newspaper rested on one arm of his chair, a rummer of brandy he'd yet to taste balanced on the other. Other gentlemen passed through the room, but if they sought his company, one look at his gloomy countenance changed their minds.

He wondered what Sophie was doing. Was it the day of her At Home? Would she welcome dozens of callers, each staying the required half hour? Did hordes of gentlemen bring posies?

Or was she out, accompanying her aunt on a tour of the homes of Mayfair? Perhaps she was even now walking along Bond Street, shopping for ribbons and bonnets, stopping to talk to friends, smiling as some charming man spoke prettily to her.

Kit's teeth ground together and his hand tightened around his glass. He closed his eyes and took a deep breath, pushing aside the images that so disturbed him.

Although why they should disturb him was a mystery. This was the outcome he'd wanted when he began this charade, was it not? He'd had no intention of making a genuine offer himself. Even had he a mind to, he couldn't have done so. Once he persuaded his father he was in earnest, he would be at University, studying to be an engineer, and in no position to support a wife any more than he could support one in his current financial state.

"Evening." Ed sat in the chair next to him. He crossed his legs, flicked an imaginary speck from the knee of his pantaloons and added, "You looked to be lost in a land all your own."

Kit gave him a half smile. "Not really." He looked down at his glass, swirling it so the liquid coated the side.

Ed watched him for a moment. "She isn't talking to me yet, either."

"She will. You're her brother."

"And you're her friend. One she's going to need if we don't confront Leo and force him to withdraw his ultimatum to her." Kit frowned and put the newspaper onto the table beside him, then placed his untouched brandy next to it. He'd thought Ed would have spoken to his uncle before now. He had the evidence, after all. He could demand the return of his money and the banishment of Pinkerton, so why had his friend not yet taken action?

"I was going to speak to him yesterday," Ed explained, sheepishly. "The opportunity never arose."

Kit gave him a skeptical look.

Ed sighed. "He's still my guardian. I've been used to deferring to him. It isn't easy to change."

"He's an embezzler, Ed."

147

"I know, but..." Ed shrugged.

"He cannot be allowed to get away with it."

"I don't want him to get away with it."

"Good."

"No, it's not. Wanting to put a stop to his activities and doing so are not the same thing." Ed rubbed his chin as if checking for signs of a beard. "I know I need the money to invest in the estate, and Sophie needs her dowry if she's to make a good match, but..."

"No!" Kit's protest stopped Ed mid-sentence. Several men stopped their chatter and glared, disapproving, at Kit. He waited until the hum of voices began again before leaning forward and saying, in no more than a whisper: "Sophie needs her dowry because it's hers, and she has a right to it. She does not need it to make a good match."

"But..."

"Any man would be honored to make her his wife, dowry or not." As Kit sat back, he realized the truth of his words. Any man would be honored. *He* would be honored. Calling her his wife would be the greatest privilege of his life.

That was when it hit him. He loved her. She was everything he wanted, and more. He needed her and he'd marry her tomorrow, even if it meant giving up his dreams of engineering.

"You're right, of course," Ed answered. "I didn't mean she could only make a good match if she had money. Damn it, Kit, you know I'm not good with words." He shrugged. "Not that it matters, anyway. As she's probably told you, she's not eager to marry. It's not just Pinkerton she has an aversion to. It's husbands in general."

148

And therein lay the rub. Sophie didn't want to marry anyone. And even if she changed her mind on that, she wouldn't consider Kit. He couldn't even get her to accept flowers.

Ed continued, oblivious to Kit's thoughts. "What I meant to say was, a decent dowry might change her mind."

Kit turned that comment over in his brain, trying to make sense of it. He could not. "Why would having a dowry change her mind?"

"It might."

Kit closed his eyes for a second. "I'll bite. Why might it?"

"Well," Ed leaned forward, resting his forearms on his thighs, "dowerless, she has no power. She must marry someone who'll put a roof over her head, and do what her husband wishes."

"That's the same whether she has money or not."

"Not necessarily. With money, the marriage contract could be drawn up to allow her more freedom to pursue her scientific hobby horse."

"It's more than a hobby horse." Kit was angry with Ed on Sophie's behalf.

"Obsession, then." Ed waved a hand, dismissively. "That's not the point. Point is, she could get a husband to agree to let her spend every day up to her elbows in mud, if that's what she wished."

"Or," said Kit, "she could remain your unmarried sister." Which was what she truly wanted. Because even the most accommodating husband would still have power over her.

Ed scoffed. "That's not sustainable in the long term."

"Why not?"

"Is that a serious question?"

"The lady doesn't wish to marry."

Ed stared at Kit for several seconds, as if weighing his words. Then he nodded. "When she has her dowry, all will be well." Kit shook his head and Ed continued, "but first, I must beard the lion in his den." There was a small hesitation. "Would you come with me?"

"You don't need me."

"But I do."

"It's your family's business."

"Which is precisely why I need you. Leo—blood complicates things."

Kit grimaced. It had been one thing to help Ed investigate, to search for evidence of Leo's wrongdoing, but to actually embroil himself in the confrontation, to be party to the inevitable argument between family members...that was too much.

On the other hand, Kit knew Ed. His friend was good-natured and always ready to see the best in everyone. He clearly struggled with his uncle's betrayal and might be unable to deal with the problem, leaving both himself and Sophie penniless. Kit could not, in good conscience, allow that to happen. "I will stand outside the door, ready to enter if you need me. No," he held up a hand to stop Ed's objection, "I cannot do more. This is something you must ultimately face alone."

Ed pulled a face. "I suppose you're right. I'll do it tomorrow. Shall we say, two o'clock?" He sat back in his chair, determination and distaste on his face.

Kit slapped his palms against his knees and stood. "Billiards?" he asked, and they headed to the library.

****

It took Sophie hours to get into Uncle Leo's study to look for something that might account for what she'd seen in the garden. She'd planned to do it days ago, but it had taken some time to find the nerve. She wasn't really made for subterfuge, and sneaking behind his back didn't sit easily with her. However, she couldn't shake the feeling that whatever was happening involved her future, and if she didn't discover it, she'd be the sorrier.

Uncle Leo hadn't left the house the first day, so she couldn't search then. On the second day, Aunt Jess insisted Sophie accompany her to buy some new ribbons. She'd tried when he went to his club yesterday, but the door had been locked. Sophie racked her brain for hours, trying to think of an alternate entrance. The windows were locked, and there were no servants' access passages, like the ones in the bedchambers.

She wished she weren't estranged from Kit. He'd have known what to do. He'd probably have come with her, helped her find a way in, stood guard while she looked. She tightened her jaw. Yes. He'd have been good at this. Hadn't he shown his capability for trickery?

"I don't need him," she said, firmly. Whatever needed doing, she'd do it herself. She would *not* be beholden to him. No matter how much she missed his laughing eyes, or the comfort of having his arms around her, or the searing kiss that had burned its way deep into her soul...

"No!" He was a—a confidence trickster.

Although, to be fair, wasn't that a touch of the pot and the kettle? She'd been prepared to lie, too. Had done so, in fact. She'd told her uncle, and her aunt, that she and Kit were...more than was true.

A lump formed in her throat. If she'd fooled anyone,

it had been herself. Had he not always been perfectly clear their courtship was a ruse? Was it his fault she'd begun to believe her own untruths? And why should he not benefit from the arrangement?

No. No, no, no. He'd taken money Ed didn't have and callously used her for his own ends.

On the other hand... Enough! Angrily, she pushed all thoughts of him aside.

Finally, on the third day, Sophie saw the maid enter the study. Sophie took one of the pearl earbobs from her jewelry case and put it into her pocket, then ran downstairs and followed her in.

"Hello, Mary," she said as lightly as she could.

"Oh, miss, you made me start." Mary picked up the kindling she had dropped and continued arranging it in the hearth.

"I think I lost my earbob the other day. I thought I'd have a look for it."

"Would you like me to help you, miss?"

"That's not necessary. I'll find it. You can go when you finish."

Mary frowned. "I'm supposed to lock the door."

"I can do that."

"The master's very particular." The girl was torn between what Uncle Leo had instructed, and what Sophie asked. Sophie felt badly for pushing her into this position, but she needed to discover what was happening.

"He'll never know."

Mary hesitated. Sophie's smile felt brittle. Somehow, she'd thought being alone in a room in her own home would be easier than this. The thought struck her that the maid's intransigence was punishment for telling lies, but she couldn't back away now. This was the best chance she'd had. Besides, she might be helping her uncle. If Lord Pinkerton was threatening him, Sophie might be able to discover how and why, and rescue him.

She rolled her eyes. She'd clearly been reading too many novels.

Trying to seem relaxed, she sat beside the fire. "The thing is," she said, reflecting how easily one lie led to another, "my uncle says I'm too careless. If he knew I'd lost the earbob—which he gave me—he'd give me such a lecture. I hope to find it before he, or anybody else, discovers it was missing." She glanced at Mary, who scrunched her face up as she thought about it.

"Are you sure you lost it in here, then, miss? Perhaps you'd do better to look in the morning room…"

"I can look there at any time." Sophie took a deep breath and pinned her smile back into place. "I'll lock up when I've finished, and I will return the key directly to you. No one else need know."

"I suppose," said Mary, uncertainly. "How long will you be?"

"Fifteen minutes?"

Mary nodded. "All right, miss. I'll come back in fifteen minutes."

"Thank you." Sophie's smile broadened and she had to refrain from hugging the maid, who finished her tasks while Sophie made a show of hunting the earbob in the carpet tufts.

"Fifteen minutes, mind. Not a minute more," said Mary, and she shut the door behind her.

As soon as she was alone, Sophie stood, dusted her hands together, and looked around the room. She had no idea what she expected to find but trusted she'd know it when she saw it. But where to look? With only fifteen minutes, she couldn't afford to waste a moment.

Uncle Leo's desk seemed the most likely place to start. The desk surface was bare, the only thing upon it the inkwell and the pens standing upright in the lacquered pot. She didn't know whether putting everything away made her uncle very tidy or very cautious.

Sophie opened drawers and rifled through the contents—ledgers filled with figures in his spidery hand, letters, none of them from Lord Pinkerton, bills and orders mostly to do with his business. Not a thing that seemed suspicious.

She pushed the last drawer shut and looked around. She was running out of time. "If I had something I didn't want anyone to find," she muttered, "where would I put it?" A cursory look inside the Chinese bureau yielded nothing. She didn't have time to search the bookshelves.

Defeat tasted bitter as she made to leave. Mary would return at any moment to collect the key. Sophie took the earbob from her pocket, ready to show the maid.

She pulled open the door, then jumped back, eyes wide as she came face to face with Uncle Leo, his own key in his hand, ready to put it into the lock.

For an instant, he looked shocked. Then his eyebrows lowered over eyes that were hard as coal.

"Explain yourself, miss."

For a second, Sophie thought to hold up the earbob and tell him the same lie she'd told Mary, but as soon as she thought of it, she knew it wouldn't work. Uncle Leo would not be fooled by such a rum tale.

A shadow moved in the corridor and Sophie saw Mary slip back into the servants' part of the house. At least the maid would not share in the trouble.

Uncle Leo grabbed Sophie's arm and steered her back into his study. "What were you doing in here?" he demanded. "This is my private study. You have no business being in here without my permission."

There was only one thing Sophie could do. She drew herself up to her full height, took a deep breath and went on the offensive. "I know what you've been doing," she said.

His eyes narrowed. "What I've been doing?" His voice was low and menacing. Sophie swallowed, hard.

"I kn-know of your arrangement with Lord Pinkerton."

For the briefest moment, panic flashed in his eyes. Then he let go of her and took a step back.

"Oh?" He smiled, his expression completely neutral now. "I've made no secret of it. He wishes to marry you, and it would be a good match." He crossed to the tantalus in the corner and poured himself a brandy. His eyes flicked toward his desk, then back to her. "I have your best interests at heart."

"I doubt that." Sophie was amazed at the steadiness of her voice, for every part of her trembled and she felt goose-skin on her arms.

"Well," he answered after a sip of his drink. "That was candid. If a little insulting. I'm not sure that's the way one should speak to one's guardian."

"You won't be my guardian much longer," she said. "You're my uncle and I have affection for you, but I won't allow you to—to—dictate my life."

"Dictate?" His eyebrows rose. "I merely wish to provide you with a future."

"I won't marry that odious man. You cannot force me."

"I beg leave to differ." He sounded almost amused, which stoked her anger. Sophie had to press her lips together to prevent saying something ill-advised and childish, which would lose her the argument.

He glanced over toward the desk again, and Sophie followed suit. He was concealing something there. If he believed she'd found it, perhaps it would unnerve him enough that he would divulge everything.

"I'm aware of everything," she said, and gave him the most insincere smile she could muster. "I know all. I will speak to Ed, and together he and I will decide what is to be done."

The color drained from Leo's face. He glanced toward the desk again, then drained the contents of his glass. Sophie waited, wondering what he would say now.

"There's no need to be hasty," he told her, at last. His lips glistened with brandy and color rushed back into his cheeks, making him look flushed. A broken vein stood out like a scar. "All can be put right in a day or two."

Did that mean he would tell Lord Pinkerton there'd be no marriage between him and Sophie? She could only hope.

"See that it is," she answered, crisply, and turned to go. Part of her was elated it had gone so well, but another part screamed caution, that his capitulation had come too easily.

She went through the door and pulled it to, behind her. Before it could close, she looked back. Uncle Leo was no longer by the tantalus. Now he'd crossed to his desk, but he ignored the drawers filled with papers. Instead, he turned his chair upside down. Sophie frowned. What on earth was he doing? She heard a click, and then he cursed and looked at the door. Sophie turned and ran, along the corridor and around a corner.

"Sophie!" he bellowed. The fury in his voice terrified her. What was hidden under the chair that would cause such rage?

"Sophie!" She heard him running along the corridor. Suddenly, she felt very unsafe. From here, she couldn't get upstairs to the sanctuary of her room, nor could she reach the front door before he caught up to her. She'd never considered him a violent man before, but he sounded violent now.

She tucked into an alcove, behind a fern, and prayed he wouldn't see her. He came around the corner, his face purple with rage. "Sophie!" he yelled again. Sophie cringed.

"For goodness' sake, what is all the noise?" Aunt Jess came out of the morning room and glared at her brother. "You sound like a costermonger, not a gentleman."

"Where's Sophie?" he demanded.

"I'm sure I don't know," replied Aunt Jess. "Although, if she's in the house she must know you're calling her. I'm surprised they don't hear you on Hampstead Heath! Why do you want her?"

His demeanor changed. He slowed his breathing and willed his anger away. "I wanted to—discuss her engagement."

"If you mean to Lord Pinkerton, it's no wonder she isn't coming. Forget that for now, and come in here. I was about to ring for tea."

"I don't want tea." He sounded petulant now, like a scolded boy.

"Of course you do. Perfect restorative. Worry about

Sophie later," and Aunt Jess steered him into the morning room. At the last moment she turned and looked straight at Sophie, winked and gestured with her head that her niece should make herself scarce. Then she closed the door.

Sophie waited a few moments to make sure her uncle didn't come out, then made good her escape.

Chapter Twelve

Kit woke at first light, thinking of Sophie. Now he'd admitted to himself that he loved her, he wanted to proclaim it to the world. Most of all, he wanted to tell her. He lay, hands cradling his head, and imagined the scene.

They'd be in her uncle's home, in the morning room. Sophie would be on the sofa, looking beautiful as ever, gazing up at him with eyes shining in hope and anticipation. He'd apologize profusely for hurting her, beg for her forgiveness, and she would give it. Then he'd sit beside her, take one of her hands in both of his, and tell her how much he cared. And she'd…

His fantasy faltered. He didn't know what she'd do or say.

In a perfect world, she'd smile brightly and tell him she loved him too. Then he'd propose and she'd cry *Yes!* before throwing her arms around him and giving him the kiss of his life.

He grinned, almost able to feel her fingers playing with his hair, her warm scent filling the air.

Then the grin faded. This was not a perfect world, and Sophie was not in love with him. She might be willing to forgive him—if he groveled enough. She might even cry friends with him, to deter Pinkerton, if nothing else. But one thing he knew for certain—she wouldn't lie to him. There'd be no declaration of love, no eager acceptance of his proposal, no warm kiss.

Sophie didn't wish to marry Kit. Sophie didn't wish to marry anyone. She wasn't avoiding Pinkerton's offer just because he was an odious blackguard. She wanted her freedom to work in her laboratory, finding ways to increase the yield from wheat and earning that medal from the Royal Academy. And after she'd increased wheat yield, there'd be something else she would want to work on. The application of science for the benefit of her fellow man was what mattered to Sophie Wilson.

Kit sat up sharply and rested his forearms on his raised knees, suddenly able to see things clearly. Sophie wasn't actually averse to the idea of marrying. She just wanted the freedom to work on her experiments. If a prospective husband was willing to give her that freedom, she might accept him.

If she only felt friendship for a man, could that be enough upon which to base a successful marriage? If she could also continue with her experiments, Kit thought it could be.

Except… Kit was in no position to keep a wife. He had no income, not even the allowance from his father any longer, and he wouldn't have any unless he capitulated and took on an estate.

An estate! A place where Sophie could experiment to her heart's content.

There'd be no studying for him, but then, that wasn't really a viable option. If his father hadn't given permission by now, he never would.

Knowing he'd never be an engineer caused a hard lump to form in Kit's throat. He would never contribute to the safety of mines. He would never save lives. But Sophie would. She would improve the crops, saving thousands from starvation.

Basking in her glory would be enough for Kit.

Tomorrow morning, before he accompanied Ed, Kit would visit his father. Then, once his future was secured, he'd seek out Sophie and offer her his heart, for the rest of his life.

Next day, as soon as the hour was reasonable, Kit went to see his father.

The earl received him in his study, and it struck Kit with a pang of sadness that they were more like business associates than family members who felt affection for each other. He stood in front of his father's desk, waiting for the earl to look up from his books, and in that moment Kit vowed, should he be blessed with a son, he would not treat him this way. The relationship between Kit and his children would be close, loving and filled with joy.

Finally, his father looked up over the top of the spectacles perched on his nose. His hair was completely gray and his skin was lined, with dark circles around his eyes, and Kit was shocked to realize, for the first time, his father was no longer a young man.

"Are you up early, or have you yet to go to bed?" the earl asked, dryly.

Kit tightened his jaw. "Good morning to you too, Father."

"I meant what I said. I will not pay your gambling debts."

"Then it's as well I have none." Kit could feel his temper rising. Why must his father always assume the worst of him? Borrowing money was not the only reason a son might visit, and it was insulting that it was the reason his father thought most likely.

Immediately, the anger turned to shame as Kit

admitted to himself that money was the only reason they ever met, and had been for some time.

The earl stood and crossed to a sideboard, where he poured two drinks. His face showed no hint of his thoughts as he handed Kit a glass and invited him to sit in the armchair beside the hearth. From the wall above the fireplace, Kit's mother smiled down on them. The artist had captured her kindness and her gentle nature perfectly, and Kit felt sorrow that she was no longer here. He wished he could share his news with her. She would have liked Sophie. The pair of them would have been thick as thieves, conspiring to run rings around him and enjoying every moment. He could almost hear their happy laughter filling the corridors of this old house, transforming it from the mausoleum it had become.

"She didn't want to sit for that portrait," his father said. "She said there were far better things to paint."

"She was wrong."

"Which is exactly what I told her." The earl held up his glass in silent salute to his countess.

"I miss her."

"As do I," whispered the earl. Then he cleared his throat, sat down, and studied his son carefully. "You've not been gambling?"

"I have no debts," corrected Kit.

His father raised one eyebrow. "You've been winning?"

Kit took a sip of his own drink. "I've learned to quit the table at a more judicious moment." The look of approval in his father's eyes lifted Kit's spirits. Warmth filled him, and his lips twitched. He worked to keep the grin from showing. He hadn't come seeking his father's approbation for doing something common sense should have taught him long ago.

"You wish me to take over the management of the Martlets estate." Father would appreciate Kit getting straight to the point. He'd never been one to indulge in idle chit-chat.

The earl studied Kit for a long moment. "May I ask what's brought on this acquiescence? You were dead set against it a week ago."

"I wish to be married. I need to be able to support her."

Father nodded. "To whom?"

"Lord Hamsey's sister."

"Hamsey?" The earl downed his brandy in one gulp, then glared at Kit. "You said before you had an understanding with her. But now I hear the barony is penniless. And what's more, the maternal family are in trade."

Kit bristled. What did it matter what her antecedents were? This was the woman he loved. But if he was to have her, he needed his father's blessing. Without it, he couldn't afford to marry. With that thought uppermost, he spoke evenly.

"I do not deny her...very successful...trade connections, Father. But you're mistaken in calling her penniless."

His father nodded. "Her uncle has settled five hundred pounds on her to try and rid himself of her without too much expense. He always was a skinflint. I dare say that's how he amassed his fortune." He pointed a warning finger at Kit. "Which is to his credit, I suppose, but it don't make him good *ton*, and it don't make his niece irresistible."

"She doesn't need him to make her irresistible,"

snapped Kit. "She's beautiful, and witty, and clever. Everything a man could want in a wife. I'd take her, with or without the five hundred pounds." He wanted to add that she'd soon be worth much more than that, but he couldn't. For one thing, until Ed had confronted Leo about his crimes, nothing was certain. For another, Kit had no intention of living off his wife, so the point was moot. On top of which, he didn't have Ed's permission to share the Wilson family news.

The earl stared at Kit, astounded. "You love her," he said.

Kit squared his jaw, waiting for the mockery. Sons of aristocrats didn't marry for love, as his father would undoubtedly remind him. They married to secure an unblemished bloodline, to enrich the family's assets, to gain land and prestige. Marriage to Sophie wouldn't achieve these goals, so Kit braced himself for the fight.

It didn't come. Instead, his father stared up at his mother's portrait, a far-off look in his eyes. "He's your son, Emily," he whispered. Then he returned his attention to Kit. "You're certain about her?"

"I am."

"Will she have you?"

"I haven't asked her yet. But I live in hope."

"And you'll take the Martlets?"

"I will." A momentary pain ripped through Kit's chest, raw and jagged, at the loss of his dream, but the thought of Sophie standing beside him soothed it, like balm on a burn. He imagined her standing on the roof of the Elizabethan house at Martlets, surveying the land, the myriad fields in which she could grow her new strains of wheat. The unadulterated joy he'd see on her face made everything worthwhile.

The vision changed and they were in the master bedroom, its dark wood paneling soaking up what light penetrated the two small latticed windows. Kit had always found the dark rooms depressing, but now they didn't seem so terrible, for Sophie would light them in a way the ancient decor could never extinguish. He held her as he unbuttoned her dress and let it fall to her feet, the soft silk shushing against her skin and making her nipples stand begging for his attention. Her fingers wove through his hair, her tongue played with his...

The images caused his trousers to tighten, painfully. He shifted in his seat, looking for comfort, and cleared his throat as he banished the fantasy until he had time to savor it.

"Very well," said Father. "I look forward to welcoming her to the family. I suppose I'll have to meet with that dreadful uncle of hers, to make the arrangements." The earl sipped his brandy. "Although, with some string pulling, I may be able to get my man to do most of it, so I'll scarcely have to see him."

Kit grinned. "Perhaps he'll leave the arrangements to her brother." After today, he had no doubt that would be the case.

Now, if only he could get Sophie to talk to him long enough to forgive him and hear his proposal.

****

Sophie sat in the morning room, staring into the hearth and thinking of very little. The day's visitors had gone, leaving nothing but a few posies and the memory of inane chatter over tea and biscuits. Aunt Jess was lying down before she dressed for dinner, and Sophie was alone in the quiet.

Today's conversations replayed in her head,

snippets of gossip about people she barely knew, catty remarks about some poor girl who had worn the same gown three times now, and how Amelia Trindon had had her vouchers to Almack's revoked but nobody could discover why. Since Sophie had always found Miss Trindon to be unexceptionable, she couldn't believe it was anything too bad and said so rather more forcefully than she intended, but then, she liked Amelia, not something she could truthfully say of the gossips here today.

"Oh," said Arabella Dinnington, on an unbecoming titter, "I commend your Christian charity, Sophie. You always see the best in everybody. Mayhap that's why you've not given Mr. Thomas a set down?"

Sophie looked at her sharply. "A set down?" she asked, cautiously.

"For pestering you. I do, of course, realize he's attractive," continued Arabella, and she gave a salacious wink. "But Mama says handsome is as handsome does, and you have to confess, the delectable Mr. Thomas has acquired his fair share of comment. He's gained quite the reputation, you know. They say," Arabella leaned forward as if passing on a confidence, "his father's cut him off."

"Do they?" Anyone who knew Sophie well would recognize the dry tone in her voice and realize the conversation annoyed her. The wise would change the subject, or shut up. Arabella neither knew Sophie well nor was she wise.

"Standing on the banks of the River Tick, my brother says."

It was the sort of phrase Ed used when talking to Sophie, and she thought nothing of it then. In fact, she'd probably answer him using the same low cant. Not that such a truth stopped her scathing reply. "Does your brother always use vulgar language in your presence? What does your mama say?"

Arabella blushed. One or two of the other young ladies smirked behind their hands, but their smiles faded when Arabella glared at them.

"You should not believe all the *on dit* you hear," Sophie continued, her tone deliberately light. "Much of it is exaggerated. Some is even woven from whole cloth." It was the nearest she could come to refuting the rumors without telling an outright lie.

Not that she cared what the *ton* thought of Kit. No, indeed. They could spread the tale that he painted himself bright blue and rode on a donkey wearing nothing but a woman's apron for aught she cared. But he was Ed's particular friend, and he'd been seen squiring her about town. It was a hop and a skip from gossiping about him to spreading stories about her and her family, and Sophie had no wish for that.

The ploy worked, and the conversation moved in another direction. Sophie listened graciously until the visit was over and she could sigh her relief.

Now it was an hour since they'd gone, and she told herself she should get up and do something useful. Sitting here, sighing like a moonstruck ninny, would help no one. With reluctance, she stood just as the door opened. A footman announced Mr. Thomas as Kit strode into the room.

He looked wonderful in his blue coat and silver waistcoat, buff-colored breeches hugging his long, powerful thighs above black boots that shone like mirrors. His hair was tousled—she suspected more from the breeze and the careless removal of his hat than from the art of his valet, since his cheeks glowed with the effects of the sun-filled air outside.

Sophie's heart gave a little leap. Irritated, she reminded herself it didn't matter how fine he looked. She was still angry with him, and his presence did not—*absolutely did not*—affect her in the slightest.

When he saw her, he stopped, seeming as stunned as she was. "Miss Wilson," he said, "I apologize. I had no idea you were in here."

She nodded, acknowledging his words, then looked away from him.

He sighed. "I can wait for your brother in the hall."

"No." She willed her heart to stop racing and swallowed, twice. "No," she repeated. "You stay and wait for Ed. I was about to quit this room anyway."

She made to leave, but stopped when his hand brushed her arm and his fingers gently circled her wrist. "Please stay." His voice was soft, and there was a pleading look in his eyes.

Sophie knew she should pull away, but the warmth of his hand against her skin was too delicious, and she doubted she could have moved from him if she tried. There was a hint of his cologne in the air, a woodsy scent mingled with the freshness of the summer air. This close, she could see the blue-black of new beard just below the skin on his jaw, and the movement of his Adam's apple above the top line of his cravat as he swallowed.

"I'm sorry," he said. He let go of her and took a step away. "About what happened. The other day," he clarified.

She nodded, her teeth clenching against the memory of that humiliation. How could she have forgotten it, even for an instant? This man, this mercenary, was not worthy to even be in her presence. "Yes," she said, her tone sharp enough to cut him. "When you tried to profit from my misfortune."

"I didn't try…"

"Or was it that I learned of your duplicity that you regret?"

"I did not try to profit from your situation." His voice was quiet, and it sent chills up her spine, making her shudder. "I was pleased to be of service."

She stiffened at his blatant untruth. "I heard you."

Kit shook his head. "Sophie…"

"Mr. Thomas," she retorted, letting him know they were no longer on first-name terms. It sent a frisson of regret through her, but she hardened her heart. The chill in their relationship had been caused by him, not her. He must now live with the consequences.

He sighed. "Miss Wilson," he said, deliberately, each syllable clear. "I am sorry, deeply sorry, that what you thought you heard caused you pain. I can only pray that, given time, you will find it possible to forgive me my part in it. For now, though, I must tell you I have not been paid so much as a farthing for spending time with you. I never sought to be paid, and I shall not be paid. On that you have my word."

She narrowed her eyes as she studied him. He held her stare steadily. Her treacherous pulse skittered.

A minute passed. Another. Then she nodded once. "I believe you."

He breathed out heavily and gave a half smile. "Thank you. So, do we cry friends?"

"I suppose we must." She tried to sound haughty and reluctant, but she knew her attitude for a lie. He was forgiven, and Sophie realized that was what she'd wanted to do from the first. She'd missed him, missed his company, the way he spoke to her as an equal and respected her dream. He made her feel valued and desirable.

"About our betrothal," he said, bringing her attention back to their conversation.

Sophie bristled. "You've no need for concern," she said. "Your sacrifice is no longer needed."

The sadness in his eyes surprised her. Surely he didn't wish to pretend they were engaged when it wasn't necessary?

That led her to ponder her own wishes on the subject. Had she been too hasty to dismiss the idea? If he was willing to— No! Absolutely not. The very thought was absurd. He had no more wish to find himself betrothed than Sophie did. Although, if she had felt so inclined, Kit would definitely be the one who…

No! He would not. He was nothing more than Ed's good friend, and she was destined to remain unmarried and take the scientific community by storm. There was no place in her life for a husband, or even a faux fiancé. There was no need of one now she'd confronted Uncle Leo. Surely, after their conversation yesterday, he wouldn't continue to force Lord Pinkerton on her.

She frowned, thoughtfully. Uncle Leo had been angry, and more than a little frightening. Sophie hoped, rather than believed, he would cease to press Lord Pinkerton's suit. As for the baron himself—he was unlikely to accept defeat graciously.

It might behoove her to continue her false courtship with Kit for a few more days, just to be sure.

"You've spoken to Ed, I take it?" Kit's question

pulled her from her thoughts. "About our betrothal arrangement?"

"No." Sophie was confused as to why she should have done. "I haven't spoken about anything to him for several days." She gave him a half smile. "You weren't the only one who angered me."

Kit nodded slowly. "Your brother cares for you."

"So he tells me." She moved to the fireplace and reached out to caress the tiny figurine of a shepherd on the mantelpiece. The porcelain felt cold beneath her fingertips, nothing like the warm vibrance of Kit's hand when it had circled her wrist. She wondered if he'd felt her quickening pulse at his touch, or noted the hitch in her breath. Her cheeks heated at the memory, and she wished there were a fire burning, that she might blame her rising color on its flames.

"As do I." He stood close enough she felt his breath against the back of her neck, his words stirring the tiny strands of hair that escaped her chignon. A shiver slithered down her spine. Her legs jellied. She barely trusted them to keep her upright.

"Lord Pinkerton isn't the only reason..." Kit touched her arm, and her muscle twitched in awareness. "What I mean—the thing is, dam—dash it, Sophie, I—I lo—I like being with you."

"And I you."

Sophie wasn't sure if she turned to him, or if he guided her around. All she knew was, suddenly, she was gazing up into a face filled with hope, affection, and a tinge of desperation.

"Then why can't we...could we...? Oh, hell!" The last words came out on a groan as he took her in his arms and kissed her.

His lips were warm and soft, his cheek slightly rough against her smooth skin. He tasted of the coffee he'd had for breakfast, its bittersweet aroma mixing with his cologne, the starch in his cravat, and that indefinable scent that was uniquely him. She heard his breath catch, and the tiny groan of pleasure, the one she answered with a groan of her own. Of their own volition, her arms wound around him, her hands pressing against his back, anchoring him. His firm chest pressed against her soft breasts. Her nipples tingled as they hardened and rubbed against the soft linen of her shift, and that strange feeling, somewhere between an itch and an ache, built between her legs.

He caressed her shoulders, her arms, her neck. He pressed closer, until she could feel his heart, beating as rapidly as her own. His hardness nudged against her stomach, and the ache between her legs grew harder to bear. She wanted him to touch her, to press against her flesh and ease these feelings that threatened to overwhelm her.

His tongue traced the seam of her lips. She opened her mouth and he slipped inside, his tongue playing with hers, thrusting back and forth. She copied his moves with her own tongue, relishing the taste of him, the feel of him inside her mouth.

His lips feathered kisses along the line of her jaw and down, onto her neck. He kissed the pulse point behind her ear and she thought she would explode.

His hand moved from her neck, slowly, over her shoulder and down to her waist. The warmth of his fingers singed her through the layers of clothes, and she wouldn't have been surprised to find her dress scorched and her body branded by his touch.

He stroked his way over her rib cage to the underside of her breast. She wanted to scream, to beg him for something more.

Outside, a dog barked and a child squealed its delight. The sounds brought reality crashing back. She'd kissed Kit in the morning room, in full view of anyone who might walk in. They risked censure, their reputations, their futures, for if anyone had come in, they would have had to marry. Sophie couldn't risk that, for both their sakes.

It took every ounce of her willpower, but she moved her hands to his chest, his safe, solid chest with the rock-like muscles, and— This could not happen! This *must* not happen.

With the last of her strength, Sophie pushed against him and stepped back. He released her, and she felt cold, bereft of the warmth of his arms, and the feel of his lips against her skin. Her heart raced and her breaths shallowed as she stared at him, noting he too seemed to struggle to catch his breath. His hair was messier than before, his eyes bright and intense. She wanted to move close to him again, to repeat the kiss, over and over.

She didn't know how long they stood, staring at each other. Eventually, her heart slowed and her cheeks cooled. Kit, too, seemed more composed with every passing second.

Finally, Sophie spoke. "I'll…" Her voice came out on a croak, and she cleared her throat. "I'll ring for tea." She turned to the bell pull.

"Ring for tea?" His shocked whisper made her frown, confused. "After that…what just happened, you will ring for tea?"

Sophie stiffened, her shoulders back, every nerve on

edge. The best defense, Papa had always said, was offense, and she employed that now. "What else would you have me do, sir? I don't generally offer brandy to gentlemen at this hour, and it's rather late for coffee or chocolate."

He flinched. "You can think of drinks after... Didn't that mean anything to you?"

Sophie looked away from him. She took another step back, fixing her gaze on the shepherd on the mantelpiece. The little porcelain man had a mischievous smile painted on his cold white face and seemed to mock her. She turned back to Kit, who still stood, looking shocked.

Why? she wanted to ask him. Had it meant something to him? If she told him the truth, confessed her feelings for him, what would he say? Would he reciprocate? Or would she be hurt and humiliated once again?

"Tell me," he said, and his voice was low and deep, "it meant nothing to you, and I'll walk away. You'll never need to see me again."

The determination on his face told her he was in earnest. The urge to run into his arms and beg him to stay was almost overwhelming. Still, a wary voice in the back of her mind whispered caution. She needed to be sure before attaching her heart so blatantly to her sleeve.

"And if it did?" she asked, carefully.

A slow smile spread across his face. "If it did," he began, then stopped abruptly as the door was opened with gusto and Ed strode in.

"Sorry to keep you waiting," he began, grinning at Kit. Then he saw Sophie, and his smile fell away. He looked from one to the other, uncertainly. Sophie willed her blush to stay away as she wondered if he could tell she'd been well and truly kissed. Were her lips swollen? Was there a rash where Kit's beard had scraped her skin? Perhaps her hair was in disarray? She resisted the temptation to reach up and check it and confirm Ed's obvious suspicions.

"I was waiting for Aunt Jess," she said, at the same moment that Kit said, "I was early for our appointment."

Both fell into guilty silence. Ed studied them, carefully.

Sophie managed a weak smile. "I don't know what can be keeping her. I'll go and find her." She gave a curtsy to Kit. "Good day to you, Mr. Thomas. Ed," and she fled the room.

Chapter Thirteen

Kit watched Sophie leave. He wanted to call out and beg her to stay. He pressed his lips together to ensure he did no such thing. Bad enough he'd been in a room with her, alone and unchaperoned, and with the door closed. Luckily, the only person who knew about that was her brother, and he wasn't going to ruin Sophie by spreading the news. But if he thought anything other than conversation had taken place...

Not that Kit regretted the kiss he'd shared with Sophie. Far from it. It had sparked something deep inside him, something he'd never felt before. His heart had missed, then scrambled to catch up, until he thought it would beat its way right out of his chest. Every nerve was on edge, everything taut to the point of breaking. He could barely form a coherent thought.

Judging from the way she'd stared at him, shocked and confused, her bosom heaving as if each breath was an effort and her color high, Sophie felt the same. Her eyes glittered too brightly, and her lips were red and swollen. He saw the outline of her hardened nipples through the bodice of her dress, and he ached to touch her again. She looked wary, frightened of what had happened between them, yet glad it had done so.

Had Ed not come in, Kit would have proposed there and then. And that, he thought now, might have been the biggest mistake of all. Because she might well have rejected him out of hand. Sophie would have assumed he was caught in the heat of the moment, that his words were a spontaneous reaction to having compromised her. She would have considered her rejection a favor to him, saving him from himself, and that would have left him a mountain to climb.

Better by far to wait until a cold moment, untouched by passion. Then she could be certain his words were thought out and planned, and sincere.

Of course, even if she knew his true intentions, she might still reject him, although the kiss gave him hope that she wouldn't. Just the remembrance of her lips on his while his fingers skimmed her warm figure and her arms surrounded him was enough to make his breeches tighten. Which would most certainly not do when he stood in front of her brother. The brother who was, at this moment, giving him a slant-eyed look.

Kit sat and crossed his legs, trying to hide the evidence of her effect upon him. The suspicion did not leave Ed's eyes.

"I would ask if she'd been berating you, but if you say yes, I shall know you for a liar."

Kit swallowed. It took everything he had to maintain eye contact with Ed, in the hope it would convince his friend there was no crime for which to answer. "She didn't berate me," he said. "She was all that was amenable."

"Yes." The single word seemed loaded with meaning. Kit looked down and plucked imaginary lint from his coat. It occupied his hands, his attention, and his mind until he could recompose himself. His thoughts raced. He wondered if he should tell Ed he planned to propose. Or would it be better to wait to make that announcement?

Before he could decide, Ed continued, "It may be better if you behave more cautiously from now on. Distance yourself from her a little."

Kit stilled. Even his breathing seemed to stop. Everything within him turned cold. "Distance myself?"

"For Sophie's sake. After today, she'll be a very eligible young lady, with excellent prospects. I'm sure you don't want to see her newfound hopes dashed any more than I do." Ed smiled, clearly trying to soften the blow. "Can't have her ruined at this point, can we?"

The hairs on the back of Kit's neck stood to attention. The muscles in his shoulders tensed. "Ruined," he repeated Ed's word. "Ruined how, exactly?"

Ed stared at him as if he was unsure whether Kit was serious. Kit knew his return gaze was hard and icy. Ed huffed and looked away, clearly uncomfortable. Then he looked back, determination in the glitter of his eyes and the set of his jaw.

"Come on, Kit. Don't play the halfwit. You know as well as I do people are talking about the pair of you."

Kit raised an eyebrow. He refused to give Ed any quarter on this. "Let them talk."

"Don't be ridiculous. I cannot. Nor would you if the shoe was on the other foot. You don't have a sister to worry over, but you must see…" Ed paced to the window and stared out at the street. His hands were clasped behind his back and his feet were apart. He looked for all the world like an angry headmaster ready to give a dressing down to an unruly student. "When Pinkerton was her only prospect, being squired about by any gentleman who wasn't him was all to the good. But now, she's going to have her pick of men to choose from, and

I would hate to… I mean…"

"I'm not good enough for her?" The anger Ed's words evoked in Kit was tempered by the truth of the statement. Kit wasn't good enough for Sophie. But then, no man was.

"I didn't say that."

"You didn't need to."

"Damn it, Kit!" Ed pushed his hand through his hair, which stood to attention, as if as tense and frustrated as he clearly was. "That isn't what I meant. I'd be proud to call you brother, and you know it. If you were truly courting Sophie, nothing would make me happier. But you're not."

Hope flickered in Kit's chest. "If I were, you wouldn't object?"

Ed laughed and turned to face Kit. "Of course I wouldn't, but the point is moot, isn't it? Since you're not and have no intention of doing so." He sighed. "The simple truth is, you're a confirmed bachelor with a certain type of reputation, and I wouldn't want that to affect my sister's renewed chances on the marriage mart. I know there's nothing to your friendship with her, but others don't. So, in future, I'd be obliged if you ensured you didn't find yourself alone with her in a room with the door closed."

Kit bristled, even though he'd been chiding himself for the very same thing just a minute earlier. "You make it sound as if I planned to ravish her."

"I didn't mean…"

"It wasn't planned." True, it wasn't regretted either, at least not by him. What Sophie thought of their encounter, he didn't dare guess.

"Well, of course it wasn't planned." Ed laughed.

"Give me some credit. You're no masochist. Why on earth would you plan to be alone with her when she's being such a termagant?"

Kit's eyes narrowed. How dare Ed insult Sophie? If he'd been anyone but her brother, Kit would have planted him a facer.

He sighed. He couldn't defend her, not without raising Ed's suspicions about his feelings for Sophie. Feelings Kit wasn't ready to share. Besides, from the way Ed had spoken, Kit wasn't certain his friend would welcome his suit, and Kit didn't wish to find himself forbidden to pay his addresses because he'd made his move too soon. Better to bide his time and discover if Sophie returned his love before he said anything. If she had no wish to marry him, there'd be no sense in losing his oldest friend as well.

He pushed a smile into place. "Well, before she can truly become eligible, as you put it, she needs to be rescued from the double threats of poverty and Pinkerton, so shall we go and find your uncle?"

****

Sophie stood outside the morning room, every nerve taut. What had she been thinking, allowing him to kiss her like that? She should have stepped back out of his embrace and given him a first-class set-down that left him in no doubt his attentions weren't welcome.

But that wasn't exactly true. She had welcomed his embrace, and his kiss. She knew it, and she suspected he did, too. His touch, the feel of his lips on hers, the warmth of him next to her, all stole her senses and left her hungry for more.

He hadn't been unaffected, either. When they broke apart, he'd been breathing heavily, as if he'd been running. There was shock and awe on his face, and he said...

What had he said? More to the point, what had he been about to say before Ed came in? Curse her brother's ill timing! If he could have stayed away another minute...

She was being absurd. Even if he hadn't been interrupted, Kit would have said nothing of import. He'd looked as if he was going to offer for her, and her heart beat frantically, anticipation building deliciously. She'd held her breath...

No! In the bright light of the hallway, with its cool, black-and-white-checkered flooring and the marble plinths supporting vases of hothouse flowers and cool marble busts, she realized how silly that fantasy had been. Kit wasn't going to offer for her. He was going to University to study engineering so he could save lives. A wife would hinder him, prevent his success. And he must succeed. The welfare of the working man was far more important than Sophie's hope of betrothal.

Not that she wanted a betrothal, of course. Although, here in the hall, with only a door separating her from the man who'd just kissed her until she wanted to melt into a puddle at his feet, she no longer found it easy to hold fast to her objections to a husband.

A man like Kit would make a fine husband, she realized. He'd understand his wife had ideas and dreams and the wit to develop them. He'd allow her to follow them, would encourage her to do so, might even join her in her quest.

Sophie sighed, heavily. There no use in dreaming of a happy ever after with Kit Thomas as her Prince Charming. The kiss they'd just shared was all she'd ever have.

She put her fingers to her mouth, savoring the memory of his lips on hers. She fancied she felt his breath, warm on her cheek, her ear, her neck. Wonderful shivers raced along her spine. In years to come, she would sit alone in her room, remembering this kiss and the way he'd made her feel.

It would have to be enough. Perhaps the day would come when she would wed, but she knew, deep in her heart, that even the best of husbands wouldn't make her feel the way she'd felt today, in Kit Thomas's arms.

She needed to get out of the house. His presence made the very air sing, and the walls seemed to close in, as if he shrank the space.

"Shopping," she whispered. She'd find Aunt Jess and go to Bond Street. By the time they'd spent an hour browsing through the establishments there, Ed and Kit would have left for wherever they planned to go.

She moved across the hall and climbed the stairs.

As she reached the top stair, Uncle Leo turned the corner from the corridor leading to the family chambers. He grinned broadly at her.

"Sophie. There you are. I was looking for you."

It occurred to Sophie that he couldn't have looked for long or he would have found her in the morning room. The thought that he might have been the one who burst in upon her and Kit horrified her. She felt her color rise, and it was a moment before she could answer him.

"I was downstairs."

He glanced at the staircase behind her. "Clearly. Your aunt thought you might be in your chamber, so I went there."

Sophie frowned. "Does Aunt Jess wish for me?" She

took a step forward.

"No!" Uncle Leo's tone startled her. He took a deep breath and said, more quietly, "No. She is...resting. It was I who looked for you."

"I see." Although Sophie didn't see at all. Her uncle had never sought her out, and he'd never been as nervous as he appeared now. More than nervous, in fact. Anxious.

Sophie thought back to the moment in his study, when he'd seemed so angry at her presence. She wondered if that was what he wished to speak to her about. Part of her wanted to turn and run and avoid the unpleasantness, but the rational part of her knew it was better to get it over and done with.

He stood silently for several seconds, studying her until she felt she was being sized up, like a horse for sale. She shifted, uncomfortably.

"Did you wish to see me for a reason?" she asked, her voice clipped by the tightness in her jaw.

He smiled, but it did not reach his eyes. "Yes, I did," he said. "Your aunt was concerned you might disturb her. She, ah, has the headache."

Poor Aunt Jess. She'd always suffered the most terrible megrims, and they left her debilitated for days. "What can I do for her?"

"Nothing." Uncle Leo smiled again. And again, it seemed strained. "She said you'd try to be of help, but she doesn't wish you to overset yourself. Her maid has prepared a tisane, and she's going to sleep."

Sophie nodded. "That will do her good." She frowned. This megrim had come on very suddenly. Usually, there was some warning. Aunt Jess would report flashes of light and strange smells that told her all was not well and allowed her to take a preventive draught.

Perhaps the warnings had been there and she'd chosen not to tell Sophie. It would be exactly the sort of thing she would do, take to her bed and suffer in silence rather than worry her niece when she was entertaining visitors.

"Thank you for telling me," she said to Uncle Leo. "I will make sure to be quiet."

That's why I sought you. You aunt was…most concerned that you should…that is, she didn't wish you to mope about the house, alone and unoccupied."

"She needn't be concerned for me."

"Which is exactly what I told her. I promised her that I'd help to fill your day."

Sophie's heart sank. She could only imagine what her uncle would deem suitable recreation for a young woman. She envisaged a day of needlework and pastel drawing, or worse, practicing on the pianoforte, an instrument Sophie had never mastered.

"When she's a little better," Uncle Leo continued, "she'll need a book to read while she convalesces. I thought Hatchard's might have something she'd like."

"I'm sure they would."

"I would go alone, but I don't know what kind of reading she enjoys. So I wondered if you might accompany me, and help me to choose something for her?"

Sophie's smile was genuine. Uncle Leo was clearly concerned for his sister's welfare. Perhaps he wasn't as grim and distant as she'd presumed. "I'll just go and change my dress," she said.

"Good. Good." He nodded and looked down the

stairs again, distracted. Sophie felt a twinge of unease. It would be the work of an instant for him to push her and make her fall. She doubted she would survive such a tumble. Although why her uncle should want to do her such harm, she couldn't fathom. She was being foolish, allowing flights of fancy to frighten her.

Nevertheless, she moved away from the step.

"Don't take too long," he said. "I've ordered the carriage, and I don't wish to keep the horses standing."

He was worried for his horses. That explained his distraction. Feeling guilty that she'd allowed her macabre imagination to malign him, Sophie resolved to make up for it by doing as he asked.

"I won't change," she said. "I'll fetch my pelisse and gloves and be with you in a moment."

Uncle Leo smiled and made his way downstairs.

Sophie hurried along the landing to her chamber, collected her pelisse, gloves, and the jaunty hat she'd decorated the other day. Her maid was in the room, tidying her things.

"I'm going to Hatchard's to find a book for my aunt," she told Mary. "She's unwell."

"Shall I come with you, miss?" It would be usual for her to do so. Young ladies did not go out alone, unless they wished to cause gossip. Sophie hesitated. Even though an outing with her uncle needed no chaperone, the maid's presence couldn't hurt. But then she'd promised to be but a moment. By the time Mary had gone downstairs to inform the housekeeper where she was going, then run up to fetch her own hat and coat from her room, Uncle Leo would be agitated about the state of his horses again. Sophie had no wish to spoil his good mood.

"No," she said. "Not today. I'm going with my

uncle. I doubt we'll be out for long." She pulled on her gloves.

Hopefully long enough that Kit has gone before I return, though.

She ran downstairs. Her uncle stood waiting and nodded his approval at her. "Punctuality. How wonderful. A sadly rare virtue in a lady."

Sophie bristled. "I am always punctual."

"Glad to hear it." He took her arm and led her to the door. She glanced at the morning room as they passed, wondering what Kit and Ed discussed in there. She hoped they didn't come out until she'd gone so she had no reason to see Kit and talk to him while pretending the kiss had never happened. Yet, at the same time, she wished he would appear. She wanted to see him, to look into his eyes and know, once and for all, if that kiss had meant as much to him as it had to her. Could they be friends once more? Or could they be something else, something much deeper?

If he appeared, of course, she'd probably color, and her tongue would tie, and that would be disastrous. Ed might not have seen the tension between them earlier, but he was not completely oblivious. And even if he were, Uncle Leo would certainly notice. Sophie didn't wish to explain to him something she barely understood herself. She hurried outside.

The sky was a dirty gray, the clouds thick and unbroken, blocking the sunshine and threatening rain. The air was hot and stifling, the kind of day more suited to sitting quietly, doing very little. Even the birdsong in the park across the road seemed languid. The light had a strange quality, bright and close, as if it were too big for the space it occupied.

"I don't have my raincoat," she said.

"We're going in a carriage, so no matter." Uncle Leo pointed at the closed carriage waiting in the street. It was of high quality, its lacquered doors gleaming. Four bay horses waited patiently, a coachman at the head of the front runners. But it wasn't her uncle's coach or coachman, and she didn't recognize the bays.

"My carriage wheel is broken," explained Uncle Leo as if he'd read her thoughts. "I've borrowed this from a friend."

"We could wait—"

"When someone has done me the honor of lending me such a wonderful team, it would be churlish not to use it." He took her elbow and steered her, gently but firmly, to the vehicle.

A footman in a livery she didn't recognize opened the door and let down the steps. Uncle Leo handed her inside, then climbed in after her.

The blinds were drawn, and with Uncle Leo's bulk in the doorway, Sophie could see nothing. She squinted, trying to make out the barest detail as she sat, facing forward.

Uncle Leo sat across from her. His move from the door allowed the briefest moment of light to penetrate the carriage, and Sophie saw there was another person within. A man, hidden in the shadows of the far corner. His clothes were dark and his hat shielded his face, so she couldn't see who it was, but his presence made her wish she'd never agreed to this outing.

The door closed and the carriage was plunged into darkness once more.

"Uncle…" Her voice trembled. The carriage lurched forward. "Uncle! Stop the carriage!"

"I don't think that's a good idea," sneered the shadow man, and Sophie swallowed hard against the terror bubbling up inside her.

"L-Lord Pinkerton," she whispered.

Chapter Fourteen

It took a moment for the truth to hit Sophie. She and Uncle Leo were inside Lord Pinkerton's carriage! The blinds were drawn so not even a sliver of daylight seeped in. A perfect vessel for abduction, she thought, and she wanted to laugh hysterically.

Instead, she scolded herself for indulging in such histrionics. Lord Pinkerton did not abduct young ladies. He was a peer of the realm, not a…a kidnapper.

Besides, he could hardly be abducting her when her uncle sat beside him, could he? Although, to be fair to herself, he'd sounded more than a little menacing, and it was so very dark in here… She widened her eyes until they hurt, as if by doing so she would see more, but the darkness was complete.

"Let me out of the coach, please," she said, surprised and relieved at the steadiness of her voice. No trace of the fear that made her heart race and her limbs rigid with tension.

Lord Pinkerton laughed, softly.

"Now, my dear, don't make a fuss," said Uncle Leo. His voice trembled, as if he, too, was afraid. Sophie bit her bottom lip and tried to think. She swayed slightly as the carriage rounded a corner, the horse's hooves ringing on the road surface, echoing in her head. She had to make these men stop the coach and let her out. But how?

Gathering all the bravado she could muster, she

lifted her chin and said, "Kidnapping is a capital crime."

Lord Pinkerton's soft, menacing chuckle turned into a genuine sound of amusement.

"No, no, my dear," said Leo. The usual authority was gone from his voice, which frightened her even more. "Nobody kidnapped you," he continued. "You got into the carriage willingly."

"I was tricked! Stop this vehicle at once and let me out."

"Now, Sophie…"

"At once, Uncle Leo." She swallowed. Maintaining the bravado was exhausting and it dried her mouth until her throat hurt, but she couldn't give in. She must persuade them to let her go before it was too late. "If you stop now, there will be an end to it," she tried. "Nothing more will need to be said." In the dark, she crossed her fingers, the way she and Ed had done whenever they told a lie as children.

Because her reassurances were definitely lies. She wouldn't be silent about this. As soon as she could, she'd tell Kit what had happened, and he… Sophie frowned. Why would she look to Kit for protection? Ed. She meant Ed. She'd tell Ed, not Kit. Although she made no doubt that Kit would want to help Ed deal with these miscreants.

"Be reasonable, Sophie." Uncle Leo's entreaty cut into her musings.

Her eyes, already impossibly wide in a vain attempt to see in the dark carriage, widened even further. Her jaw dropped in disbelief and anger rose, replacing her fear. "Reasonable? What in this entire situation is reasonable?"

"I dislike hysterics." Pinkerton's voice was soft and

calm. It made her shudder. "I suggest you desist, for I won't tolerate them in my bride."

Sophie's breath caught in her throat. Her voice deserted her.

"You brought this upon yourself," he continued. "If you'd accepted me in the first place, we could have done this in a more conventional manner." His seat creaked as he leaned forward. She felt his hand caress her knee. She pulled her leg away and shrank back into the corner of her seat.

Uncle Leo spoke again. He was clearly emboldened by Lord Pinkerton's cold control and Sophie's momentary speechlessness, because he sounded more confident now. "Where is the ledger?"

For a moment, Sophie thought she'd misheard him. The question made no sense to her, a complete non sequitur, totally divorced from the situation at hand.

"Pardon?" She sounded stupid to her own ears but was at a loss how else to respond.

"It isn't in your rooms, so where did you put it?"

"My—rooms?" An image came to mind of her maid, tidying her room. Sophie had thought little of it at the time; Mary was merely doing her job. But now, in her mind's eye, Sophie saw the clothes, rumpled and disturbed, the perfume box open, and her trinket case skewed. Even her bed curtains had been untidy, not tied back neatly as they usually were.

"You were in my room," she whispered. He'd searched her rooms, disturbed her things, and destroyed her privacy. For some ledger she knew nothing about? She swallowed and shook her head, willing sense to return. "What ledger?"

"Don't play me for a fool, miss." His customary

anger had returned. "I know you have it, and it must be returned."

"I don't know what you mean." She'd hardly finished saying the words before he leapt forward. His seat protested, its squeak more alarming than the soft creak of Lord Pinkerton's more controlled movement of a few moments ago.

Uncle Leo made a grab for Sophie's shoulders. In the dark, he missed and hit her chin instead. The clunk sounded loud to her and knocked her head back against the squabs. For a moment she was stunned. He found her shoulders and gripped them, painfully and tightly, and he shook her until her teeth rattled, and her senses, already reeling from the blow to her chin and the nonsensical conversation, were completely scrambled.

"You took it from my study," he cried. "I want it back!"

Sophie pushed at him, trying to loosen his grip on her shoulders, but he held her too firmly. "You're hurting me!" He shook her again and flashes of bright green and orange filled the darkness around her head.

There was a whisper of cloth, and she was pulled forward. She braced herself, trying to pull back, then fell against the squabs when Uncle Leo suddenly let go of her. At the same moment she heard a sharp crack, as if somebody had been slapped. Uncle Leo cried out.

Sophie righted herself on the seat and tried to make herself small and distant so he couldn't grab her again.

The opposite seat creaked, presumably because he'd thrown himself into it. It moaned again, without so much protest, and she surmised that was Lord Pinkerton taking his seat. He must have pulled Uncle Leo away from her. She breathed a sigh of relief, which turned halfway through into a gasp of shocked despair when the baron spoke in a cold, low tone. "If you ever lay hands on my bride again, I'll kill you." The silken threat should frighten her uncle, because it absolutely terrified Sophie. She pushed herself back farther, willing herself to disappear completely.

It was a full minute before her mind processed his words. He'd called her his bride. Sophie shook her head, then felt stupid, for no one would see the movement in this darkness.

She could not let his statement stand unchallenged. He couldn't think, even for a moment, that she accepted his claim. If he did, she knew instinctively it would be impossible to escape from him.

"I am not your bride." Her voice was tiny, the squeak of a mouse, and the words held no power. Even Sophie didn't believe they meant anything, or that they would persuade Lord Pinkerton of their truth.

He didn't reply, but in her imagination she saw him sitting comfortably in the dark carriage, relaxed and grinning at her. She swallowed and pressed even farther into the corner of her seat. Her breathing was shallow, each breath barely there. The inside of her mouth was dry and rough and felt like the sand the maids used to clean the stone surrounds on the fireplaces. Her mind whirled, dizzying her, and her thoughts tumbled one over another until they were tangled in an incoherent heap. The only word her befuddled brain could make sense of was "Escape!" She heard it, banging against her skull, trying to get out, repeating itself over and over again.

Escape! Escape! Escape!

She took in a deep breath through her mouth. The warm air in the carriage tasted of old cigars and fresh cologne, worn leather, and men. Sophie shuddered.

Escape, she silently told herself again.

But how? replied the more lucid part of her. She turned her head toward the door. The dark blinds must be fastened to the frame, for even the jostling and bouncing over ruts in the road did not make them move, and no chink of light entered from anywhere.

She didn't need to see, though, to know she couldn't jump out at this moment. The carriage was traveling far too fast. If she managed to open the door and make the leap, she'd likely kill herself. At the very least, she'd break a leg, and then she'd be as caught as she was now, and in pain to boot.

Sophie caught her bottom lip under her top teeth and tried to think of another solution, one that was more likely to work.

Someone sniffed. Someone else clicked their tongue against their teeth in irritation. The next sniff was louder and more pronounced. Was Uncle Leo crying?

"Pull yourself together, man," said Lord Pinkerton, his voice low, annoyance shivering through his words.

"What am I to do?" Uncle Leo's answer was a soft whisper.

Lord Pinkerton sighed deeply. "She'll tell me where it is," he said. "And I shall inform you." He sounded so calm, so certain of himself. Sophie's heartbeat stepped up.

"But in the meantime…" Uncle Leo began, but he stopped when Lord Pinkerton scoffed.

"In the meantime, it is safe."

"You cannot know…" This time Uncle Leo's words ended on a startled squawk. He seemed to choke. Was Lord Pinkerton throttling him? The first tears spilled from Sophie's eyes and slid over her cheeks.

"I can know," murmured Lord Pinkerton. "And so can you. If you cannot discover its hiding place, despite your compelling reasons to do so, then it is well hidden and unlikely to come to the notice of anyone else."

The choking ended on a cough and a wheeze. "I pray you're right," said Uncle Leo, his voice hoarse, his breathing heavy.

A soft, rhythmic drumming sounded on the roof. Sophie guessed the rain had started. That could be good for her, in that her uncle and Lord Pinkerton might not be so ready to chase her through the wet streets. But it could also be a bad thing, for after some days of dryness, the rain would turn the pavements slick and it would be hard to keep her balance.

Her head ached now, and the skin around her eyes felt stretched and sore from trying to see. Her chin stung where Uncle Leo had caught it, and her shoulders were stiff and bruised from the way he'd clawed them. She was grateful to Lord Pinkerton for stopping the assault— No! She shuddered. She would feel nothing but disgust for the man who had abducted her and wanted to force her to marry him.

She swallowed, willing away the bile that rose through her. There were ways a man could force a woman to be his bride—Aunt Jess had said so when she warned Sophie never to be alone with a man. Besides, Sophie was a country girl, and she'd seen enough of the animals on her father's estate to have an inkling as to what would happen. The thought of Lord Pinkerton doing that to her... The bile reached the back of her throat, and she was suddenly cold and clammy. She put her hand across her mouth to stop herself being sick.

She'd been alone with Kit and he…well, he kissed her. Thoroughly. Her lips tingled at the memory of it, even now. But he hadn't hurt her, he hadn't compromised her, and he certainly hadn't done anything she didn't wish him to do. The thought of him now calmed her, pushing the nausea down and allowing her thoughts to reorder themselves. If he were here, he'd make sure Lord Pinkerton received his just deserts for this.

But he wasn't here. And since he had no way of knowing what had happened, he wasn't going to be here. It was up to Sophie to save herself.

I will do it. She breathed in slowly and repeated those four words in her mind, building determination and pushing away the paralyzing fear.

"You've only yourself to blame," said Lord Pinkerton, cutting into her thoughts. For a moment, Sophie thought he spoke to her, blaming her for his actions. Anger surged through her and she prepared to tell him what she thought of him, but before she could say anything, he continued, "Only an idiot would keep a ledger such as that."

The ledger! He was berating Uncle Leo, whose breath shuddered on a sob. Sophie had no idea what that ledger recorded, but it was clearly incriminating, and its loss had panicked her uncle.

He thought she had it. What would he do when he discovered she didn't? More fear flowed, icing her veins. She felt the color drain from her face, and the back of her eyes stung with tears. She blinked most of them away, and swiped from her cheek the one that escaped. The leather of her gloves felt warm against her cold face.

She needed to escape before they discovered she

knew nothing about it. Once Uncle Leo knew she couldn't help him, he'd search elsewhere, and Sophie would be left to face Lord Pinkerton alone.

Oh, why had she not stayed in the morning room with Kit and Ed? If she'd been with them, none of this would have happened. She shook her head. That logic was wrong. None of this would have happened *now*. If Uncle Leo and Lord Pinkerton had determined to abduct her, they would have done so, even if they'd had to delay it.

In fact, a delay might have been worse. Taking her at three o'clock was one thing. She made no doubt she'd soon be missed. When Aunt Jess awoke—if indeed she was even sleeping, for Sophie only had her uncle's word on that—she'd look for Sophie and, not finding her, would raise the hue and cry. Whereas, had this action been delayed until after the house retired for the night, who could say how long it might have been before her disappearance was discovered? Long enough, Sophie was sure, to ruin her. Lord Pinkerton's plan would have succeeded then, for certain. Even Aunt Jess would insist the wedding must go ahead.

Her thoughts, and her mood, began a downward spiral. It could be hours before Aunt Jess looked for her, even during the day. Hours in the company of these men. Hours when her control over her future slipped steadily away.

She had to escape. And she had to make the men realize how futile their intentions were.

If only her "betrothal" to Kit had been public. At the very least, she wished Uncle Leo had been aware of it, because then he'd have realized there was no point to this.

Wait! There was no reason Sophie couldn't make him aware of it now. If he thought she had a fiancé, someone who would look for her and refuse to believe she left willingly…

She could pretend Kit had made her an offer, and she'd accepted. He'd certainly kissed her like a man about to make an offer. She put her fingertip to her lips, feeling once more the press of his mouth against hers, the wonderful scent of him surrounding her, the taste of him threatening to overwhelm her.

As a beau, Kit Thomas was all too real. Her betrothal to him might be false, a means to an end, but it no longer felt that way to Sophie. It felt true, and more desirable than anything had ever felt before. Even the work in her laboratory, the dream of a medal at the Royal Academy, even those things faded into insignificance beside him. Could she make claim to him now and then relinquish her hold on him when the danger was passed? Or would she be tempted to cling to him, causing heartbreak and misery to him? And, ultimately, to herself. No one was happy forever, giving unrequited love.

That was a bridge to be crossed when she reached it. For now, the most pressing issue wasn't her future heartbreak. It was the deterrence of her would-be suitor, and the withdrawal of her uncle's support for him. All other considerations must wait.

Taking her courage in both hands, she prepared to tell them. She bit her bottom lip, anxious. She needed to say it in exactly the right way, or they'd know she was lying.

Fear raised its ugly head once more. Sophie had seen the way other gentlemen reacted to Lord Pinkerton. Her uncle wasn't the only one who seemed terrified of him. If she made him angry…

Surely, though, he wouldn't hurt a woman, would he? *Oh, Kit. Find me. Please.*

A deep breath. Another. Then, with her hand on her chest as if, somehow, that would calm her racing heart, she said in a clear steady voice, "Stop this coach at once and let me out."

Lord Pinkerton laughed. Uncle Leo's seat creaked. Sophie's pulse raced.

"I don't think that's a good idea," said the baron. "You'd catch your death out there in that rain." Sophie looked up at the roof. The drumming was harder now, more insistent. No doubt the heavens had opened fully, and everything was being soaked. She didn't care. Compared to being here, at the mercy of these men, being in the rain was of no consequence at all.

"Let me out," she repeated. "I am not your bride." She spoke the words slowly and clearly, as if talking to a child who was particularly slow to learn. "Nor shall I ever be your bride."

The baron's voice had lost none of its humor. "I beg to differ, my dear."

"I am not your dear."

"You will be."

Here it was. The moment of truth. Or should that be "of lie"? The moment that mattered. She closed her eyes and delivered her coup de grace. "I fail to see how," she said, proud of her matter-of-fact tone, "when I am already betrothed to someone else."

She thanked God for the darkness of the carriage, because the burning in her cheeks could only mean they were as red as the scullery maid's hands.

There was a moment of absolute silence. The tension within the carriage grew until she felt that, if she reached out a hand, she could pluck notes from the air, as one would pluck a harp's strings. Did this mean the ploy had worked? Would he realize he'd been bested and let her go?

Then she heard her uncle, gurgling and choking once again. Sophie gasped in horror. She had meant Lord Pinkerton to release her, not for him to murder Uncle Leo!

"Stop! Let go of him," she cried. If she launched herself at the men, would she stop Uncle Leo being strangled, or would she put herself in more danger?

"I swear," said Uncle Leo, his voice tight, every word a struggle, "I didn't know." He gurgled again. "I gave—no—permission. I swear."

The gurgling was replaced by spluttering and coughing, and deep, heaving breath, as if he couldn't get his fill of air. Sophie stared into the darkness, terrified as, for the first time, she believed Lord Pinkerton was capable of doing both of them severe physical harm. She regretted the lie she'd just told, regretted that she hadn't foreseen its consequences. The heat left her face and her mouth dried until it was difficult to swallow.

Kit, please find me. Find me before it's too late!

The seat across from her creaked and she knew Lord Pinkerton had leaned forward. She felt the air shift as if to make room for him, smelled the warm musk of him, the cigars and brandy stale upon his breath. She imagined him fixing his glare on her, his eyes no more than slivers. His hand touched her knee. She flinched.

"Mr. Thomas, I suppose," he said, quietly. The words landed on her face like blows. "Well, we shall see." He patted her knee. She moved her leg, trying to escape his touch. It didn't work.

"He's a troublesome gnat," he continued. Behind him, Uncle Leo drew in a deep, greedy breath.

Sophie swallowed. Having defied the baron, she must now keep at it, or she was lost. "He's more of a man than you are."

If she thought he'd be goaded by the statement, angered enough to make a mistake, she was wrong. He merely laughed. "Is he now?"

"He'll be looking for me," she said, head held high in an effort to bolster her courage. If only her words were true.

"Let him look."

"When he finds me, he'll make you sorry."

The sneer was evident in his voice as he answered. "By the time he finds you, it will be too late."

He moved like a viper. One minute he was talking at her, his manner almost languid. The next instant, he struck.

His lips pressed against hers, wet and cold. She tried to lean back, to get away from him but his hand clasped the back of her head, dislodging her bonnet, and his fingers dug painfully into her scalp as he held her in place. His tongue pressed against her, seeking entry. She pushed her lips together tightly, and held them firm. She could smell his body odor under his cologne, and the stubble on his face scratched her cheeks.

Kit! She prayed that, somehow, Kit would hear her silent scream.

Chapter Fifteen

Sophie squirmed, trying to pull away from him, but he was stronger, pinning her in place like a butterfly on a collector's board. His hand rested against her breast and his fingers fumbled with the buttons on her pelisse. Strength born of terror surged through her and she pushed him away, but an instant later he was back for more. His lips curled against hers in a grin. He was enjoying this!

Briefly, Sophie wondered if she should stop struggling. If he enjoyed the fight, might he be put off by a placid, still creature?

She'd never know. Her instinct was to fight, and fight she would.

He breached the pelisse. Cold air hit her chest. There was a tearing sound and the bodice of her dress slackened. She squealed in alarm, the sound muted by her lips being pressed so determinedly together. Her fists beat ineffectively at him and she tried to kick out, but he pushed against her, holding her legs down with the weight of his body.

His fingers reached inside her shift and he pinched her nipple, hard enough that she cried out in pained surprise. He took his chance, pushing his tongue through her lips and deep into her mouth. She tasted cigar smoke and brandy, and she gagged. Twice.

With a grunt of disgust, he moved away. Blessed air

rushed between them. Hard coughs wracked her, as if her body did all it could to expel the sour taste of him, the nauseating smell he left on her skin.

When Kit kissed her, it had felt wonderful, like nothing she'd ever felt before. When Lord Pinkerton did it… No. She would not dwell on it, would not allow him room in her thoughts. She would push his kiss, his touch—him—completely away.

Sophie closed her eyes and thought of Kit, of his kiss. His lips had been warm against hers, soft, yet firm, tormenting, teasing, not enough and yet too much. His breath had caressed her skin, her throat, her breasts. She clung to the memory of it now, pushing away the horror of the moment.

"You have a lot to learn about pleasing a man," said Lord Pinkerton, his voice a low growl, his breathing heavy. "I shall enjoy teaching you."

"I say!" Uncle Leo sounded shocked. Sophie glared at him, even though the darkness meant he couldn't see her contempt.

"You'll say nothing." Lord Pinkerton told him.

"You promised me she wouldn't be harmed," protested Uncle Leo.

"She won't be." Lord Pinkerton gave a low chuckle. "Unless she forces my hand."

The seat creaked. Sophie thought her uncle moved, though whether it was to shield her, she couldn't tell. "Now see here…"

"Quiet, I said." Lord Pinkerton's tone brooked no argument, and Uncle Leo didn't give him one. The seat creaked again as he sat back.

There were three short raps as someone—she suspected Lord Pinkerton—signaled to the driver.

Sophie jerked to the side as the carriage slowed, then tensed as she wondered what this might mean for her. A chance to escape? With the carriage slowed, or even stopped, she might scramble out and run as though the devil was on her tail—which he would be.

Even if running wasn't an option, all hope was not lost. If she screamed and yelled for all she was worth, might a passerby hear? Although, surely, Lord Pinkerton would have thought of that?

He might have discounted the possibility, thinking her too afraid of ruin to bring attention upon herself. A lady's reputation was so fragile, anything outside the normal bounds of behavior could tear holes in it, even when that behavior was not hers and the repercussions not her fault.

Well, if he or Uncle Leo thought Sophie a scared mouse who valued what Society thought over her own wellbeing, they were in for a rude awakening. Reputation be hanged! All that mattered was that she escape this carriage before something worse could happen.

Besides, the people whose opinions mattered would stand with her. Ed and Aunt Jess. And Kit. He'd remain her friend, and he wouldn't blame her.

And if she was wrong about that, wrong about him…another bridge for the future.

"Go to your club," instructed Lord Pinkerton, tersely, as the horses slowed to a walk. "Make sure you're seen. Then, when you go home and discover your niece is gone, act the distraught guardian. Send out a search party. Blame Thomas."

"But—"

"Do as I say." It sounded like those words were squeezed between closely gritted teeth.

Sophie knew a moment of hope. This part of the plan, at least, wouldn't work. No one who knew them would believe Uncle Leo would be distraught over her loss. And nobody would believe Kit had a hand in this. Would they? She closed her eyes and prayed he'd been in Ed's company constantly since she left the morning room.

The men fell silent. The carriage wheels hissed over the wet road surface, the harnesses jingling and the struts wheezing as it slowed to a crawl. Now was her chance. Sophie leaned forward, outstretched fingers finding the door panel, looking for the latch.

There wasn't one! Frantically, she ran her hand over the entire width of the door. No indentation. No string to pull or wood to lift. Nothing but smooth leather which undoubtedly matched the upholstery on the seats.

That made no sense. How could there not be an opener of some kind? There must be one. Otherwise, how would passengers free themselves? She ran her hand across the panel again. Nothing.

What had she thought earlier? A perfect vessel for abduction? The notion didn't seem quite so absurd now. Panic crowded her, seizing her lungs so she could barely take a breath.

The carriage rocked as the horses stopped. The movement jolted Sophie from the horror threatening to engulf her. The coachman would open the door, and when he did, she'd dart past him and run. She could be several hundred yards away before he gave chase, or before Lord Pinkerton could get past him to come after her himself.

She lifted her skirts to free her lower legs, and tensed, ready.

The coachman spoke soothing words to the horses. They snorted a reply. Their harnesses jangled. The carriage dipped slightly as he climbed from his perch. Inside the cab, Uncle Leo's breath was fast and shallow. Sophie could smell his fear. It mixed with the malevolence oozing from Lord Pinkerton, fouling the air. Sophie shuddered and took small, quick, breaths through her mouth so she would not inhale the scent of them. Her fingers bunched tighter around her skirt and she gripped her reticule, ready to use it like a club, though how effective it might be she couldn't imagine. Her heartbeat quickened until it was almost one long unbroken note, whooshing past her ear.

The door rattled. She leaned forward, ready…

Lord Pinkerton grabbed her arm as he sat beside her on the forward-facing seat. "Your uncle will leave us now," he said. "You and I will stay in here and make our way to Scotland. A marriage over the anvil is not what I'd have chosen, but needs must."

She pulled away, but he was too strong. His arms encircled her, clamping her firmly to his side.

The carriage door flew open and light spilled inside. Instinctively, Sophie squeezed her eyes shut against it and tried to turn her head away, but she couldn't move with him pressed so close to her.

The wind blew the rain inside the carriage. It splashed against Sophie's face, the cold of it bringing her to her senses. "Help!" she yelled. The baron clamped his hand across her mouth, his fingers digging into her cheek. She cried again, but only a muffled sound came out.

A footman let down the steps and the carriage swayed as Uncle Leo moved. Sophie glared at him, pushing all her hatred and anger into that stare. Regret and sorrow filled his eyes, and he looked as if he might say something, but he glanced at Lord Pinkerton and suddenly fear was the only emotion she saw. He lowered his head and didn't look at her again.

She screamed into Lord Pinkerton's hand, but the sound was tiny and wouldn't be heard outside the cab. She squirmed and fought and kicked. Her boot connected with Uncle Leo's calf. He cried out and stumbled, but he didn't stop. And then he was gone. The door closed and they were in darkness once more. The carriage dipped under the weight of the footman returning to his seat, and they moved off.

"I never thought we'd be rid of him, did you?" asked Lord Pinkerton. "But, at long last, it's just the two of us." He let go of her and moved along the seat to give her room.

Sophie wiped her mouth, as if that could somehow rid her of the feel of his hand. Her cheeks were sore, and she could taste the leather of his gloves. She wanted to be sick, but she wouldn't give him the satisfaction. Instead, she raised her head defiantly and said, "I will not marry you."

His answering chuckle was soft, and all the more frightening because of that. "I think you will. When it becomes common knowledge that you spent the night with me, you'll have no choice."

"There's always a choice." That wasn't quite true, and Sophie knew it. If word got out—and she made no doubt that it would—that she'd been with him all night, she'd face ruin. The only thing that would save her would be marriage. Ruination and ostracism from Society would destroy everything. Oh, she'd be free to go back to the country and work on her wheat seeds, but she could never present her findings to the Royal Academy under her own name. No one there would receive her or her experiments with any kindness whatsoever.

Worse than that, though, was that she wouldn't be the only person to suffer. Ed's prospects would be damaged. He'd find it difficult to make an advantageous marriage, or to find friends to help him restore the family fortunes. And poor Aunt Jess would be beside herself with shame.

She could not, however, allow Lord Pinkerton to cow her into submission. She'd fight him every step of the way. And she wasn't ruined yet. She'd be rescued long before that happened.

She hoped.

The baron was not as clever as he thought he was. Uncle Leo wasn't a man of strong character. When she was missed, it wouldn't take much for him to break down and confess. It would be easy to track them on the road to Gretna Green. With fast horses and determination, Kit and Ed would probably reach them before their first change of horses.

The baron made a tutting sound. "I know what you're thinking," he said. "You're thinking your uncle will tell them where we're going, and your knight errant will ride to the rescue."

Disconcerted at how easily he read her thoughts, Sophie said, a little uncertainly, "He will."

"Indubitably."

Sophie frowned. Was he mad? He knew his plan would be thwarted, yet he didn't seem to mind.

"There are flaws with your thinking," he continued.

"You see, I have every expectation that your uncle will stay silent. The evidence I hold against him could see him hang, and he is unlikely to sacrifice himself to save you. Besides, who will suspect him of knowing anything? He has been at his club, as several gentlemen will attest, should they be asked. Since nobody knows you left with him, no one is likely to question him."

"My maid knows," retorted Sophie. "She will tell the household."

There was a moment of silence. Then he rapped on the roof of the cab and they slowed to a halt. The noise of the rain was incessant now, and when the footman opened the door he was soaked through.

"Miss Wilson's maid," said Lord Pinkerton. "Get rid of her."

"No!" Sophie lunged for the door. Lord Pinkerton caught her around the waist and held her against himself. She kicked and heard the grunt as her boot found his shin. The door closed and the carriage moved off, but still Sophie fought, scratching, kicking, biting. She screamed and he put his hand over her mouth, so she bit him hard enough that she tasted the warm copper of his blood. He yelled, spun her around, and slapped her hard. She fell to the floor, her ear ringing and her cheek on fire.

She wiped her hand across the end of her nose and sniffed. Silent tears trickled down her cheeks, making her skin itch. This monster had sent someone to hurt Mary. The poor maid had done nothing wrong, yet she would pay because Sophie had betrayed her. Why had she told him? She was so stupid!

Her breath caught on a sob.

"Enough histrionics," he said, in a bored tone. "I want my bride to be happy."

"I am not your bride. You'll never get me to Scotland. If my family doesn't catch you, I will make certain other travelers know what you've done, my reputation be hanged." Her voice was soft, broken by the sobs she couldn't hold back, but she meant every word.

Lord Pinkerton laughed. "Then it is a good job we are not going to Scotland."

"But…"

"I leave nothing to chance, my dear. I don't think your uncle will betray me, but should he do so, they will hare off up the Great North Road. By the time they realize they have been had, you and I will be wed, and you will be safely tucked away in Pinkerton Hall. And no one will be able to do anything about it."

Chapter Sixteen

Ed led Kit toward his uncle's study. The house seemed extraordinarily quiet considering it was the middle of the day. No servants busied themselves nearby, and there was no sound of the ladies. To Kit, the heels of their boots seemed loud against the checkered tiles, and he had the absurd notion they too should be quiet.

At the study door Ed turned, uncertainty plain on his face. "Do I knock and wait for him to call 'Enter,' or do we catch him off guard?"

Kit shrugged. "Does it matter?"

Ed gave a tiny nod, then rapped sharply on the door and tried to push it open. It didn't move. He tried the handle twice more, putting his shoulder to the door, but it didn't budge.

"It's locked." He sounded disappointed, yet at the same time relieved. Kit understood. Family dynamics were complicated and daunting.

"If you'd rather not do this…"

"It's not what I'd rather," answered Ed, the temptation to leave clearly displayed on his face. "It has to be done."

"You pay people who could do this," Kit pointed out. "No one would blame you. I'd hate to have to confront my father on something like this."

"But you would do so."

Kit wanted to refute that assertion, but he couldn't. They both knew, if called upon, Kit would stand and do what he thought he must, no matter how unpleasant the task. Which meant there'd be no shirking this responsibility for Ed, either.

"It's a damn nuisance," said Ed. "I was certain he'd be in. This is his day for paperwork. He's always here."

"Perhaps he hasn't gone far."

"Hmm." Ed paced the floor in front of the study. His steps were quick and agitated, the sound of them echoing through the house. "I should have made an appointment with him, but I wanted to catch him unawares. I worked out what I needed to say, and how to say it. Damn it all!"

On Ed's fourth turn about the tiny section of the corridor, Kit raised his hand and touched his friend's shoulder, stopping him midstride. "You're making me giddy."

"Sorry." Ed straightened. He bounced up and down on the balls of his feet, his heels clicking the floor. Kit looked pointedly at him. He apologized again and made the effort to be still. It was plainly a struggle.

"We shouldn't stand here like a couple of naughty boys at the headmaster's door," said Kit. "Shall we return to the morning room and await his return?"

Ed didn't look convinced. "We won't hear him. We won't know he's come back."

"We will if one of your servants comes to tell us," and Kit steered Ed back along the corridor. As they reached the stairs, he couldn't help but glance up. Sophie wasn't there. He hadn't truly expected she would be; she was hardly likely to be skulking at the top of the staircase, waiting for him. Even so, he felt a twinge of disappointment.

He sat Ed down, poured him a brandy, and rang for attention. Moments later, the butler entered. Mr. Leo was, he informed them in his most regretful tone, away from home. He did say he expected to be here for dinner, so he couldn't have gone far, but no, the butler had no idea where he'd gone, nor his expected time of return.

Ed swore and downed his brandy, then poured himself a second glass. If Kit didn't keep his mind on something other than the meeting, he'd likely be too drunk to confront his uncle today. And he must do so. The longer the task was left, the more difficult it would become, until it assumed gargantuan proportions in Ed's mind. Kit couldn't let that happen.

"Well," he said, slapping his hand against his thigh and springing to his feet, "it seems we have two options. We can either spend the day here, twirling our thumbs until he comes home, or we can make use of the time and visit Archie Hammond. It's a few days since I saw him, and I'd like to know how he fares."

Ed grinned sheepishly. "I'm driving you mad, aren't I?"

"To Bedlam. You're like a fish on a hook, wriggling and fighting."

Ed apologized, and they headed out. As he walked to the front door, hat and gloves ready, cane under his arm, Kit took one more surreptitious look up the stairs. She wasn't there. He cocked his head and listened but he couldn't hear her, either. He sighed and followed Ed out of the house.

The day, which had been bright, was now overcast. Angry gray clouds hung low, threatening to soak the world at any moment. The air was heavy with anticipation of it, the heat of the last few days fighting to stay and the humidity weighing everything down. The leaves on the trees in the park opposite seemed a deeper, clearer green, and everything was cast in sharper relief than usual.

"We're in for a thunderstorm," said Ed as he squinted at the sky.

"Aye," said Kit. "All the more reason to hurry to Archie's. We don't want to be soaked by the time we get there."

They spent an hour with Archie, whose cuts and bruises were already fading. It would be some time before he left his room, but he was looking a lot better than he had the last time Kit saw him. He had books to read and letters to write and a lighthearted maiden aunt who had taken it upon herself to keep him company. Satisfied he wouldn't expire from loneliness and boredom, Kit and Ed took their leave.

The rain was lashing down now, making the streets shiny and filling the roads with tiny puddles. Carriages swished through, splashing water onto the pavements. Kit and Ed waited in the hallway of Archie's apartments while a servant ran to find a cab. Ed was grim-faced.

"Oh, come now, Ed," said Kit, trying to lighten the mood. "It's only rain. Though I grant you, it's of Biblical proportions."

Ed gave him a sidelong look. "Archie didn't deserve that," he said. "Bloody Pinkerton. Someone needs to take him down a peg."

"He'll get what he deserves."

"Meanwhile, I wish he'd leave my sister alone."

Kit gritted his teeth. "He will." Whatever it took, he'd make sure of that.

"Damn him to hell! And damn Uncle Leo for

throwing her at him."

"She's managed to avoid him quite well," Kit replied. "And in less than three months, when you've attained your majority…"

"Let's pray she can keep him at bay until then."

She will, vowed Kit, silently. He studied Ed for a moment. *But will you give me permission to marry her? Will she have me?* Doubt and trepidation made his heart skitter. He might well do some praying himself.

The servant returned and held an umbrella over them as they hurried from the doorway to the cab. The rain beat on the roof, fast and booming, like a drum announcing an opera was about to open.

In the half light of the cab, Ed turned to Kit, his face earnest. "Thank you for your help in thwarting him so far."

Kit shrugged and hoped he looked more nonchalant than he felt. "What are friends for?" *And what would you say if you knew thwarting him was only part of my reason for being with her?*

His memory replayed Ed's words to him, just that morning—*When Pinkerton was her only prospect, being squired about by any other gentleman was all to the good. But now, she's going to have her pick of men to choose from… You're a confirmed bachelor with a certain type of reputation, and I wouldn't want that to affect my sister's renewed chances on the marriage mart.*

"Watch your back," said Ed, cutting into Kit's thoughts. "Archie only spoke to Sophie, and look what happened to him."

"I'm not so easy to ambush. And I expect it, which helps." Kit settled back against the squabs and watched Ed, who gazed out the window at the drab streets, his jaw clenched, frown deep.

Would this be a good time to let Ed know Kit's feelings for Sophie had changed? That his desire for a betrothal with her was now real? How was Ed likely to take such news? It was one thing to let a friend spend time with your sister. It was quite another to welcome his amorous intentions toward her.

She's going to have her pick of men to choose from.

Ed knew Kit had no prospects. He wasn't going to inherit the Markham title or its fortune. He had only what his father chose to give him. Which didn't exactly make him the catch Sophie deserved.

What would happen if he made his feelings clear now? Would Ed be angry? Incensed, even?

It wasn't something Kit felt able to ask plainly. Instead, he tried to take a roundabout route. "I wonder," he said, as innocently as he could, "what your uncle will say when I present my suit and announce my intention to marry Sophie."

Ed turned to him, confused. "He won't say anything," he replied. "He won't be able to. Not when we show him what we've found." He tapped his cane gently on the carriage floor and added, "Besides, you won't need to do so, will you?"

"But say I did. For argument's sake. How would you react? If you didn't know our agreement, I mean? If I came at you unexpectedly, and asked you?"

"If I thought you were serious, you mean?" Ed grinned. "I'd plant you a facer and hope that would be the end of it."

Kit raised an eyebrow. "Bit drastic."

"No offense, Kit. You're my best friend. I'd die for you. But give you my sister?"

"You've got to give her to someone."

"Ye-es." Ed drew the word out thoughtfully. "But she can do better."

"Thanks very much." But there was no real anger in Kit's words. Ed was only saying what he'd acknowledged moments ago.

"Oh, come on, Kit. You've been cut off by your father, and you're going to University. You can hardly support a wife. And you'd never be content to live on her dowry. You're not that kind of man."

Kit sighed. "No, I'm not." There was a moment of silence. Kit looked out the window. The streets were gray, the buildings blurred and misshapen by the rain. One or two brave souls hurried along the pavement, heads down, bent forward against the wind and rain.

"That's your objection, is it?" he asked, eventually. "If my pockets weren't to let, you'd be happy with me?"

Ed shifted in his seat, clearly uncomfortable. "Why? Hypothetical questions just take up time when we could be doing something more useful."

Kit turned back to the window and watched two raindrops racing each other diagonally from top to bottom as he pondered why Ed wouldn't be happy to allow him to court Sophie. His reputation was less than stellar, granted, but Ed knew that wasn't the real Kit Thomas. If anyone should know the true person beneath the charade, it was his best friend. So what was wrong with Kit that Ed didn't wish him among Sophie's suitors?

Finally, he could stand the wondering no longer. He glowered at Ed. "Why?"

Ed looked startled. "Why what?"

"Why wouldn't I be suitable for her?"

Ed opened his mouth to answer, then closed it again, clearly nonplussed.

"Given that, before I pressed my suit I'd be certain I had a decent income and could care for her. Why wouldn't I be suitable?"

"For God's sake, Kit. We're talking about my sister. A man doesn't like to think of his best friend and his baby sister in such terms."

She's not a baby. "So it isn't me, per se?"

"Of course it isn't you. Look, if it makes you feel better, I'd be happy to have you as a brother. But since I know the last thing you want is to be leg-shackled to anyone, I won't take your constant harping on the subject as an indication that an offer is about to be made. Satisfied? Are we going to the club? Or do you want to see if Uncle Leo has returned home yet?"

Kit hesitated. If they went to Ed's home, his uncle might be there and they could get everything sorted. On the other hand, if he hadn't yet returned, they'd be forced to sit in the house waiting for him. Then again, that might afford Kit a glimpse… He shook his head, annoyed with himself. When had he become such a love-stricken moon-dreamer?

Yes, he loved her. He wanted to marry her. But Sophie had given him no indication she returned his feelings or that she'd welcome his suit. In fact, she'd made it plain she didn't wish to marry at all. All she wished was to be left alone to conduct experiments. She'd probably view Kit and his offer with the same horror that she'd viewed Pinkerton's.

Yet he had to try. Surely, it was better to have been courageous and beaten back than to wonder if he might have scaled the heights.

Perhaps he could persuade her that getting married to him wouldn't be a fate worse than death. He'd tell her she might experiment as much as she pleased. He'd set up a laboratory on the estate his father gave him. He'd buy her all the equipment she needed, support her ambition in every conceivable way.

Would that be enough? Would the promise of such freedom bring her round? And if it did, would Ed still voice reservations?

On that, at least, Kit felt easier. If Sophie accepted his offer, he didn't think Ed would stand against it for long. He would want his sister to be happy.

But if Sophie rebuffed Kit's advances... Would he turn back to his dream of University? Kit didn't think he would. Without her, that dream, too, would be empty. No. He'd agreed to manage Martlets, and he'd do so. With her, it would be perfect. Without her, it was the perfect place to nurse a broken heart.

He pushed the subject away as they reached Ed's home.

Leo still was not there, although he couldn't be out much longer if he intended to eat dinner at home. Ed invited Kit to join them, offering him a suit of clothes so he didn't have to go home to change. His nervousness at the coming confrontation and his reluctance to chance being alone when it happened were obvious, so Kit accepted the invitation and they headed upstairs to change.

They were almost at Ed's chambers when Lady Jess appeared. She looked flustered. "She's gone," she said, breathlessly. "I can't find her anywhere."

Kit's eyes narrowed as he studied Ed's aunt. She was pale, her face strained, and she wrung her hands in her apparent distress.

"Who's gone, where?" asked Ed, although Kit had the awful feeling he knew the answer. His stomach did a strange, unpleasant flip, and he prayed he was wrong.

His prayers were not answered. "Sophie," said Lady Jess. "I can't find her anywhere. I thought she was in her room, but there's no sign of her there."

"She's not downstairs," said Ed. His aunt bit her bottom lip nervously.

Kit took a deep breath, trying to control the rising panic as his heart beat louder and faster and his stomach churned. A few hours ago, she'd been with them. Surely she couldn't have gone far. By the time she'd changed her gown, then fetched her coat, a bonnet, and gloves, she couldn't have walked more than a street or two.

But why had she gone out in the first place? When he'd come across her earlier, she'd been in no hurry, mentioned no errand—and he felt sure she would have done, using it as an excuse to escape him.

Besides, if she'd wished to go out, she'd have done so before now. It was almost four o'clock, far too late to begin visiting friends and neighbors, and an unfashionable time to shop. But then, if she planned to go shopping, she'd have asked her aunt to go with her.

It was too early to drive in Hyde Park. Not that she'd have accepted any invitation to do that without mentioning it to her aunt. Young ladies didn't leave their homes with gentlemen callers without informing their chaperones.

But then, young ladies weren't kissed to the point of ravishment in their uncle's drawing room, either. Kit couldn't forget her look as she pulled away from him. She'd been shocked, perhaps even frightened by what had happened between them.

They'd been so close. He could still taste her on his lips, the mint of her toothpowder, the tea she'd drunk, the tiny grains of sugar from her biscuit. Even now he fancied he could feel her warm breath mingling with his, the soft skin of her cheek beneath his rough fingers, the trembling of her heart, and the urgent need to put his arms around her, draw her closer, and hold her till the rest of the world disappeared.

He grimaced at a sudden thought. Had he scared her? Caused her to flee?

She hadn't seemed overwrought at the time. She'd kissed him back, sending shivers of desire through him that rode straight to his groin, making him impossibly, painfully hard. Had he groaned? Had she? Had it given her a disgust that sent her running?

"Calm yourself," Ed said. It took Kit a second to realize Ed was talking to his aunt and not to him. "I'm certain she's all right. She probably went for a walk with her maid. Have you checked the park?"

"I have." Lady Jess bristled, probably at Ed's patronizing tone. "She's not there, and if she was, her maid wouldn't be with her. The housekeeper says Mary left about thirty minutes ago, and Sophie wasn't with her. Some emergency with the girl's family."

Kit and Ed exchanged glances. An alarm bell clanged, loudly and incessantly in Kit's head.

"What emergency?" he asked.

Lady Jess shrugged her shoulders. "I don't know. Somebody came to the back door for her. The housekeeper said she was a little upset and asked if she might take the rest of the day off, and then went out. What does that matter? It's Sophie I'm concerned about."

So was Kit. That she would have left the house seemingly without a chaperone, while less than half an hour later her maid was summoned to an emergency, did not sit well with him.

"You say you've searched the entire house?" asked Ed.

"Every conceivable corner. And the gardens. And the park." Lady Jess's knuckles shone white, so tightly did she wring her hands. "I cannot begin to guess…"

She stopped speaking as a cry of alarm came from behind the door that led to the kitchens. Someone screeched, "Mercy me! Whatever next?"

Kit ran down the stairs, along the corridor, and through the baize door. Ed was close on his tail, and his aunt brought up the rear, calling, "What is it? What's happened?" as she tried to keep up.

The kitchen was in a set-to. The boot boy and a scruffy young girl Kit assumed was the scullery maid stood by the hearth, eyes and mouths open wide in shocked disbelief. The housekeeper directed two men to lay a limp woman on the table, which was being hastily cleared by two other maids.

A watchman stood at the back door, feeding the brim of his hat through his fingers, and the cook stood near the stove, her hands pressed to her cheeks.

"Is she dead?" she asked, voice shrill. "We'll all be murdered in our beds!"

"I doubt that very much," the housekeeper answered, "since your room is on the top floor. An intruder would have to be very determined to get that far. Make yourself useful. Make tea. Frederick," she pointed at one of the men, "go for the doctor. You," she turned to the watchman, "come in and shut the door. It's pouring with rain, and I don't want a wet floor on top of everything else."

Kit smiled in admiration. The woman was magnificent. If she'd been in Wellington's army, the French would have been routed within a month.

"What's happened?" asked Lady Jess as she bustled through the door, almost colliding with Ed. "Oh, my word! Mary!" She sat heavily on the nearest chair and fanned her face with her hand.

The watchman stepped forward. "I'm afraid, my lady," he said, "she was attacked."

"Don't know what the world's coming to," muttered the cook.

"Is she dead?" asked the boot boy, eagerly. The cook cuffed his ear.

"She isn't dead," answered the watchman. "No thanks to her attacker. Had his hands round her throat, squeezing the life out of her." He bowed to Lady Jess. "Begging your pardon, my lady."

He went in to a long, blow-by-blow account of how he'd been summoned to a right to-do in an alley three streets away, where poor Mary had been dragged and throttled. Kit could see the ugly bruises forming on her neck. They looked like obscene, oversized caricatures of the smudges one's finger left on a glass. The maid's breathing was rasping and labored, and she was unconscious.

"Lucky for her, the butcher's boy saw what was happening," continued the watchman. "He yelled fit to be heard on Hampstead Heath. Frightened the attacker off. One gentleman gave chase, another stayed with her, and the lad came for me."

"Decent folks robbed in broad daylight!" The cook's face was alight with relished horror.

"I don't think it was a robbery." The watchman glanced, uncomfortably, at Lady Jess, who rolled her eyes.

"I was married for a good many years. My sensibilities will not be overset by anything you have to say." She studied Mary. "Although if that was his motive, he didn't get far. Her clothes aren't torn, nor particularly disheveled."

No, thought Kit. They weren't. Which indicated the attacker hadn't intended to violate the poor girl. He'd simply wanted to kill her. Which made him fearful for Sophie.

Lady Jess looked at Kit and Ed. "What now?" Ed shrugged. Kit massaged his eyelids with a thumb and forefinger and wished he knew.

Mary groaned and tried to move. The housekeeper held her shoulders down, murmuring soft reassurances. Kit stepped forward. He had every sympathy for the girl and knew she needed tender care, but he had to question her. Sophie's life might depend on it.

He leaned over her and spoke softly. "Mary?" Her eyes fluttered, and she stared at him, confused. He smiled reassuringly. "Was Miss Wilson with you?"

Mary shook her head and groaned at the movement.

"She went out," she whispered. It seemed to cost her a great deal of effort. Guilt filled Kit for making her talk, but he had to know.

"Do you know where?"

"Hatch." The maid heaved and a panicked look came over her, as if she didn't think she could find enough air. Kit put his arm under her shoulders and lifted her into a sitting position. Her breathing eased. "Books."

"Hatchards?" Mary nodded and swallowed. "Was she alone?"

"Uncle." Mary took a deep, labored breath.

"Is she going to die?" asked the boot boy as he ducked out of reach of the cook's fist.

"No, she's not going to die," said Lady Jess in a voice that brooked no opposition. "She's going to bed. Not in her usual room. Put her in Miss Wilson's dressing room, where she'll be more comfortable. You, sir," she addressed the watchman, "sit and have tea. I daresay her attacker is well gone by now." She pursed her lips. "Where is that blasted doctor?"

Kit gestured with his head that Ed should follow him back to the main part of the house. "Sophie went out with your uncle," he said, as soon as they were alone.

"Then she should be safe."

Kit didn't share Ed's confidence. Ed raised an eyebrow. "Uncle Leo has no reason to harm her. And let's face it, we all lose track of time at Hatchard's."

"Hmm." Kit thought for a minute. "I'm going to find them," he said, and he headed for the front door. Ed followed him.

An hour later, they had established that Sophie and her uncle had never reached Hatchard's, nor any of the other book shops in the area. They checked the milliner and the glovemaker also, but neither had seen her.

"Where do we look now?" Ed asked after they'd tried Gunter's. The tea shop was, as usual, packed with members of the *ton* enjoying their ices, but Sophie wasn't among them.

"All we can do now is return to your home and see if they're there. If not…" Kit shrugged. If not, he wasn't quite sure what to do next.

Chapter Seventeen

The absolute darkness inside the carriage was disorienting. Sophie had no way of knowing how much time had elapsed, or in which direction they drove. She did know the storm outside was heavy; the dreadful pounding of the rain on the cab's roof convinced her of that. It made chance rescue improbable, since nobody would be on the streets in such a downpour. She heard the cracks and bangs of nearby thunder and the rumble of it when it struck farther away, but she never saw even the slightest spark of lightning.

The sound of the wheels changed from a soft hum over well-maintained city streets to the harsh grate of poorer surfaces. The carriage bounced and swayed over ruts and pot-holes, throwing Sophie about, even though she tried to brace herself. Lord Pinkerton cursed and banged on the roof, yelling for the coachman to be steady and have a care.

By the time the carriage stopped, Sophie was exhausted. Every muscle ached from the effort of staying in her seat. Her shoulder hurt where she'd smashed into the side of the carriage. Her neck muscles burned, her head ached, and she felt sick. She might have found some satisfaction in casting up her accounts over the baron, but pride outweighed it, so she took deep breaths through her mouth to make the nausea subside.

The door opened. The coachman let down the steps

and stood aside, holding an umbrella over the doorway, while water sloshed in the brim of his hat and dripped from the cape on his coat. Lord Pinkerton stepped down, then turned and held out his hand for Sophie. Sophie did not move. He wiggled his fingers, encouraging her, then clenched his jaw, took a firm hold on her wrist, and pulled her. She pulled back but was no match for him, and she tumbled through the door, missed the steps, and would have sprawled in the mud had he not held onto her, pulling her into his embrace.

He grinned. "We should at least go inside, my dear."

Sophie glared at him. He grasped her upper arm and led her toward a small house. The light was strange, not the black of midnight but not fully day, either. Sophie couldn't decide if it was dusk or if the storm made it seem so.

She stepped in a puddle and freezing water spilled over the top of her half-boot, soaking her foot. Rain beat deafeningly on her bonnet and ran down the back of her neck. She shuddered.

Lightning struck, illuminating the house. The sign said Cherry Tree Cottage, a charming name for a building that looked ready to collapse. Its walls were misshapen, its windows dark, and the roof sagged.

Lord Pinkerton swung the cottage door open and pulled her inside, while the coachman lit a candle lamp on the table. It coated the room in light, chasing the shadows to the corners, where they crouched like monsters awaiting their chance to strike. The table in the middle of the room was covered in a thick film of gray dust, the hearth and the walls were black, and there was a smell of old grease, decay, and lack of care.

Lord Pinkerton pushed her, harder than was

necessary, into a chair. Sophie put out her hand to stop her fall and dislodged dust on the table. It flew into the air and made her sneeze, while other bits stuck to her wet glove. He tugged at her bonnet, catching her hair and forcing the wet ribbons into her throat. She felt a moment of panic before the ribbon tore free and her bonnet came off while most of her hairpins scattered onto the sunken red pantiles on the floor. Her last remaining hatpin stayed in her hair, digging into her scalp.

"Remove her boots," the baron commanded, and the coachman knelt to do so. Sophie kicked him, but Lord Pinkerton grabbed the back of her neck and squeezed painfully. "Behave," he hissed, "or face the consequences." Sophie saw the icy threat in his eyes and let her boots be pulled from her feet. In truth, though she would never admit it to him, taking them off was wonderful. They were cold and wet and uncomfortable, leather already stiffening and chafing at her toes and heels.

The baron peeled away her pelisse, then dug his fingers painfully into her upper arm and wrenched her to her feet, across the kitchen, and up a set of wooden stairs. At the top he pushed her into a bedroom, where there was a bed, a dresser with a pitcher and bowl on it, and an age-spotted mirror. The room smelled cold and damp. Involuntarily, Sophie shivered.

Lord Pinkerton ordered the coachman to remove the bowl and pitcher. "Can't have you throwing them at me." He grinned.

Oh, God! What was he going to do? She tugged against his hold on her, and fought the hysteria threatening to overwhelm her. Bile burned her chest and throat. *Kit! Please come!*

Her breath caught on a sob as she realized he could not. He had no clue where she was. He might not even know she was in trouble. And by the time he did know, it would be too late.

The thought of him strengthened her resolve. It couldn't be too late. She must escape and find her way home, to the safety of his arms. Even though stolen kisses and clandestine embraces were all they could ever share, even though he didn't love her and planned to leave her to pursue his dream. That didn't matter. Sophie would rather risk scandal in a temporary love with Kit than have a lifetime of respectability with anyone else.

Especially Lord Pinkerton. She braced herself, ready to give him the fight of his life.

He curled his lip in disgust. "Credit me with a modicum of honor," he said. "I've never yet married a woman who wasn't a virgin, and you won't be the first." He looked her up and down, and his eyes took on a lascivious gleam. "I have a special license. We'll marry tomorrow. I can wait one more night. Although, in that wet dress and looking like that…" He took a hank of her hair and held it in his hand, admiring it. Sophie snatched it away, ignoring the sharp tug at her scalp. He snarled, spun on his heels and left the room. The door slammed behind him, and a key turned in the lock.

The instant he was gone, Sophie looked around for an escape route. There was a fireplace, old ash in the grate. Sweep's boys went up chimneys, didn't they? If they could, could she? She shook her head. The grate was tiny, the chimney opening narrow. Even if she was able to climb up into it—and she doubted that—she'd never fit up there. She looked for something else.

The window was nailed shut. *Nailed shut? How*

often does he bring women here, that he would be so prepared?

Sophie closed her eyes and rested a hand on her stomach until the panic subsided, then scolded herself. This was no time to become hysterical. If she was going to escape the fate Lord Pinkerton planned for her, she must free herself quickly, and this window was the only possible way out. But how? She couldn't open it, and she had nothing to break the glass with. Even if she did have, the noise would alert her captors. Besides, when she leaned her head against the pane and peered out, she could see there was no way to climb down. In all the novels she'd read, there was always a tree growing conveniently near the window for the heroine to climb down. "So of course there's not one in real life," she muttered.

Sophie rested her forehead on the pane of glass, her hands on the sill, and stared at the darkness. In her misery, it took a minute to realize her fingers were wet and a small draught played against her wrist where her glove ended. A quick inspection showed a hole between the window frame and the wall. If Sophie could work on that, make it bigger, perhaps she could remove the window. Then, once she was outside, she could worry about getting to the ground.

She tried scratching with her hands, but all that did was tear her gloves. She looked around, but there was nothing in the room that might help her. With a growl of frustration, she pushed back a lock of hair that swung across her face...and caught her finger on the hatpin that hadn't fallen when her bonnet left her head.

She took a deep breath and blew it out, hard. Then she set at digging through the wall with the pin.

****

Ed and Kit walked into the house to hear Lady Jess's voice coming from the morning room. She sounded shrill, and that they could hear her in the hall gave an indication of her distress. They glanced at one another and hurried to see what was amiss.

She stood, hands clasped at waist height in front of her, her shoulders trembling visibly. Her color was high and her eyes sheened with angry tears. "Don't give me your claptrap, Leo Farnham," she said, and her voice quivered. "She went out of this house with you. Mr. Thomas had nothing to do with it."

Leo stood at the hearth, a drink in his hand. He looked smug. "I've been at my club. You can check. Plenty of people saw me there…" He broke off as he saw Kit and, with his free hand, pointed accusingly at him. "There's your culprit, I make no doubt. What have you done with my niece, you good-for-nothing miscreant? Don't think that luring her away will make me accept any offers from you."

"Don't be absurd," said Lady Jess at the same moment Ed said, "Kit's been with me all day."

Leo glanced at Ed, uncertainty in his eyes, then raised his chin, defiantly. "You'd lie for him with no regard for your sister, would you? It's good that Lord Pinkerton isn't a man to care what the *ton* says. If he were, poor Sophie might have lost a most advantageous offer because of this…this…blackguard."

Kit rolled his eyes and turned to Lady Jess, to ask her what she'd learned. Before he could say a word, however, Ed shouldered past him, grabbed his uncle by the lapels and hit him hard enough for the smack of knuckles against jaw to reverberate around the room.

Leo staggered back and would have fallen if Ed had let him go.

"That's for impugning my sister's name," he hissed, and then he hit Leo again, this time square on the nose. "And that's for questioning my friend's honor."

Leo covered his nose with his hand. "You broke my nose," he wailed.

Ed let go and stood back. Leo sank into the nearest chair and rocked back and forth, holding his nose. Blood flowed between his fingers. Ed turned to his aunt and gave a curt bow. "My apologies for my actions, madam."

Lady Jess grinned. "Nothing to apologize for. I'm only vexed someone didn't do it years ago."

Leo looked up at her, eyes wide. "Jessica!" His nose was already swelling. He was soon going to have a hard time seeing.

"You deserved it. Now, where's my niece?"

"I told you, I don't know. I haven't seen her today." Ed grabbed his uncle's lapels again and forced him to his feet. Leo squealed in terror. "I swear, I don't know."

"Ed," said Kit, quietly, and he touched his friend on the shoulder. There were better ways to get to the truth, ways that wouldn't involve physical pain or the letting of blood, especially in front of a lady.

Ed glared at Kit for a second, then nodded and stepped back. He swept his hand through his hair, pushing it back from his forehead, where it had tumbled out of place. "Do you have it?"

"It's in my greatcoat. I'll fetch it." Kit left the room, conscious of three sets of eyes watching him. Ed's were full of anger at Leo and concern for Sophie, while Lady Jess was puzzled and Leo wary. As well he should be, thought Kit. The man had no idea of the trouble about to fall upon him. Trouble that, big as it was, would seem small and insignificant if Kit learned he'd harmed Sophie in any way.

A minute later, he returned to the room, the ledger in his hand. When Leo saw it, the color drained from his face and his cravat bobbed up and down with the force of his swallowing.

"I see you know what that is," said Ed.

Leo's gaze didn't waver from the book in Kit's hand. "She gave it to you," he whispered.

"What have you done with her?" Ed's voice was steady, a lot steadier than Kit's would have been. He could feel the fear rising through him, chilling him. His heart beat too fast and there was a sick feeling deep in his stomach.

Leo glanced at Ed, then back to the ledger. "I've done nothing. She's unharmed." He looked at Kit and nodded so furiously his jowls quivered. "He promised. She won't be harmed."

Lady Jess stared at each man in turn, her expression a mixture of confusion and fear. "Who promised?"

Leo didn't answer but Ed and Kit said together, "Pinkerton."

A red rage descended upon Kit. He thrust the ledger at Lady Jess and sprang forward to grab the terrified Leo by his shirt front. Linen ripped and Leo shrieked. "Let me go! Let me go! Edward! Jessica!"

From the corner of his eye Kit saw Ed fold his arms. Leo obviously saw it too because he cried out again. "Don't hurt me! Let me go and I'll tell you where Pinkerton took her."

Kit pulled Leo closer. The tiny veins on the man's cheeks stood out, stark against the pallor of his skin.

Beads of sweat glistened on his brow, his eyes were agonizingly wide, and spittle wet his slack lips.

"You tell me where he took her," countered Kit, his voice low and calm and dangerous, "and I won't kill you."

Leo looked up at Ed, his eyes begging for help, and then he tried to see past Kit to Lady Jess. Neither moved. Seconds passed. They felt like an eternity. Kit bunched the fabric in his fist tighter, and Leo squealed. "Don't hurt me! I'll tell you! They're on their way to Gretna."

Within fifteen minutes, Ed had arranged for Leo to be locked in his room, then gathered every able-bodied male servant and instructed them to ride north in pairs, checking every inn, every back road, leaving no stone unturned. Ed's valet had packed his clothes so he could follow, while Lady Jess paced, wringing her hands in distress. "You have to find her," she said, over and over. "Oh, what will happen to her? Why did he take her?"

"Because he could." Ed's voice was hollow, his face grim.

While Ed raced to make arrangements to search for Sophie, Kit stood at the window, staring out into the storm. Rivulets of rain ran down the road, and the trees in the park swayed and bent, their leaves shaking loose and swirling everywhere. Now and then, streaks of lightning turned the dark sky white, and the ensuing explosions of thunder rattled the windows.

Something wasn't right. It was too easy. If Pinkerton had headed to Scotland, it would only be a matter of hours before they caught him. He had to know that, had to know he could never get as far as the border before he was stopped. Why risk it? And if he hadn't risked it, where was he? What had he done to Sophie?

The image of her, trapped, alone, helpless, caused a sharp pain inside his chest. "I will find you, Sophie," he promised, silently. And when he did, he just might kill Pinkerton.

"Will you come with me?"

Kit turned and shook his head. "They're not going to Gretna."

"But my uncle said…"

"Your uncle would save his own skin before he'd keep Pinkerton's secrets. Pinkerton knows that, so why would he tell him where he was going and make it easy for us?"

"What are you trying to say?" asked Lady Jess. "Where else would he…"

Kit saw the moment Ed realized what he was thinking, and he nodded. Together, they said, "The cottage."

"What if you're wrong?" Ed asked. "If he headed north and we delay in order to go to Chelsea…"

"You take the Great North Road. I'll go to Chelsea. If she's there, I'll get her out. If she's not, I'll catch up to you."

Lady Jess sat heavily on the sofa, too distressed to speak. Ed studied Kit for a moment, then nodded.

"And Ed? Just so you know, I'm going to marry your sister, if she'll have me."

For a moment both Ed and Lady Jess stared at him in amazement. Then Lady Jess sighed and smiled. Ed grinned, nodded, and headed out to search.

Chapter Eighteen

Sophie prodded the hole with the now-blunted hatpin and scraped away the loose chips of brick and wood. Her fingers hurt from the unnatural position they'd held for the last few hours, and the tiny cuts in her skin stung. Dust stuck to her, and the cold sent a strange numbing ache into her wrist and thumb.

Outside, the storm howled. She thought more rain made its way into the room now, though she was already so cold and damp she couldn't be sure. It was fully dark, broken only by flashes of lightning that made the air crackle and filled her nostrils with the acrid smell of burning.

She scratched the hatpin through the hole once more. There was a definite draught, so she pushed her fingers in and pulled, as she had done every few minutes since the gap had become big enough to try. Every other time, the window frame had stood firm, but now, finally, she felt it give. She pulled again. It creaked and moved. Almost crying with a combination of relief at having done so much and frustration that it still didn't ease away smoothly, Sophie pulled the frame again. This time it began to come inward. She braced herself to take its weight.

A loud crash of thunder sounded right over the cottage, and lightning forked the sky, hitting a tree in the yard. Sophie startled and lost her grip on the frame. She tensed, expecting it to hit the floor.

It didn't. Instead, it swayed back and forth, then toppled outward in a strange slow motion, and crashed to the ground outside. Its landing thud and the smashing of the glass panes were swallowed up by a second crack of thunder, followed immediately by a third.

Rain drove in, soaking Sophie. Her dress pasted to her body and her hair hung limp against her skull, water dripping from it and pattering against the floor.

She listened over the howl of the wind and the drum of the rain. No boots thundered up the stairs, no shout raised the alarm. It seemed the storm had hidden the crash of the window completely.

"Thank you, God," she whispered. She sucked in air, only now realizing she'd been holding her breath, and she leaned out into the filthy night.

Lightning struck again, and by its light, Sophie confirmed there were no trees within reach of the window. She'd have to rely on courage, faith, and ingenuity if she was going to make good her escape. "Well," she said in a voice that sounded much more confident than she felt, "so be it."

Carefully, she felt the wall outside the window. It was cold and wet, the stones slick with rainwater, although the mortar between them had crumbled, leaving spaces big enough to make footholds and handholds.

Another flash of lightning, and her heart missed a beat. It was a very long way to the ground.

Sophie took a deep breath. Another. *Please, God, don't abandon me now, get me out of here*, and she swung one leg, then the other, over the window ledge.

As soon as her fingers clutched at the first break in the mortar, Sophie wished she'd picked up her gloves.

Tattered as they were, they would have provided some protection from the harsh lime. Still, it was too late now. They were on the bed where she'd thrown them, and she couldn't go back for them. If she did, she doubted she'd have the courage to climb out again.

The first few handholds scraped the skin from her fingertips and broke her nails. Her feet slipped, and she slammed into the wall, knocking the air from her lungs.

Six feet from the ground, her foot slipped on the soaked stone and her hands couldn't find purchase enough to cling on. As she fell, she twisted and got her feet under her. The shock as she hit the ground jarred her spine and made her teeth rattle, and the air whooshed from her.

It was a moment before a dozen sharp stabs let her know she'd landed, bare feet first, in the shards of glass. She bit her tongue against the searing pain, which worsened when she put her weight on either foot. "A curse on you, Lord Pinkerton," she whispered, as tears came. "I hope they hang you and you rot in Hell."

Bearing her weight on her heels and twisting her feet awkwardly to avoid putting the glass-filled soles to the ground, she hobbled over the yard to the woods that grew thick around the cottage perimeter.

Once she was safely within the trees and hidden from the cottage windows, Sophie sat down and tried to pull the splinters out. She felt along the sole of each foot, searching for shards, gasping in pain at the pressure of her fingers on them. She quickly realized she couldn't dig out any but the biggest ones. She was going to need the expertise of a doctor, working in daylight—if she hadn't pushed them in so far that even a medical man couldn't extract them.

Meanwhile, she knew she couldn't stay here. As soon as he realized she'd escaped, Lord Pinkerton would look for her. She had to get as far away as possible. She wished there was someone, anyone, nearby, who might help her.

An image of Kit came to mind. He'd help her. He'd move heaven and earth to reach her, and he'd make sure Lord Pinkerton never hurt her again. But Kit wasn't here. He didn't have the first idea where to look for her. That thought brought fresh tears and a heavy lump to her throat as she hobbled away, wincing at every step.

****

Kit rode carefully over the pitted lane that led to Pinkerton's cottage. Every instinct told him to hurry, to reach her before the swine laid a finger on her, but he forced himself not to do so. He'd be no help to her if the horse he needed to get her home was lamed.

He reached the cottage and looked around, carefully. A light shone through the grimy window of what he knew, from his previous visit, to be the parlor. Another light shone from the kitchen window. Kit dismounted and tied his horse to the handle of the water pump in the yard, then crept nearer to the house. He passed a dilapidated stable and peered inside to see a carriage and two unharnessed horses. They whickered nervously as thunder rumbled overhead.

He ran across the yard, his feet sliding on the muddy cobbles. A glance through the parlor window showed Pinkerton, sitting alone, reading a book and nursing a rummer of brandy. In the kitchen, he saw the coachman who'd told him and Ed of this place. The man sat at the table, boots off, picking at his feet.

Kit did a quick tour of the perimeter. No other lights

shone and, as far as he could see, there were no other men on guard. He burst in through the back door, into the kitchen and the coachman jumped up, frightened.

"Wasn't me. I just drive for him." His words were rushed, as if he suspected he wouldn't get them out in time to save himself.

"Where is she?" Kit's voice was low.

The coachman swallowed hard and pointed upstairs.

"If she's been harmed..."

The coachman shook his head, frantically. "No. She hasn't." The look Kit gave him made him cringe. "Screw this," he said. "He doesn't pay me enough for this." He grabbed his boots, bolted through the door, and disappeared into the rain.

Kit ran up the stairs, taking them two at a time, and threw open the first door. It led into a bedroom with a bed, a dresser, and a garderobe. A fire burned in the hearth, reducing the chill. Nobody was here.

The door to the other room was locked. Kit used his body like a battering ram against it. It took three attempts, but finally the wood gave with a loud crack, the frame split, and he fell into the room.

It was cold and wet. The wind howled through where the window should be. A flash of lightning showed a soaked bed quilt, the tattered remains of a woman's gloves on it. Fury burned through him at their sight.

"Pinkerton!" he yelled, and he flew down the stairs and stormed the parlor.

The baron leapt up, dropping his book and sloshing his brandy so it spattered his clothes. Outside, the wind shrieked like a coven of excited witches, and thunder crashed, drowning out Pinkerton's startled shout. Even had the coachman not fled, Kit doubted he would have heard his master's yell.

"Where is she?" Kit shouted the words at the top of his lungs. They sounded like a whisper against the rage of the elements. Pinkerton snarled and attacked.

Kit blocked the first blow, and the second, and managed to get in a jab of his own, which made Pinkerton stagger back. The baron recovered quickly and threw himself at Kit, and both men went down, wrestling, each trying to hold the other at bay while getting his own blows to count. They might have fought for a minute or for an eternity. Furniture overturned. Glasses shattered. A decanter fell and the sickly smell of brandy filled the air. Kit hit Pinkerton in the stomach and felt, rather than heard, the baron's breath whoosh from him. Pinkerton grabbed Kit's hair and yanked it, forcing his head back, then butted him with his forehead. Kit saw stars.

His vision cleared enough to see the brass poker Pinkerton clutched. Kit tried to dodge the blow, but he was still groggy from the head butt. He felt the crunch at his temple, his eyes lost focus, and he went down like a sack of coal.

It took him a moment to get up, and when he did, he staggered awkwardly. His head spun and he grasped the chair to hold himself steady. Cautiously, he touched his temple and winced. The skin was already tightening over the tender lump, though he didn't feel the sticky wetness that meant blood. He blinked hard and stumbled from the room.

Pinkerton ran upstairs, his face contorted by rage. His mouth formed the shape of Sophie's name, though the words were lost on the storm. Seconds later, he came down so fast Kit wondered he didn't break his neck. He grabbed Kit by his coat.

"Where is she?" he yelled. His eyes glinted with maniacal rage, and spittle collected on his teeth and at the corner of his lip. His breath smelled of stale brandy and cigars, and the beard growing beneath it darkened his cheeks.

He hit Kit squarely on the jaw, sending him sprawling. Pinkerton grabbed his own coat and rushed from the house.

By the time Kit got to his feet and gave chase, Pinkerton had untethered Kit's horse, mounted, and taken off at a faster pace than was safe. The dark road seemed to swallow him.

Kit pushed water back from his face and ran to the stable. It would take time to harness the horses, but riding the coach would be better than trying to walk and, in this storm, much safer. Streams already ran along the road, fast and furious and deep enough to cover Kit's ankles. Not that sitting atop the carriage would be any dryer, but he was less likely to be swept over and drowned, and when he found Sophie she could ride inside.

He glanced into the stable and cursed. The carriage and horses were gone, no doubt taken by the coachman when he deserted his master. Kit fought the urge to bellow at the injustice of it all.

"Sophie!" he yelled. The wind tore his words away, unheard and unheeded. He would try again once he reached the relative calmness within the woods. Wearily, his coat growing heavier every moment, water dripping from the ends of his hair, and his feet sliding in his waterlogged boots, he began the long walk back to town.

****

Sophie moved through the woods, holding on to one cold, wet tree trunk after another. Dead pine needles stuck to her feet, although by now the injuries from the glass had reached a kind of pinching numbness. She could still feel the splinters pressing on her flesh, but the pain of them barely registered any more. The cool thick mud soothed her, even if it did make each step harder.

The latest rumble of thunder faded, and she heard the pulsating throb of horse hooves on the road. She pressed closer to a tree so the rider wouldn't see her. A moment later, she almost cried with relief at her invisibility when Lord Pinkerton rode by, slapping the reins and urging the horse to greater speed as if the devil himself was on his tail.

Sophie shrank back. He'd obviously discovered her escape, although at that speed, he didn't appear to be carefully searching for her. Still, she grimaced. If only he hadn't discovered her gone until the morning...

Her mother's smiling face seemed to float into her view and her sweet voice sang an old lullaby.

"Oh, how I wish, I wish that if only,
if only was nought but a pretty little pony.
Then the law would always take my side,
and every beggar man would always ride."

Mama knew about "if only," thought Sophie. "If only" she'd pursued her dream instead of marrying Papa, she might have gone on to great things. "If only" she'd resisted the pressure to be a good wife and mother, and not sacrificed her work, she might have been happy.

Her mother's image shivered and distorted, as if seen through a rain-spattered window. The smile faded, and sadness filled Mama's eyes. Her soft voice melded with the steady patter of rain on leaves, and the water rushing down the road. *Marriage to your father was my dream. All else is garnish.*

The image shimmered and disappeared. Sophie grasped at the tree trunk, clinging as if it were all that prevented her from washing away with the mud and stones and twigs. The sounds of the storm faded, although lightning still flashed and floodwater still flowed over the road. The wind still bullied the trees, but Sophie didn't hear it.

The garnish?

Suddenly, images of her mother tumbled one over another. She moved from the scientific experiments she'd loved to her husband's embrace and the joyous games she played with her children. She kissed Papa and smiled. He held her while she used the equipment in her laboratory.

"He knew." Lightning flashed as Sophie spoke. Papa had known about Mama's science. He hadn't prevented her doing it, he'd embraced it as a part of her, an aspect of the woman he loved, and who loved him. "But he forbade me to…"

Sophie stopped dead. The wind tugged at her skirts, threatening to knock her down. Locks of hair fell over her face and she swept them back, oblivious to all but her epiphanic moment. Papa hadn't forbidden her to work in the laboratory. He'd never once said she couldn't.

From the furthest recesses of her mind, she retrieved memories of herself, a small child in his arms, both of them watching proudly as Mama showed them what she'd discovered.

There'd been a fire. It consumed Mama's workspace so quickly, destroying her experiments, her notes, and her. Papa buried her and pulled down what was left of the laboratory. And at night, when he thought Sophie and Ed slept, he'd sat on the chair in Mama's chamber, and he'd sobbed.

Tears mixed with the rain on Sophie's cheek, warm water with cold, and the salt in her tears made her skin itch. She'd been so blind, so caught up in what she believed had happened, she hadn't been able to see the truth. "And you call yourself a scientist!" What irony! Here she was, insistent on experiment and provable evidence, and she'd thrown that all away and jumped to conclusions when the truth had mattered most.

"Sophie!" The voice startled her. For an instant she thought her father was calling her. To admonish her for her false conclusions and express his disappointment with her?

"I'm sorry, Papa," she whispered. The winds carried her words away. She prayed they'd reach him.

"Sophie!"

She frowned. That wasn't Papa. But it was a voice she knew. A voice she trusted.

Released by relief, the tears flowed freely, reducing her vision to almost nothing as she staggered and stumbled out of the woods, her feet catching on bramble and her hair snagging on low branches.

Sophie reached the road, and Kit pulled her in so close she felt she was part of him.

"Thank God," he murmured against her ear, and he held her tighter than she'd ever been held before.

Chapter Nineteen

Sophie pressed into Kit. Her skin was the lifeless ice of marble, smooth next to the harsh roughness of her torn dress. Her hair flopped over her face and fell haphazardly down her back, and there were scratches on her cheek where she'd collided with trees in the dark.

He embraced her tightly. He felt her heartbeat against his chest, rapid and frightened like a bird. Her fingers clutched his coat and her breath tickled the skin of his throat. He nuzzled her hair, cherishing the smell of rain and leaves. His thighs hardened, and an ache began low in his belly.

She shivered, bringing him to his senses. What the hell was he doing? He was no better than Pinkerton, lusting after her when she needed only rescue and the safety of home. A home he couldn't immediately get her to. Without transport, in this weather, she'd probably expire from lung fever long before they reached civilization. Panic clawed his chest at the thought of what could happen. He tamped it down, determined it would *not* happen.

But he had to get her out of the rain, quickly. He needed somewhere dry, preferably warm; somewhere away from the wind, where she'd be safe until help arrived.

Pinkerton's cottage. It was half a mile back along the road, and it was dry and warm, thanks to the fires

Pinkerton had lit. There was, no doubt, food and drink there, and Ed would find them.

But what if Pinkerton returned? Kit pressed his lips together, determined. He'd be ready for the blackguard. If they fought again, he'd expect his tricks. He wouldn't be bested again.

Still, the niggling voice in his head persisted, *What if he brings help*? Pinkerton had a dozen men he could call on, all of them thick with muscle and ready to use it against whomever their master decided they should. If a few of them joined the fray, Kit could make himself as ready as he liked. He wouldn't come out of that fight victorious.

If he brings men, we'll do the only thing we can. We'll hide. Honor be damned.

"We need to get out of the rain," he told Sophie, putting his mouth close to her ear. The feel of her skin beneath his lips lit a fire inside him and set his pulse galloping. Kit closed his eyes and told himself to behave.

Sophie slipped her hand into his. His heart jumped and his breathing stalled. Jaw clenched so tight it hurt, he led her back toward the cottage.

They'd gone just a few yards when Kit realized she was limping badly. He turned to her and frowned at her grimace of pain. She took another step and he saw she wasn't limping at all. She was hobbling, trying not to put her weight fully on her feet. What had that dastard done to her? If Pinkerton had been there now, Kit would have killed him.

He scooped her up into his arms. She put her arms around his neck and huddled against his torso, and desire shot through him. He could feel it in his blood, like the sharp bubbles in champagne. He bit his bottom lip, willed his erection to subside, and prayed she hadn't noticed it. He should concentrate on her safety, not the feel of her curves in his arms, her round bottom nestling against him, her breasts scant inches from his fingers. He took a deep breath. He was in more trouble than he'd realized.

The journey back to the cottage seemed to take forever. Sophie wasn't heavy, even when drenched, but Kit was mindful of her in his arms, and terrified that if he stumbled, he might drop her. He became aware of every rut and hole in the road. His feet froze in his stiff leather boots. The wool of his breeches chafed at his legs and his coat weighed him down, but he was buoyed by the weight of her against him, her head on his chest, her arms around his neck. Her embrace helped to steady her in his arms, he knew, but he longed for her to cling to him for another reason, one that had nothing to do with safety and balance but which allowed her fingers to play in his hair, to pull his head closer to hers, his mouth nearer…

He jerked and nearly dropped her. What was the matter with him? When had his common sense disappeared? He had challenges enough for one night— getting her to the cottage, keeping her warm and dry, and safe. The last thing Kit should do was lust after her. And yet…

Kit bit the end of his tongue and forced his mind away from carnality.

Finally, he reached the cottage. The main door was open, as he'd left it when he pursued Pinkerton. Rain had soaked the floor in the hall and the wind had snuffed the candle in the wall sconce, leaving the hall lit only by the sputtering candles in the parlor. Long shadows made strange shapes up the wall, the flickering light that created them also bringing them to life. Sophie clutched him more tightly.

He murmured something at her. He didn't know what he said, and he didn't think it mattered. The tone of his voice calmed her as he carried her into the parlor and set her down in the chair nearest the fire.

"Don't leave me," she whispered, as he stood up.

"I won't," he promised. Gently, he extricated himself from her grasp. There were things he must do for her safety and wellbeing. He couldn't simply sit and hold her all night and hope for the best. But he saw the terror in her eyes. She needed him, his physical presence, beside her. So he hurried to close and lock the cottage doors. The locks were old and feeble, and they wouldn't keep out Pinkerton's thugs forever, but they would provide Kit with valuable moments when he could hide Sophie.

After locking the kitchen door, he stoked the fire in the stove and set a pan of water to boil. They'd need it to wash off the rain and warm themselves, and if he managed to find a box of tea, so much the better. If not, there was always brandy. It would warm her from the inside, although Kit would abstain. He needed his wits at their sharpest tonight.

The weight of his coat pressed down on him, the wet wool suffocating. It took a lot of effort to peel it from his shoulders and set it over the back of a chair. The heat of the kitchen would dry it somewhat, although it would probably shrink and pull it out of shape, too. Hopefully, Ed would rescue them in a carriage so Kit didn't have to ride into London in his shirt sleeves. Now *that* would excite the gossips!

Cool air made him shiver. Sophie would be cold too. He went upstairs to the master bedroom, stripped the blankets from the bed, and took them to the parlor for her.

She sat on the chair, staring at the hearth where the embers glowed red for a fleeting moment, then faded as if the effort to stay alight was too much. Candles flickered, giving off a soft glow that coated her face in a pale lemon-gold and made her eyes seem huge. Her dress was tattered, a rip at the sleeve exposing the ball of one shoulder and the soft mound of her breast. Underneath the dirty, soaked material her nipples stood at attention, drawing his gaze. Kit swallowed and struggled not to stare.

"I...have...blankets," he said, and all but threw them at her. She didn't move. They slid from her lap to the floor. He wished the same would happen to her wet clothes.

Wet clothes! "I'll...do...fire." Averting his gaze, he moved past her, picked up the poker, and thrust at the logs in the fireplace. One split, revealing the white, unburned wood within. Embers flared and grabbed eagerly at it. When he'd coaxed a flame out of hiding, Kit reached over to the basket on the hearth and fed more logs to it. The room warmed, its light a soft blush, the air filling with the scent of pine cones mixed with that of wet linen and of stale brandy, and the coppery tang of...blood?

Kit turned to Sophie. She stared at the fire, her bottom lip clamped beneath her top teeth. She shivered, her breath short and ragged. Her dress clung to her, showing off the perfect mounds of her breasts, her flat stomach, the way her hips flared... The fall of his trousers was increasingly, uncomfortably tight and there was a pulsing ache within him. His mouth dried as his eyes moved to take in every inch of her. Her legs were long and slender, the wet dress molding to them so perfectly he could see the shape of her thighs, her knees, her calves. The hem of the dress was black with mud, which seemed to highlight her tiny ankles, and bare feet smeared with soil and leaf mulch, rain and…

"Good Lord," he whispered, horrified at the long jagged cuts surrounded by angry, swelling skin. He knelt and lifted her foot, cradling it gently in his hand. She flinched at his touch, then relaxed slightly and let him examine it.

"It was the glass," she explained, her voice soft. "From the window. I broke it. I… couldn't avoid it when I…"

"Oh, Sophie." He cursed the horror and pain she'd endured. When he caught up to Pinkerton… Kit pushed away the rage he felt for the villain. Sophie didn't need his anger now. It could wait.

He caressed her foot, his fingers barely touching her, yet he was more aware of her than of anything he'd ever touched before. Mostly, her skin was cold, the sole of her foot wrinkled from the wet. Mud slicked under his hands, soft and smooth but for the occasional piece of grit. Some of the sores on her feet were hot to the touch, the skin around them tight and the embedded splinters of glass hard beneath. She winced at each one he found.

"They have to come out," he said. She nodded, her teeth chattering. *Oh, for the love of God, what was the matter with him?* Of course she was shivering. She must be frozen, and sitting in a wet dress would not help her one iota.

He pulled her into his lap, grabbed a blanket, and wrapped it around her like a massive shawl. Her wet hair slid over his wrist, making his pulse race as he held the blanket in place, his face close to her ear, every nerve within him alive and at attention.

Sophie turned her head at the same moment he moved to say something to her. His mouth was almost on hers, their breath mingling. He saw the silver flecks in her eyes, alive and brilliant, sparking like fireworks. Each individual eyelash was clear, every soft freckle stood out. Kit wanted to kiss them, one by one. Instead, he held her tighter.

"I should…" she whispered, then licked her lips. His heart skipped a beat and the jolt went straight to his groin. "I'll… I don't want a chill."

A chill? Kit thought he was more in danger of spontaneously combusting.

"I cannot…" She blushed a beautiful shade of deep pink. "My clothes are wet."

"Yes."

"I…should get out of them."

Every fiber of Kit's being quivered. He wanted to punch the air and yell, "Yes!" He had to bite the inside of his cheek to keep his wits and ensure he didn't shout out loud.

"Will you…help me?" Her words were a barely audible whisper but, to Kit, they were cannon, firing from all four corners of the world. "I…cannot undo the buttons," she continued. "The rain's made them… impossible. I need…" She blushed again. Heat radiated from her cheeks and she lowered her eyes.

It took every last ounce of Kit's resolve to keep his gaze above her shoulders. He wanted so much to remove those clothes, open every delicious inch of her, slowly peel back the layers of dress and shift and petticoat, and kiss every newly exposed piece of her…

He couldn't. She'd just dealt with Pinkerton. The last thing she needed now was some other dastard taking advantage of her.

He deserved to be horsewhipped. He set her down on the chair, stood and turned his back on her, eyes closed, hands on hips and breaths coming sharp and shallow while he willed his erection to subside.

"Kit?"

He turned and saw the pleading in her eyes. She again caught the edge of her bottom lip behind her top teeth and Kit almost groaned out loud. All he had to do was reach out, pull her to him, kiss her…

No! She was Ed's sister! She blinked. He swallowed, hard. Ed's sister, and so much more. The woman he loved. The woman he would marry.

Sophie's eyes darkened with a mix of innocence and wanton desire. "I don't want to catch pneumonia," she said.

"No," he agreed, and he surrendered.

****

Sophie saw Kit's resistance crumble. She wondered, fleetingly, what she was unleashing, but she couldn't have stopped this if she wanted to. Her lips were suddenly dry, and she traced them with the tip of her tongue. His gaze fixed on her mouth. She touched her tongue to her lips once more. He swallowed. He looked as if his cravat was tied too tightly.

She shivered, though she was no longer cold. The warm fire caressed her, and every nerve stood to attention. The tiny hairs on her forearm crackled, as if lightning passed through her, filling her with energy and leaving her on edge. A warm wetness grew between her thighs and a strange aching sensation made her need…she hardly knew what, but the need grew stronger with every throb of her pulse.

The fire filled the room with woodsmoke and the clean, fresh scent of pine cones. The steam rising from her dress smelled of linen and rain and outdoors. And then there was Kit. Woodsy cologne, the musk of wet hair and the indefinable smell that was uniquely Kit. She wanted to breathe it in, to put her lips against his skin and taste it.

Kit's arms went around her, and a small groan escaped her. His fingers moved deftly as, one by one, the buttons gave and her dress fell open. His breaths, as short and ragged as her own, feathered her neck. His lips brushed her skin, once, twice, and then he nibbled her ear lobe. His hand was warm against her skin, his hard chest pressed against her breasts, setting her nipples aflame.

His mouth joined with hers, soft at first, tentative, then firmer. She parted her lips and he pushed inside, thrusting his tongue along the length of hers. She pressed closer to him, wanting to feel him on her, around her, in her.

Her dress hit the floor with a soft rustle. His hands explored every inch of her, heating her skin and feeding the strange restlessness within her. He pulled her onto his lap, never once breaking the kiss as he stroked her shoulders, her arms, her back, her stomach, the undersides of her breasts. Sophie wanted to shout, to tell him what she wanted, though she barely knew herself. All she knew was that if he didn't stop teasing her, she would likely die from the wanting.

His fingertips brushed her nipples and she arched her back, pushing them into his hands. He smiled against her lips and massaged her breasts, gently, maddeningly. Her pulse skittered, and every breath was a fight. She didn't know what she wanted, yet at the same time she knew exactly.

Sophie's fingers splayed against his head, deepening the kiss. His hair was soft and cold, his skin warm, his flesh firm, and…

She needed his clothes gone. Now. Fingers fumbling, she tugged at his shirt and cravat, then huffed her frustration when neither came away.

Kit chuckled. "Allow me." He leaned back. The loss of his skin on hers made her groan, although she enjoyed watching him untie his cravat and remove his shirt.

He sat naked to the waist, and all Sophie could do was stare. He was magnificent. His shoulders were broad, his chest flat, covered in a smattering of hair that narrowed to a dark line tracing down over his well-defined stomach muscles and disappearing below the waistband of his trousers. Her eyes widened when she saw the fall of those trousers standing to attention. Her cheeks heated and she looked away, flustered.

There was a moment of silence. Then Kit said in a strangled voice, "We can stop."

"No!" Sophie's cheeks grew hotter, and she made a conscious effort to steady her voice. "No."

Kit watched her, as if he expected her to say something more. But what more could she say? She had no idea. Surely, a lady wasn't supposed to tell a gentleman she enjoyed the way he touched her, loved the kisses they'd shared, kisses that made her feel in a way she'd never felt before. Ever.

He leaned back in the chair, creating distance between them. His eyes were hooded, their color hidden. His jaw was clenched, his mouth taut, and a strange panic filled her. This could not end like this. She leaned forward, closing the gap again. He swallowed.

Sophie had liked how it felt when his fingers moved on her nipples. Would Kit like her to do the same to him? There was only one way to find out, she thought, as her hand covered his flat breast. His nipple hardened. He gasped.

"Are you sure?" he asked, hoarsely. "Don't start what I may not be able to stop."

Sophie smiled. "I don't want you to stop."

A growl began deep in his chest. He pulled her to him and kissed her. His hands wandered over first one nipple, then the other, before moving lower, skimming her stomach, making her quiver. Her arms and legs felt heavy, and the ache between her thighs seemed to grow and spread until she could hardly bear it.

Her shift came off, leaving her naked. He eyed her, appreciatively. "Beautiful," he murmured.

"So are you," she answered, and taking her courage in both hands—literally—she reached down and unbuttoned the fall of his trousers. He sobbed as he sprang free and she stroked her hand along him. That part of him was unlike anything Sophie had seen or touched before. Warm, yet cool, hard yet soft, the skin velvet over iron. She touched the tip and his hips bucked, almost unseating her. Startled, she drew back. "I'm sorry. I didn't mean... Did I hurt you?"

"Oh, Sophie, you're killing me," he groaned, and he took her in his arms and carried her to the hearth rug, where he gently laid her down and kissed her again, his fingers moving, light as a butterfly's wing, across her side, her hips, her thighs. She quivered where he touched, with a wonderful tingle in her nerves and a delicious jump of her muscles. Then he reached her most private place...and Sophie forgot to breathe.

His mouth left hers. She gave a tiny moan of displeasure, which changed halfway through to a sigh of contentment as he nibbled his way along her jaw and over her neck. He suckled at the pulse point behind her ear before he moved down, over her shoulder, her collar bone, the soft mound of her breast. He took her nipple into his mouth, rubbing his teeth over it. It grew, and she cried out in feverish delight. He released the first breast and paid attention to the other one until she cried out again. She wanted him to stop. She wanted him to never quit. She felt every part of her would explode, that she would shatter into a million pieces. And all the time, his fingers played, stroking the sensitive spot between her thighs. Warm honey filled her and she bucked, trying to press herself against his hand.

"Please," she begged, though she didn't know what for. Acting on instinct, she reached for him, and her fingers curled around him, hoping to keep him with her, doing what he was doing.

Then, suddenly, she fell over a cliff edge. She soared and swooped, her stomach dropping, heart racing and legs trembling with every pulsing, vibrating moment. She screamed and held on to him for dear life.

****

Kit held her while she came apart, savoring every second of her pleasure. He was so hard it was painful, and every beat of his heart threatened to carry him over. He'd never felt so good, so...complete before, and he hadn't even had his own release yet.

Nor would he. Showing Sophie the wondrousness of love was one thing. Ruining her to satisfy his own lust was quite another. When she agreed to marry him, it would be because she chose him, not because all choice was gone. He could not, would not do that, even if it meant standing outside in the cold rain until the craving subsided and the pain of wanting her faded away. If it ever did. At this moment, he had his doubts.

Sophie lay on the rug beside him, her eyes half closed, a soft smile playing on her face. "I never expected... I never dreamed..." She frowned. "But what about you?"

"I'm fine."

She glanced at him, at his manhood. It was harder than it had ever been, his balls tight, ready to burst. She reached out to touch him, and he tensed. "You're not fine," she argued. "You're still..." She struggled for the words but failed to find them. "That."

"I'm fine," he repeated. She wrapped her hand around him and began to stroke him. He hissed and clenched his jaw.

"Sophie. Don't."

"Don't you want to?"

His laugh was filled with pain and little humor. "Of course I want to. But..."

"Then do." She caressed him again.

"I can't. There are rules."

"Forget the rules. I want it all."

"Damn it, Sophie. I'm only a man."

"I know." She ran her thumb along his length, once, twice, three times.

He groaned and gave in, positioning himself

between her legs, his tip at her opening, one hand playing with her again, bringing her back to ecstasy before he thrust inside her. There was a moment of tension, resistance, and she cried out. He stilled immediately.

"I'm sorry," he said.

Sophie smiled through tears. "I'm not." She thrust her hips up to meet him.

It took everything he had to make the moment last until she'd peaked again. His muscles ached with the effort, and every sinew strained. If he gritted his teeth any harder, they would crack.

Then finally, finally, he cried out, and followed her into the deep.

Chapter Twenty

When Sophie woke, it was light. The rain had
stopped and a weak sun shone, turning the clouds from
gray to a soft blue. The fire had died to embers and a
damp chill in the room stroked her shoulders. The rest of
her body was comfortably cozy beneath the blanket Kit
had lovingly wrapped around her after they'd made love
for the second time.

She smiled at the memory. After the first time, he'd
made her feel so cherished. He'd fetched warm water
from the kitchen and bathed her, then carefully washed
her feet before wrapping them in bandages made from
torn strips of the linen sheet from the bed in the master
chamber. He'd held her and they talked.

When he'd taken her the second time, it had been
long and slow. He kissed her until her skin tingled and
her nerves sang, and he brought her to completion twice
before entering her.

She'd slept in his arms then, the warmth of his body
comforting, the soft evenness of his breathing relaxing
her, making her feel safe.

She knew she wasn't safe, of course. They were
miles from anywhere, in a cottage belonging to Lord
Pinkerton. If he returned with enough men to overpower
Kit, there'd be nobody to help. That Kit would do his
utmost to protect her, she made no doubt. He'd fight
tooth and nail for her, even to the point of dying, and that

terrified her.

Thinking such dark thoughts made her wonder where he'd gone. He may have needed the necessary, she supposed, or perhaps he'd gone for more water. But what if Lord Pinkerton had returned and Kit had gone to face him… Her heart thundered in her ears and bile rose at the thought. She needed to find him.

Her clothes were draped neatly over a ladder-backed chair as near to the fire as possible. Her boots stood on the hearth, her pelisse folded over them. His thoughtfulness brought a lump to her throat. He really was the most wonderful man.

Sophie reached out and felt her dress. It was still slightly damp, though nowhere near as soaked as it had been last night. Damp or not, it would have to do, because she couldn't spend the day wearing nothing but a blanket.

It wasn't easy to put on. The wet fabric was cold and heavy and clung to her skin, twisting itself so that it took three attempts to pull it down.

She couldn't pull her boots past the bandages on her feet, and there was a sharp pain every time she put pressure on her soles. She gave up trying and instead crawled to the chair beside the fire and pulled herself into it. If she stretched, she could poke the fire and build its warmth, then sit back and wait, poker in hand in case it was Lord Pinkerton who came in rather than Kit.

A few minutes later, Kit returned, carrying a tray on which were tea cups and a pot, thick hunks of bread, and wedges of cheese. He wore his breeches and shirt, but no coat or cravat, his neck and throat on show, revealing the dark hair at the top of his chest. His sleeves were rolled up, showing lean, muscled forearms. His feet and legs below the knee were also bare. Sophie stared, committing every inch of him to memory for when they returned to their dull, ordinary lives.

"Good, you're awake." Kit smiled. "I hoped you'd be up and dressed before Ed arrives." He put the tray onto the table.

Sophie felt the color drain from her face. "Ed? My brother?"

"Unless you're expecting someone else with that name?" For a moment, she stared at him, nonplussed. Then he grinned.

"Oh, you!" she scolded, relieved beyond measure that he'd been teasing her. Of course Ed wasn't coming. How would he? He didn't even know this cottage existed.

Which led her to wonder how Kit had known about it. He hadn't arrived here by chance. Before she could ask, though, he horrified her again. "Of course I meant your brother, you goose."

Sophie swallowed. "But...how? Ed doesn't know about this..." She gestured at the room.

Kit nodded. "He does. We came here when we were looking for Pinkerton once. Yesterday, Ed took the Great North Road and I came here. Whichever of us didn't find you would come for the other. I should think he's well aware by now that you didn't go north."

"Ed's coming here." She whispered the words, but she didn't feel they came from her. They were soft and devoid of emotion, and did nothing to convey the panic rising within her. Ed would know she'd spent the night, unchaperoned, here. Worse, he'd know she and Kit did...what they did. It would surely be written in her eyes. Ed could read her like a well-known book. She'd never been able to keep anything from him.

Although, if anyone suspected anything about last night, it was probably better that it was Ed. He loved them both, and he knew neither wanted to marry. Rather than make them miserable, he'd surely be inclined to allow them some leeway. He wouldn't force...

Kit spoke again, and his words made her think he'd read her mind. "You don't need to worry," he said. "Ed won't cause a commotion. He won't want a hole-in-the-wall wedding for you, with suspicion and whispered rumors spoiling your reputation."

Sophie sighed her relief.

"No," continued Kit. "Our wedding will be at Saint George's, with no hiding and no unseemly rush as if we should be ashamed of it."

"What?" Sophie stared at him. He looked back at her blankly, as if he couldn't see what had her so aghast. She took a deep breath. Then another. Then, as calmly as she could manage, she said, "Our betrothal isn't real. I'm not going to marry you, and you will not marry me. We agreed."

Kit frowned. "But after last night..."

"No." Her voice was forceful. He stared at her in disbelief, so she went on, "Last night was..." She struggled to find the words. Wonderful? Magical? The best night of her life? None of these descriptions would help now. She couldn't describe their lovemaking in any way that would help. So she changed tack. "Well, I can tell you what it wasn't."

"Sophie..."

"We agreed. We don't want marriage. We both have other dreams. You want University."

"No, I—"

"And I want my wheat."

"You can still…"

"We cannot throw all of that away because of one night."

"Damn—dash it, Sophie. This isn't just about last night."

She frowned, not sure she understood him. He pushed his hand through his hair, then faced her squarely. His gaze radiated sincerity, and her heart did a little skip.

"This isn't how I imagined it." He flashed her an uncertain smile. "I had it all planned, you see. For one thing, it would take place in your uncle's home, not in Pinkerton's trysting place. I'd have gone down on one knee, which I still could do, I suppose." He looked doubtfully at the floor, then shrugged and got down. "Sophie Wilson, I love you. Will you make me the happiest man alive by agreeing to become my wife? My real wife?"

For an instant, hope flared within Sophie. She quickly tamped it down. Kit Thomas was an honorable man and he was trying to do the honorable thing. She knew he said he'd planned this before her kidnapping. He said that because he thought it would crumble her resistance. It wouldn't. She would not be responsible for shattering his dreams. If he didn't study engineering, he would come to resent her, perhaps even hate her. She shook her head. "The answer is no, Kit. But thank you."

****

Kit was furious. He'd offered her everything, and she'd refused him. More, she looked as though where he'd hoped she would love him, there was only pity. How dare she? The last thing he wanted was her pity.

Unable to face her, or the sorrow in her eyes, he gave a curt nod and stormed from the room, then stalked to the kitchen where he'd put his clothes. His coat was beyond hope, but his cravat and his stockings should be nearly dry now. His ruined boots were fit only for the rubbish, but they'd suffice for the journey home. He'd put them on at the last minute to avoid waterlogged feet.

It took him four attempts to tie his cravat. He told himself it was because the linen was damp and wrinkled, but he knew that wasn't the true reason. The true reason was in the morning room, wearing a ruined dress, her hair in knots, nursing a cup of tea and paying no heed to his broken heart. The only woman he'd ever had such feelings for, the only one with whom he'd not only contemplated marriage, he'd actively sought it and truly wanted it.

And she'd turned him down. Flat.

He would have expected her to do that if she thought the proposal was in response to last night, but he had made it plain he'd intended to ask her before. Which meant her refusal was not a spur-of-the-moment reaction. He just had to face it. Sophie didn't want him.

The sound of wheels squelching through the muddy yard pulled him from his sulk. A glance through the window told him the coach belonged to Sophie's family. Better yet, Kit's horse was tied to the rear. The return of the animal, mud-splattered but otherwise seemingly unharmed, lightened his mood a little. He pulled on his boots and opened the door in time to see Ed disembark, followed closely by Sophie's aunt.

"Where is she?" cried Lady Jess, the strain of the last few hours evident in the black rings around her eyes.

"I'm here, Aunt," said Sophie, and her voice broke

on the last word. She stood awkwardly, weight on her heels, the bandages bloody.

"Oh, my poor dear!" Jess bustled over and wrapped her arms about Sophie, murmuring soft words to soothe her. Knowing he couldn't comfort her, that he'd never again hold her in his arms, caused a sharp pain in Kit's chest. He gritted his teeth and tried to ignore it.

"You caught him, then?" he asked Ed, and nodded at the horse. Truthfully, he didn't much care what happened to Pinkerton, although he was glad to have the horse back, and asking Ed what had happened was better than watching Sophie sob on Lady Jess's shoulder.

It should be my shoulder. He pushed the insistent voice inside him away and concentrated on Ed. "What happened?"

"A smiling of fate," said Ed. "We'd realized Gretna was a red herring and were coming back when Pinkerton ran into us. Literally. He didn't see us until it was too late. There was a tangle, and your horse threw him."

"I always did like that animal. Was he hurt?"

"Only his pride and his…" Ed glanced at the ladies, now seated at the table. Sophie's sobs had subsided into sniffs, and Jess gripped her hands as if she was afraid that if she let go, Sophie would disappear again. "We arrested him for stealing your horse."

Kit nodded, and Ed grimaced. "Not that I think that particular charge will come to much. Member of the Lords and all that. They'll call it hi-jinks and slap his wrist." Ed grinned. "I persuaded the constable to leave it a day or two before taking him up before the beak. Won't hurt him to cool his heels."

Kit understood. Although kidnapping was a serious crime, Pinkerton would never be charged with it.

Sophie's family wouldn't wish the news to get out, which meant they couldn't call Pinkerton to account. A few days in a cell for stealing a horse was all the satisfaction they would get.

"Leo's gone," said Lady Jess. "Skulked away in the night, the villain!" Kit's eyes met Sophie's but he couldn't tell what she made of the news.

"I suspect he headed for the coast," explained Ed. "Took advantage of the fact that all the menservants came with us. From what I can see, he took his clothes and about £500 in ready cash."

"Man in a hurry." Kit nodded. "Have you sent anyone after him?"

Lady Jess snorted. "Good Lord, Christopher Thomas, use your noddle for something other than a hat stand." The insult made Sophie giggle. Kit glared at her, but there was no heat in it, and his own lips twitched with the urge to laugh as well. In truth, it was good to see her smile again.

"Why on earth would we send anyone after him?" continued Lady Jess. "We don't want him back. Good riddance, I say. Now, we must get Sophie home to a warm bath and dry clothes before she catches her death. Looking at the sorry state of that," she pointed at Kit's ruined coat and made a face of disgust, "you cannot ride in public either. So it's into the carriage with us all." The smile she gave Sophie was beatific. "We brought hot bricks, so you'll be cozy on the way home."

Sophie gave a wan smile and tried to stand, then hissed with the pain. Kit was beside her in a heartbeat, lifting her into his arms. Lady Jess raised her eyebrows, and maybe he had been a little too eager to hold her one last time, but…

"She has glass in her feet and cannot walk," he said. Sophie's aunt nodded and said nothing. She didn't even point out that it would have been more appropriate for Ed to carry his sister. For which Kit was more than grateful.

He carried Sophie to the carriage, savoring every second.

She was warm in his arms. This close he could see the flecks of silver in her blue eyes, and the faint freckles on her nose. He breathed in the scent of her, a mixture of rainwater and woodsmoke and sex, and committed every part of her to memory. He had a feeling he'd be re-examining these memories many times in the months and years to come.

Chapter Twenty-One

A fortnight passed. Sophie's feet healed enough that she could stand for some minutes and even walk a few paces, although stairs still proved painful. Friends called daily. They'd been told she'd injured herself in the conservatory, where she'd put her feet through a pane of glass. It astounded her that people accepted this explanation without demur. She'd have considered anyone who put both feet through a pane at the same time stupid. Yet no one seemed to think that of her.

Of Kit, she'd seen and heard nothing. For the first few days, of course, she hadn't expected to. She was confined to bed and no gentleman, bar Ed, could visit her. But now she spent her days in the morning room, and she'd hoped he might come.

She missed him. Not that she'd ever admit it, but she spent far too much time thinking about him, wondering where he was, what he was doing, whether he thought of her. At night, he featured in her dreams, his smile beckoning her as he hovered on the edge of her sensibility, just beyond her reach.

Today, she sat in the morning room, embroidery untouched in her lap. The day's callers had been in, apprised her of the latest *on dit,* and moved on. Outside, the sky was gray-white, not quite sunny but not promising rain either. The first brown leaves scuttered along the road and dust kicked up on the brisk breeze. A young boy fought a losing battle to sweep away that dust.

In the morning room, the air was warm and heavy with the scent of the logs burning in the fireplace. The flames crackled, sounding as though they laughed at Sophie, sitting here so alone.

She hadn't needed to be alone, she reminded herself. She could have accepted Kit's offer. He'd have been here with her now, preparing for their wedding and planning their lives afterward.

Would it be so terrible to be his wife? He was, she knew, a good man, the kind of man who could have made her happy. For one thing, he wasn't threatened by a woman's intelligence. He'd have no qualms about allowing her to continue with her experiments.

Besides, Sophie had come to understand that her scientific work was only one aspect of her life. An important aspect, yes, but not the most important. And hadn't Mama proven a woman could be a mother, a wife, and a scientist all at the same time? Of course, a wife wouldn't spend as many hours in the laboratory as a single woman might, but then, she wouldn't wish to. The quality of the work achieved was more important than the quantity of time spent on it. If her husband was willing to permit it, even a married woman could change the world. That's what Countess Ilive had done. It was what Mama had tried to do. And Sophie could do it too. Kit knew that. He would never have prevented her going after her dream.

But what about his? He dreamed of studying engineering. He couldn't do that and take on responsibility for a wife. Even her unexpected dowry wouldn't help for, Sophie knew, Kit would never be comfortable living off her income.

And if she married him, knowing he was sacrificing his dream, she'd be no better for him than Lord Pinkerton would have been for her.

Although why she wasted time pondering the question was a mystery. It was too late for that. She smiled sadly at the embroidery. She'd refused his offer and he hadn't renewed it.

A spark cracked the wood and escaped, dancing on the warm air before flying up the chimney. Even though she'd never be his wife, she thought, suddenly hopeful again, she could still try to help him pursue his dream. All she needed…

She pulled herself out of the chair and hobbled to the escritoire. There, she took out a sheet of paper and wrote, before pulling the bell-rope. A footman came and Sophie handed him her note.

"Please take this to the Earl of Markham and wait for a reply," she said. When the footman had gone, she called for the maid. If she was to go out today, she'd need to change her gown and do her hair.

Two hours later, she sat in Hatchard's, a book open on her lap. Her footman had given her his arm as she entered the shop, and now she sat alone while he and her maid stood nearby.

A clock struck five. The book shop wasn't busy. Most of its clientele had gone to be seen in Hyde Park during the fashionable hour. That suited Sophie very well. The fewer people who knew of her meeting, the better. Indeed, if it hadn't been highly inappropriate and likely to give the earl a disgust of her, Sophie would have suggested they meet somewhere much more private.

As the clock made its final chime, the earl appeared. He bowed to her, then indicated the chair nearest hers, eyebrows raised to ask if he might sit. She nodded. Her heartbeat raced and her breath caught in her chest. This was either the best thing she'd ever done…or the worst. Unfortunately, until she committed to her course, she had no way of knowing.

She saw Kit in his father. It wasn't just a physical likeness, though the two men shared eye and hair color, and the shapes of their chins and noses were similar enough to remark upon. It was also in the way they held themselves, the straight back and proud shoulders, and the tilt of the head. Sophie wondered if they knew how alike they were.

The earl sat, and Sophie began.

"Thank you for seeing me, my lord."

He smiled and his face softened. "I'm always happy to visit Hatchard's, and I'm not fool enough to forego the company of a pretty young lady." Sophie's face heated, and he gave a tiny huff of amusement. "How may I be of service, Miss Wilson?"

"It's about your son, my lord." She swallowed hard. She needed to say this quickly, before her nerve failed her. "It isn't my place to speak of him to you, but I nevertheless feel compelled to do so. I beg you will listen to what I have to say and not hold against me—or him— my boldness in coming to you. It will be your decision on whether to act upon my words or ignore them, but I cannot in good conscience stand back and not say them."

The earl studied her for several seconds, then nodded. "Go on."

She took a gulp of air. Breathed out. Took in another gulp. "Your son, as I'm sure you know, is a good and wonderful man who wishes to make better the lives of other men. Given the chance, he could save hundreds, thousands, of men through his knowledge and talent."

He stared at her, disconcerting her. His jaw was tight, but his expression was neutral, neither smiling nor scowling, and giving no indication of what he thought. Sophie swallowed again and hurried on.

"If you insist that he manage your estate and he gives his word to do so, he will do it to the best of his ability. I make no doubt the estate would prosper, for he doesn't have it in him to make a bad fist of it. But even as he does a wonderful job, he will be desperately unhappy. He'll wither away until he is no more than a shadow of the man we know today. And while you and your tenants thrive because of his labors, there will be no satisfaction in it. As his father, my lord, you must surely wish him happy, which is why I beseech you to reconsider. Let him study. Let him follow his heart."

The earl did not answer. He studied her until she longed to squirm under his intense scrutiny. She combatted her discomfort by staring back at him, defying him to scold her for speaking to him on this matter.

But she'd had to try.

Not by one flicker of an eyelid did he betray his thoughts or emotions. Finally, he asked, "Is this why you refused his offer?"

Sophie's blush burned hotter. She raised her chin and hoped she looked proud and defiant rather than petulant and disrespectful. "I won't be responsible for crushing his dreams."

The earl nodded. "It was pleasant to see you, Miss Wilson. I wish you good day." He stood, gave a curt bow, and strode from the shop.

Sophie's bravado crashed, leaving her uncertain that she'd done the right thing. It had seemed so sensible and straightforward when she'd thought of it. Now, she prayed she hadn't made Kit's life even more difficult.

****

The next morning, Kit called while she was at breakfast. As a frequent guest of the family, he was shown into the breakfast room without ceremony, and he bowed and sat beside Sophie while the footman poured him a cup of coffee.

Sophie's heart did a tiny pitter-patter, and she fought the urge to smile eagerly at him. She felt sure her pleasure showed in her eyes. She could feel their sparkle. And she didn't believe that was a fanciful notion at all.

Surreptitiously, she glanced at him. He wore a dark blue coat over a blue-and-silver waistcoat that shimmered in the light, and a snowy cravat held in place with a silver stickpin on which was mounted a sapphire. His hair was tousled and his face clean shaven, with no hint of new beard beneath the skin. He didn't look angry, which meant he either had no knowledge of her meeting with his father or he didn't mind it.

Over ham, sausages, eggs, and bacon, they spoke of the weather and the difference in taste between eggs in the country and eggs in London. He inquired after her injuries and expressed his relief that she was recovering.

Finally, breakfast was finished. He gave her his arm and helped her to the morning room, where they were alone, although he left the door ajar. He led her to a chair and sat across from her. He seemed restless, crossing and then uncrossing his legs, flicking invisible lint from his lap. Finally he stood and looked into the fire. As it warmed him it seemed to release the scents of him—the wood-smoky scent of fresh morning air, the coffee he'd drunk, his cologne.

He cleared his throat. "I spoke with my father last night."

Sophie looked away, guiltily.

"He tells me you met with him yesterday."

She glanced at him and whispered, "Yes."

"Gave him a piece of your mind." She looked up, horrified. He held up his hand to stop her protest. "His words, not mine."

Sophie shrugged. "I wouldn't have called it that."

There was a moment of silence. She chanced another glance and saw him watching her, his face serious, his eyes intense. Sophie bit her bottom lip. She'd hoped to help. She'd never meant to cause him pain. She prayed he'd see that. She searched her mind for the right words to make him understand.

Before she could say anything, though, he continued. "He says you love me. Is that true?"

Startled, Sophie almost blurted out what was in her heart. *Of course I love you, you idiot!* She pressed her lips against the words and wondered what she should actually say for the best. If she told the truth, he'd renew his offer. Much as she wanted him to do so, much as she longed to accept, she knew she could not. Offering for her would mean sacrificing his dreams, for no man could support a wife on the income of a University student.

On the other hand, to say no, she didn't love him, well, that would be a lie. She looked up at him, wondering which would be the lesser evil, yes or no, and was surprised to see him smiling at her.

"I'm being unfair," he said. "Before I asked that question, I should have told you what my father and I discussed." He turned to stare into the fireplace, resting one foot on the raised hearthstone, his hand on the mantelshelf as if he needed it to hold him upright.

"He asked me about the mines, the problems, the reason for my passion." He smiled wryly. "He's never shown interest before."

His words filled Sophie with hope. Had her talk with the earl softened his stance on his youngest son's choice of career? "Is he willing to let you attend University?" she asked.

He shook his head, and her spirits fell. Lord Markham hadn't listened to her, then. Or rather, he had, but had chosen to ignore what she said. How she wished he'd chosen to ignore other things, for now he'd told his son she loved him, Kit would renew his offer on terms she could not, would not accept. She wouldn't stand between him and his chance to become an engineer.

She was so caught up in misery and frustration, she almost didn't hear Kit's next words. Indeed, she was absolutely certain she'd misheard them. "I beg pardon, what?" she asked him.

He grinned. "We came to a compromise. One that suits us all very well, I believe."

"Compromise?"

Kit nodded. "I've agreed to manage an estate, on which he will build a laboratory for you."

"But…"

"Meanwhile, he's spoken to a friend of his, Mr. Hetton-Smith. Mr. Hetton-Smith worked with George Stephenson and has agreed to teach me engineering, physics, and mathematical mechanics. He will tutor me for five hours a week to begin, with the option to increase that if I show aptitude for the subject and a willingness to apply myself. Which you can be sure I will do."

Sophie gave a little squeal of delight and stood. Kit

was immediately at her side, holding her and ensuring she didn't put all her weight on her feet. Sophie could have told him his concerns were unfounded, as her well-bound feet no longer caused too much pain. But if she did that, he might let her go, so she stayed silent and savored his embrace.

"So," he said, "I get my dream, you get yours, and my father gets what he wants. Although there is one unnegotiable condition."

She frowned and pulled away, her shoulders sagging. "I knew it was too good to be true. What does he want?"

"Not him. Me." Kit smiled. "I can't build a laboratory for you on an estate where you won't be living, can I? That makes no sense."

"No, I suppose it doesn't."

"And you cannot live on my estate unless we're married, can you? Well, you could, but not without setting tongues a-wagging and very probably causing Ed to call me out."

"That wouldn't be a good thing."

"So, to prevent me building a useless laboratory, to save yourself the disapprobation of Society, and to ensure Ed isn't forced to put a ball into me, I must ask that you agree to my one condition." He knelt. "Sophie Wilson. I love you. Please will you marry me?"

She grinned. "When you put it like that, how can I possibly refuse?"

He breathed a huge sigh of relief, and kissed her.

A word about the author...

Caitlyn Callery lives in Sussex, southern England, near the Regency towns of Brighton and Tunbridge Wells. She is passionate about writing and suffers withdrawal symptoms when she takes a few days away from her work.

Before becoming a full-time writer, she worked in banking, as a waitress, in the motor repair industry, in a call centre, and for a charity. As part of this last job, she helped build a school in Kenya, and drove a vanload of wheelchairs from the UK to Morocco.

She also loves reading, knitting, walking by the sea, the theatre, and spending time with her family.

Visit her at:

CaitlynCallery.com

Thank you for purchasing
this publication of The Wild Rose Press, Inc.

For questions or more information
contact us at
info@thewildrosepress.com.

The Wild Rose Press, Inc.